apa Michele

DEADLY NIGHTS ON THE ISLAND

Michael Chirichella

MICHAEL CHIRICHELLA

Deadly Nights On The Island

Michael Chirichella

ISBN: 978-1-54398-406-4

Chapter I

Leah was drunk. Drunk and high on cocaine. Of course that's what she came down the shore to do; it was senior weekend after the prom. She had planned on staying in the crowded motel with every other senior from West Sheffield High School, until she met Darrell. Tall, dark-skinned, muscular, and of course wealthy. She had come back to the beach house he was renting with his friends, one of the new three-story ones. After the best sex of her life, he had gone downstairs to party some more but she just wanted to stand out on the balcony and smoke a cigarette. That's when she saw her: a girl already standing on the balcony. She looked about Leah's age, thin, but very tall with unbelievably pale skin, almost translucent. The girl's jet black hair was pulled back into a tight bun and she regarded Leah with a strange expression.

"How did you get up here?" Leah demanded.

"You did cocaine. Drugs kill, you know," the girl said in an even tone.

"What? Who even are you?"

"In this case," the girl said with a hungry, almost mischievous smile, "I guess I'm drugs."

Before Leah could even register what was happening, the girl grabbed her, sinking her long fangs into Leah's neck, and swinging both of them backward over the balcony. The girl caught the balcony's railing with her feet, holding them both upside down. Leah tried to struggle and scream but all she could manage was a faint gurgle as she lost consciousness, the blood that should have been rushing to her head instead rushing into the girl's mouth.

The girl was Felicity, and Felicity was, of course, a vampire. This was her preferred method of killing her victims – upside down. It let gravity do all the work. Once Leah's body was completely drained of blood – Felicity hadn't spilled a single drop – Felicity skillfully climbed down from the house and went to the beach, not even a block away. She had put her boat on the shore before coming to the beach house. This wasn't Felicity's first kill, or even her second. She had been born in 1926, and turned in 1944. She had been doing this a long time, long enough to know how far out she had to row her boat to ensure the tides would not be bringing this body back to shore. Just to be safe, Felicity tied a biodegradable sandbag to Leah's body using biodegradable rope and tossed her overboard. Felicity hated pollution, especially near her beach. That's why she had chosen Leah – she was pollution.

Felicity had grown up on this small island, located just four miles off the mainland. It had originally been a quaint, quiet vacation spot where Felicity's family had run a small tavern, classy and cozy, from the back of their home. The island had remained a quiet vacation spot for families until the late seventies when more and more tourists had begun to pour in, and with them, crime. A small gang had even tried to set up turf here, selling drugs to tourists and locals alike. The fools soon came to realize that this island had already been claimed by a vampire, one who did not like her home being poisoned. She had killed them all, and when another gang, realizing that the first one was gone, had come to set up shop, she killed all of them, too. No more gangs came after that and the few drug dealers who attempted to deal on her island were quickly exterminated. Felicity killed three humans a year, draining them completely of blood. She always chose people who partied excessively, partially because she hated people who brought such vile acts to her island, and partially because no one questioned their disappearances. Darrell would assume Leah had gone back to her motel and her friends at the motel would assume she had spent the night with Darrell. When she was reported missing in the next few days, there would be a search and it would be assumed that she had been too intoxicated and had accidentally drowned. No murders reported, no trouble. Because the island was so safe, partially because it was a small, easy to police island, and partially because Felicity did a good job eliminating troublemakers, no one used security cameras outside their stores or houses, which allowed Felicity to hunt her prey with complete freedom.

Felicity rowed back to the island. Motors made too much noise and her vampiric muscles were immune to the effects of fatigue. She rowed all the way back to the dock where she normally kept her small rowboat. She climbed out and walked back to her home. She used the front door and was greeted by her best friend, Cara.

"So, how was it?" Cara asked, turning off the television, a dim lamp now the only light in the room.

Although Felicity had perfect night vision and didn't need it, she clicked the lamp one more time and it brightened. "The first kill of the season is always my favorite. I feel alive again."

"Boy or girl?" Cara asked.

"Girl. Asian. Tiny thing, maybe five feet tall. Cocaine user, smoker, drinker, had sex right before," Felicity said matter-of-factly.

"At least she went out happy," Cara said, a hint of sorrow in her voice. She loved Felicity, but the fact that she had to kill to survive was still something she hadn't gotten used to.

"You know, I could stop telling you about them if that makes it easier," Felicity offered, as she always did. Cara was actually the great-granddaughter of her childhood best friend, Connie. Felicity had given her family home and tavern to Connie's family in exchange for living rent-free in her bedroom forever. Connie had eventually married and had a daughter, Helen, and Felicity had become friends with her. Since physically Felicity was perpetually eighteen years old, she became the best friend of each new generation of Connie's family. Connie, of course, had passed away and Cara's mother, Sarah, and grandmother, Helen, had been her best friends as well. It was an odd friendship but a true one.

"What are we going to do the rest of the night?" Cara asked.

"We? Don't you think you should be in bed?"

"I'll have you know that this is considered prime time for college students."

Felicity groaned. Cara going off to college was one of the hardest things Felicity had had to endure. Cara's mother and grandmother and great-grandmother had never done that to her. Cara looked thoughtful for a moment.

"Tell you what Fel, I'll go to bed early tonight but only because this weekend there's a big party going on and I want you to come."

Felicity looked at her, confused. "Like a birthday party?"

"What? No! Like a *party* party. All the lifeguards are coming back to the beaches tomorrow and there's going to be parties all over the island. It's officially summer!"

Felicity frowned, "You do realize that I hate parties, right?"

"I do, I do, but Fel, come on! Have you ever actually been to a party?"

"No," she replied, crossing her arms and giving Cara a haughty look. "Back in *my* day, we didn't engage in such frivolity."

"Back in your day there was a war going on."

Felicity didn't have a response for that. She stood there silently for a moment, berating herself for not having a better retort. "Fine. I'll go." Cara smiled at her and, standing up, walked over and hugged her goodnight.

Once Cara was in bed, Felicity changed her clothes, throwing her murder-wear in the washing machine. She was fairly certain she hadn't spilled any blood on herself but just in case, she was going to wash her clothes, which wasn't usually necessary as her body didn't produce sweat anymore. She let her long raven locks down and shook them out, then put them up into a ponytail. She changed into a bathing suit and ran out of the house.

Assuming she drained her victim completely of blood, she needed to feed every seven weeks. Every year she had her last "full meal" in September. After that, she survived by occasionally feeding on Cara's family – a pint here or there was all she would take. She would supplement that with the blood of coastal birds and fish she caught, and sometimes, if she got really desperate, the blood of the rats which can be bought in a pet shop as snake food. Fall, winter, and spring were like torture for Felicity, always hungry and weak. But now that it was May and she had consumed a full meal, she felt fantastic. She was going for a surf, her absolute favorite thing in the world. The big island surf competition was a couple of months away, and Felicity always won. It was time to practice. The waves were amazing, or at least they felt amazing. In actuality, they probably could have been breaking a little better but she didn't care. She was in her element and the summer had begun. She surfed until the waves stopped being surfable and calmed down. She put her board in the sand and dove into the water. She swam around for another hour before getting out, and turning her head, looked down the beach. It was completely empty since it was four-thirty in the morning. She looked out at the horizon, imagining she could see England like her grandfather had always told her she could if she looked hard enough.

She smiled and shook her head. *Oh grandfather.* Her smile turned melancholic, as her smiles often did. Oh, to be human. She remembered it fondly, her family had been small but tight-knit. Her father and brother had died in the war and her mother passed away in the forties from the flu. Connie's family had been all the family she had known since. She shook her head, causing her wet ponytail to slap her face. Now wasn't the time to be lamenting her immortality, now was the time to be happy. She made her way back home, put her surfboard on the rack with her other two boards and hopped into the outdoor shower.

She loved outdoor showers. She didn't know why, but she knew she did. The scents of her shampoo and body wash were especially important to her for two reasons. The first was that scents stayed on her a little longer than on a normal person since she had no natural oils to her skin to mar the scent, and second, because with her vampiric sense of smell, whatever scent she used would be overpowering, nauseating even, if it wasn't a pleasant one. After showering she went back into the house, taking one look at the sky as it was illuminated by the rising sun. She could stand to be in the sun at sunrise and sunset but once the sun was a few degrees up into the sky, she would ignite and burn to ash. It was best not to risk it but sometimes she couldn't help but admire the view for a few seconds, the weak sunlight feeling like the noon sun on her skin. She went inside toward the kitchen. Everyone else in the house was asleep – Cara's mother, Sarah, and Sarah's husband, John, shared a bedroom while Cara's grandmother Helen slept in another. Cara had her own room, as did Felicity, although Felicity's room was actually a very large walk-in closet that she had repurposed as a bedroom since it had no windows for the sun to sneak through.

Felicity went to the tavern's kitchen and began the day's cooking. This was the perfect setup as the kitchen was also windowless and Felicity never tired so she could use her vampiric dexterity and speed to prepare all the food that would be eaten that day in the tavern, as well as breakfast for Cara's family. She stretched her long limbs, which in life had been gawky and awkward but now possessed a grace and poise that was unrivaled by any living human.

"Let's get cooking," she said to herself. She began to prepare the food, which was, of course, delicious. She did possess decades of experience in the kitchen, after all. While most of her dishes were family recipes passed down from Europe, she had a few that she had created personally. Once the vegetables were cut, soups were on the stove, and the eggs and bacon were made for her family, she turned and waited.

Helen entered the kitchen and poured herself a glass of orange juice, which she diluted with water from the sink. "Good morning, Felicity," the old woman said, looking up at her with a smile.

"Good morning. I made breakfast." Felicity took the plates, balancing them all perfectly and stepping through the door in the back of the kitchen, which led into the house. She set the food on the table and sat down.

"John and Sara won't be up for a few hours," Helen said as if Felicity didn't know that already.

"I know. I can make their food when the time comes. I do expect them to be up before the first customers get here. I can't be a waitress, for obvious reasons."

Helen let out a slightly raspy laugh. "They'll be up. Who are the other eggs and bacon for? You don't eat."

"Oh right, the college students who rented out the extra room upstairs asked for this at six-thirty. Could you bring it to them?"

"Well aren't you cruel, making an old woman do all this work."

Felicity's jaw dropped with indignation, "Hey! I'm older than you by a good twenty-two years, missy!"

Helen laughed her raspy laugh again and took the plates. She could walk fairly well for a woman her age, but Felicity could see she was definitely getting slower, wobblier. The big downside to being immortal was watching your loved ones slowly waste away. She shook her head again, and walked up the stairs to the top floor. There was the master bedroom, her closet, and then a door which always remained locked from this side. On the other side of the door was a small hallway with another room and a bathroom. Throughout the summer people would rent this room, sometimes in advance and sometimes on the spot if they found they had drunk too much at the tavern. Felicity hated drunkenness but it was how she had a roof keeping that awful sun from burning her down to a pile of ash so she had to be grateful, she supposed. She flopped down on her small bed and shut her eyes. As a vampire, she didn't need sleep although she was capable of it. She dozed for forty minutes before sitting up and walking down to the kitchen to whip up more eggs and bacon for John and Sarah. She poured some coffee and placed everything on the table just as they came down the stairs.

"You are an angel, Felicity," John said gratefully.

"I'm about as far from an angel as a creature can get," she said, completely deadpan. It had taken her a long time to warm up to John. Connie had married a good man; his name had been Steve and he had been best friends with Felicity's brother. They had left at the same time to serve in World War II together. Steve had returned, but Felicity's brother had not. Helen's husband had fancied himself something of a bad boy when they had first met. Felicity hated that, but when soldiers were being drafted to go fight in Vietnam, his number wasn't called. He had been so irate about it that he enlisted. He died over there and while Felicity would never admit it, she was saddened by the loss. She hadn't liked him, but he had earned her respect. John had met Sarah when he was vacationing on the island. He had actually met the two of them at once, and had fallen immediately for Felicity. When he realized she wanted nothing to do with him, he had gone for Sarah. He had been tall, broad-shouldered, with thick brown hair, perfectly styled. Sarah gave him a chance and, much to Felicity's chagrin, they hit it off. Over the years John had shown himself to be a loving husband and caring father. Felicity had grown to care for him as she did for the rest of her little family.

"The weather's supposed to be great for the rest of the week," John said, looking at the report in the paper, "I'm guessing you're going to win the big surf competition again this year?"

Sarah laughed, "Of course she will. She's got super balance and reflexes."

Felicity gave a half smile. "I need them to make up for the fact that I surf in head to toe gear. It's a lot harder than it looks. I doubt I could even get up on a board without the super vampire dexterity."

"Any idea who's sponsoring you this year?" Sarah asked. To keep from getting roasted alive by the sun, Felicity wore a special head to toe surf suit. Every year different businesses paid her money to put their logos on her suit.

Felicity shook her head.

"I'm sure you'll find people," Sarah assured her.

"I'm not too worried about it," Felicity replied nonchalantly. She opened her mouth to say more but John held up a hand silencing her.

"I already know what you're going to say: Tavern opens in five minutes, hurry up."

Felicity looked sheepish and Sarah laughed so hard she almost fell out of her seat.

"Be careful," Helen warned, entering the room with a smile. "She's strong enough to rip your arms clean off."

"Mom!" Sarah whined.

John smiled good-naturedly. "She would never. She loves me too much."

Felicity rolled her eyes but couldn't quite hide the smile playing at her lips. She looked at the clock and then walked into the kitchen. The wait staff greeted her as they entered. She worked the kitchen as the usual breakfast run of people came in, many of whom were high schoolers who probably went to school with Leah. Felicity hummed an old tune from the forties as she prepared the food. She was the only one working in the kitchen, which was just how she liked it. No one to get in the way, and more importantly no one to see her unnaturally fast movements. If a waiter was about to enter, she would hear them coming and slow down. Around eleven-thirty she began cooking eggs and bacon for Cara who would be waking soon. When they were ready, she set them on the table and began her prep for the lunch rush.

After Cara ate, she joined Felicity in the kitchen. "I could watch you cook every day for the rest of my life and still not stop being amazed at how you move," Cara told her, staring wide-eyed at the blades that were currently filleting fish.

"I'd invite you to, but you're already late for work," Felicity informed her.

Cara sighed. "Oh, lighten up, Felicity. It's the first day. No one will care if I'm a little late."

Cara worked as a badge checker on the beach during the afternoon. People visiting the beaches had to buy little badges, this was one of the ways the island made its money.

"Come on Cara, those badges aren't going to check themselves."

Cara scoffed at this and turned to leave.

"Wait, turn and open," Felicity commanded.

Cara turned, her mouth already open and Felicity launched a small piece of onion with her knife. Cara caught it skillfully and then hurried off to work. Felicity smiled to herself and continued her work.

Cara came back at around seven o'clock to find her parents and grandmother sitting at the dinner table. Felicity entered the room carrying their dinners and set them out on the table, and then sat down.

"I'm pooped," Cara said sitting down between John and Felicity. "I'm gonna need a nap before tonight." Her family eyed her curiously. "All the summer workers are back today! It's party time!"

"When will you be home?" Sarah asked.

"I don't know! It's a party. Whenever it's done, I guess."

"Hmm."

"I'll be fine! Besides, Fel's coming."

All eyes turned to Felicity, who looked displeased but stayed silent.

Helen was the first to break the silence. "Felicity will keep her safe."

"Of course I'll keep her safe," Felicity snapped. "I just hate parties."

Sarah laughed and patted Felicity's shoulder. "She must be going soft in her old age. When I was your age, Cara, Felicity wouldn't be caught dead at a party."

"I'm always sort of dead," Felicity grumbled, crossing her arms.

After dinner, Felicity walked with Cara to the ice cream parlor on the end of the street and they watched the sunset together. Cara licked her cookies and cream cone as she watched her friend stare out at the horizon contentedly.

"Summer suits you," she noted.

Still staring out at the horizon, Felicity replied, "It's always been my favorite season. Too bad I ignite in the sun."

"Are you sure? Like have you ever tested it?"

"Once," she said bitterly. "Just the tip of my finger."

"Sorry."

"I'm not."

"Really?"

"Yeah, I get to live in my favorite place forever, watching each new generation of my favorite people."

"Am I still one of your favorite people even though I'm making you go to this party?"

A small child ran up to them and quickly pulled up a line with a soggy, chewed-up piece of chicken on the end of it, then dropped it back in. Disappointed, the boy turned and began to walk away.

"Young man," Felicity called.

The boy turned, looking startled, "M-me?" he asked in a shaky voice.

"Yes you! Is that your dropline?"

The boy puffed out his chest proudly. "Yes it is."

"Want me to show you a trick that I learned to catch more crabs with a dropline?"

"OK!" the boy ran over and Felicity took the line carefully in her hands

"The trick with a dropline is to go slowly," she explained. "So slow that the crab doesn't even know he's being pulled in. See?" There was a crab greedily eating the chicken. She dropped the line back down.

"Why did you drop it back!" the boy wailed. "There was a crab!"

Felicity cocked her head to the side. "You're not ready to catch him."

"I'm not?"

Felicity laughed. "You don't have a net!"

The boy looked embarrassed.

"Crabs are Greedy Gusses," she told him. "If you run home and get a net, I bet he'll still be there when you get back."

Perking up, the boy turned and started to run. "Thanks lady!" he called back to her.

Cara threw her arms around Felicity who looked at her, confused. "You're so cute, Fel."

"That boy was engaging in good wholesome fun. I encourage that," Felicity responded.

They walked back. Cara took a shower and began getting ready for the party. She looked through a few of her outfits. It was supposed to be warm tonight, but not too humid. She settled for a figure flattering white dress. Her shoulder-length, chestnut hair was brushed out perfectly, and she wore a small gold rose on a thin chain with matching earrings. She walked into the living room to see Felicity standing there in a floral sundress. Felicity never bothered with makeup, with the exception of a little bit of blush to make her face look like that of a living person.

"How do I look?" Cara asked excitedly.

Felicity considered her seriously for a few moments. "It's a little form-fitting don't you think?"

"That's kind of the point."

"You're not going to get the attention of a good man like that."

"Stop. You sound like a grandma. Everyone dresses like this nowadays."

"In all fairness," Felicity retorted with a hint of a smile, "I'm old enough to be your great-grandmother."

They walked to the party as it was only four blocks away.

"At least you wore sensible shoes," Felicity observed, pointing at Cara's flats.

"I need them to keep up with your super speed," Cara teased.

Felicity slowed her pace slightly. Even in life she had been a fast walker, and it didn't help that Cara was a solid six inches shorter than her.

They arrived at the party, which Felicity found way too loud for her vampiric hearing.

Cara turned to her, "I'm going to grab a drink. Do you want anything?" Felicity made a face that Cara knew from experience meant, "That's a dumb question but I'm too nice to point it out." Cara's eyes widened and she flushed with embarrassment. "Right, sorry, I forgot. You can't drink normal stuff," Cara said apologetically.

Two boys who looked like they were in their early twenties approached the pair.

"Hey, you guys want us to grab you some drinks?" asked one boy. He was shorter than Felicity but rippling with muscle.

"Sure! I was just about to get some," Cara responded enthusiastically.

"You want a beer, wine, or a mixie?" his friend asked, who was just shy of six feet, with a scraggly beard and a slight Puerto Rican accent.

"We can get our own drinks, thank you," Felicity told them curtly, dragging Cara to the next room with her.

"What was that about?!" Cara exclaimed, "Those guys were going to give us free drinks!"

Felicity looked at her patronizingly. "This is a party, Cara. All of the drinks are free,"

"I— Well— But still!" Cara fumbled.

"Eloquent as ever," Felicity said deadpan as she poured some box wine into a red Solo cup and handed it to Cara. "Here. Don't take drinks from strange men. It's not safe."

"Come on Fel, you worry too much."

"Terrible things can happen at a party like this, trust me I know." Felicity flashed a smile at her friend, revealing massive, sinister fangs where her canines should have been. Horror flashed in Cara's eyes and she took an involuntary step back. Felicity didn't often show her fangs and when she did, it reminded Cara of just how different the two of them were – like predator and prey different. She shook her head and looked up to see Felicity looking at her inquisitively.

"Sorry, was that too far?" Felicity asked her, the slightest hint of amusement creeping into her voice. "Look, I hope you have a great time tonight. Yell if you need anything. Just, be careful is what I was trying to say."

Cara hugged Felicity and when she let go, she turned and almost knocked over another boy, this one tall and lean with green eyes and sandy blond hair. He looked down at her but his eyes occasionally darted to Felicity. Cara didn't notice this, but Felicity could tell he was trying to figure out between the two of them who seemed more likely to be into him. When she was younger, she had always been insecure about her figure, or lack thereof. People at the time called her a "beanpole." Then, a few generations later, her super thin figure was in and Sarah's curves had been out. In the modern day, the pendulum hadn't quite swung back to either side so for once in her life, she and her friend were both sought after. Of course she had no interest in men. She was many decades older than anyone here, not to mention the fact that she was basically a different species. She ate people; dating one would probably be like a human dating a cow. She sighed and tapped Cara on the shoulder. "I'll be around," she said as she walked away. Even she had to admit the boy was handsome. She wouldn't deny Cara a little bit of fun, just not too much fun. Cara went off to dance with the boy, who introduced himself to her as Andrew. Felicity scoffed and rolled her eyes. Dancing for this generation was a lot of grinding and touching. Basically sex on the dance floor. Disgusting. She missed the class, the elegance, the technique of her day.

"You don't dance either?" a voice asked, interrupting her thoughts.

She turned and saw a pale boy with dark messy hair. He was wearing basketball shorts and a shirt with a character on it.

"Your shirt, it's from one of those Japanese cartoons. The ones with the person name, right?" she asked him, trying to remember what they were called.

"Person name?" he asked, confused. Then his eyes widened in comprehension. "Oh! Are you thinking of anime?"

"Yes!" she exclaimed. "Anna May."

He began to laugh, so hard that he almost fell over.

"What's so funny?" she demanded.

"You think it's Anna like the name, May like the season, don't you?"

"Y-yes," she said defiantly, crossing her arms in an attempt to cover up her embarrassment.

He smiled at her reassuringly. "It's not Anna May; it's anime. A-N-I-M-E."

"That's dumb," she said grumpily.

"It's the Japanese term for animation."

"OK, perhaps I'm the dumb one," she relented.

"N-no! No, not at all. I didn't— You're not—" The boy waved his arms in front of him frantically.

She studied him, an amused expression playing on her face. "You're very awkward," she said matter-of-factly.

"I, oh, uh, sorry," he said, looking a little put out.

She smiled and put a hand on his shoulder. He looked at it like it was the first time a girl had ever voluntarily made physical contact with him. She sort of felt for him. Even in life she had always been reserved, although less so than she was now. "I'm Felicity."

The boy extended his hand and she shook it. "I'm Basil. Ooo, your hands are really cold."

"Maybe yours are just warm," she retorted. "And to answer your original question, I do dance. I just don't do dances that make me look trashy."

"What do you dance to?"

She considered it for a moment. "Well, I haven't danced in many, many years. But a swing dance is always nice."

"I'll be right back!" He scurried off and a few moments later she heard the music stop. Everyone looked around.

"Yo! Turn the music back on!" someone yelled.

Felicity's eyes widened as she heard a drumbeat and horns start to play over the speakers. She pushed aside two pairs of angry dancers and began a flawless swing. Granted, she had to alter her moves slightly since she had no dance partner but she made it work. She was about to add a flip to her next move when the music stopped.

"What do you think you're doing?" a condescending voice called to her.

"I think I'm dancing actual dance moves to actual music. What about you?" she replied icily.

The girl stepped forward. Her name was Penelope Smith. Her father owned the biggest real estate agency on the island. She was petite, and without the six-inch wedges she would likely have been around five feet tall. She had striking green eyes accentuated with winged eyeliner, and long platinum-blonde hair, worn in a pouf. Penelope sauntered over to Felicity, flanked by an Indonesian boy in a tank top and his twin sister, who wore a more feminine tank top of the same color. Both of them had dyed their hair bright blue, although the boy's had started to fade. Penelope stuck a stubby finger, with a long fake nail in Felicity's face. "I made this playlist, no one touches it or they get thrown out. Those are the rules," she said, her voice not quite matching her tiny body.

"You're like the ghost of a middle-aged woman who possessed the body of a middle schooler," Felicity informed her.

Penelope's cheeks flushed. "Out! Get out!"

"This isn't your house. You have no authority to kick me out," Felicity told her, not moving.

"No, but this is our house," the blue-haired girl screeched, gesturing between herself and her brother. "So buh-bye."

"Fine," she said, looking around for Cara. She spotted her and walked over. "Come on."

Cara looked mortified. "I'm not going with you."

"What?" Felicity asked, genuinely confused.

"I'm staying here. I didn't get kicked out; you did."

Felicity stared at Cara, shocked. Her friend was really choosing this stupid party over her? A hand closed around her arm and she turned. Putting her hand on the chest of the poor boy who had been foolish enough to try to forcibly escort her out, she shoved him clear off his feet and onto the ground. Everyone stared at her, shocked, and she flipped her hair, smacking Cara in the face with it as she did and walked out. As soon as she was clear of the property, she broke into a run that would have put an Olympian to shame. She made it home and immediately took off her dress, changing into a bathing suit. She was hurt and upset. How could Cara do this to her? She mentally berated herself. She had shown too much of her strength at that party. Hopefully no one asked too many questions. It wasn't like anyone knew who she was anyway. Since she only went out at night, she had kept a pretty low profile all these years. She shook her head, telling herself she just needed a good surf. She grabbed her board and hurried off to the beach. Moments later, her feet hit the sand. She ran into the water with her board and not even a minute later, she was up on a wave and all the stress and irritation from before washed away with the seafoam.

Felicity hit wave after wave; the surf was perfect tonight. She was in her element, content to do this for all eternity. She inhaled the salty air and blinked in surprise. She smelled the faintest hint of blood. She also heard laughter, voices. Scanning the beach, her keen eyes spotted figures on the sand egging on a boy who threw off his shirt and dove into the water. Maybe one of them had a cut? No, the smell was definitely not coming from the land. She followed the boy's movement through the water with her eyes and they widened in shock. There was blood in this water. Lots of it. The boy couldn't tell, of course, but she could. She could also see that there was a shark. She aimed her board toward the boy. Being a predator herself, she could spot an animal on the hunt anywhere, and this shark was definitely on the hunt. She wouldn't make it in time, she realized. It was about to kill this boy. She was going to regret this, she knew. In one swift motion, she released her board from her leg and launched herself through the air. She could see the shark's eyes roll to the back of its head as it attacked. Felicity managed to get between the boy and the shark's jaws, which led to her flesh being wedged between the shark's upper and lower jaws. The shark shook its head violently from side to side, its teeth slicing and tearing through her side. Felicity convulsed in the water, her body wracked with the worst pain she had ever felt in her life. The shark had ripped out her bottom two rib bones, all the way down to her hip bone. She managed to drag herself out of the water as another boy helped her.

"Oh my God," he gasped when his friend shined a flashlight from his phone onto her.

"Call the police! Call an ambulance!" the boy she had saved yelled.

As the boy with the flashlight tried to dial 911, her hand snaked out and smacked the phone out of his hands and into the water. She let out a shriek of pain and writhed in the sand.

"We need to get her to a hospital," one of the boys said, though she couldn't tell which through the searing pain.

She felt hands trying to move her and she lashed out with her fist, which connected with a thud and a gasp as the wind was knocked out of the boy and he landed on his back. She screamed once more in pain and stood, limping toward the street.

"Wait! Miss! You're hurt bad; you need to go to the hospital," one of them called.

She ignored them and they had the good sense not to try to follow. The walk that would normally have been a brisk, pleasant one was now torture. Every step caused her more pain. After what felt like an eternity, she arrived home. Her ordeal was not over yet. She entered the outdoor shower and grabbed the soap on a rope that John always kept hanging on a hook. She turned on the water. As the ice cold spray hit her face, she closed her eyes and bit down on the rope. She used a washcloth to scrub the sand out of her wounds. The last thing she needed was her innards being full of sand. After what felt like an eternity, her wounds were clean. She dried off and limped back to the house. She collapsed onto the couch and let out a wail. Sarah, John, and Helen all rushed out to see what was going on. Sarah fainted at the sight of her on the couch, soaked and torn open. John brought Sarah to

Cara's bedroom and placed her in bed, then rushed off to grab disinfectant. Helen tottered over to her and sat down on the couch, placing Felicity's wet head in her lap. She began to stroke her arm and whisper soothing words. John rushed back in with a box of Band-Aids, a bag of cotton balls, and a bottle of hydrogen peroxide.

"If you dump that in me I will – ahhhh!" Felicity felt pitiful. She couldn't even finish her threats.

Helen waved John away. "She's a vampire. She can't get infections. She just needs time to heal."

Felicity nuzzled closer to Helen. At least her oldest living friend knew her well enough to know that she would heal from this. Felicity healed at a rate about one hundred times the speed of a human. A papercut that would normally take a day to heal took her only a little over fourteen minutes. She would be fine in a few days, but to regrow the bones the shark had bit out would be an excruciating process, not to mention the parts of her internal organs and skin. She had read once that crying helped to relieve pain. Oh God, she wished she could cry right now. She had lost that ability along with all of her other bodily functions when she was turned. She closed her eyes and tried to sleep, but her efforts were futile.

Later in the night – it may have been an hour, it may have been several minutes, Felicity could no longer tell – Cara came home, slightly intoxicated. She did a double take, her eyes widening when she realized her senses were not deceiving her and her best friend really was lying on the couch with a sizeable piece missing from her. She rushed over.

"Oh my God, what happened to Felicity?!"

"We're not really sure," John said, entering the room and hugging his daughter.

Cara kneeled down and put her hands on Felicity's arm. "Fel, I'm so so so so so sorry." Cara began to cry. "I was such a bitch. This is all my fault… please don't die."

"Why don't you brush your teeth and put on your pajamas? This could take a while," Helen told her gently.

Cara tearfully brushed her teeth, threw on her pajamas, and sat down on the floor in front of the couch. She took Felicity's hand and immediately regretted it as the vampire had a very strong grip, one she didn't hold back on when waves of pain wracked her body.

Chapter 2

Cara opened her eyes. She had no idea how long she'd been asleep for but her grandmother was gone and Felicity was asleep on the couch. Her wound still looked gnarly but it was no longer the ghastly chunk it had been when she had arrived.

She stood up and Felicity's eyes began to open, then went wide. She tried to jump up off the couch but Cara dove on top of her, hugging her. "Fel, oh my God. I'm so sorry, you have to believe me."

Felicity sighed. "It's ok, Cara. But I need to get up. Someone needs to run the kitchen."

"No," Cara told her. "You can't go. I was so worried last night! You almost died."

Felicity gave her a look like she had said something dumb but she was too nice to say anything about it.

"What? Why are you looking at me like that?"

"Cara, you realize that I'm a vampire, right? Like an immortal, cannot be killed, just regrew part of her ribcage in a single night vampire?"

"So what was all that yelling and thrashing around last night! You had us all worried sick!"

"She can still feel pain, dear," Helen said, entering the room. "And Felicity, don't worry about cooking today. We have it covered; you just worry about getting better."

Felicity tried to stand but Cara put all of her weight on her. "The only way I'm letting you stand up is if you promise to go right to bed," Cara told her firmly.

"Fine, help me up the stairs."

"Nonsense!" Helen exclaimed. "You'll sleep in Cara's room until you heal fully."

"Have you replaced her curtains? I don't feel like getting reduced to ash so soon after getting bit by a shark," Felicity said a little snarkily. She didn't appreciate being told where to sleep by all these youngsters.

Helen gestured around her and Felicity noticed that there were black-out curtains on every window.

"When you live with a vampire, you learn how to prepare to keep out the sun," Helen told her smugly.

Cara helped her up and into the bedroom, then gently onto the bed. Cara sat down on the bed with her back to the wall, her legs resting on Felicity's legs. "Fel, what happened?"

"I got kicked out of that stupid party. I was mad, so as I always do when I'm mad, I surfed. It was great, waves were perfect. The weather was perfect."

"And?" Cara prompted after a few moments of silence.

"Something didn't feel right. It still doesn't, but I can't figure out why. Anyway, I noticed blood in the water and I heard voices. Some boys. Three of them. They were laughing. They dared their friend to go night swimming, I think. They had no idea about the blood. Or the shark, but I saw it, I knew. I knew it was blood-lusted. It had been feeding on whatever was bleeding. I tried to surf toward them but I just couldn't get there in time, so I jumped and I managed to intercept the shark just as it was about to bite into him. The rest, well, I think you can figure that out on your own. Why are you crying?"

Cara wiped her eyes. "You wouldn't have been there if it wasn't for me. It's all my fault you got bit."

Felicity reached over and squeezed her friend's hand. "Hey, I got kicked out of that party on my own. You had nothing to do with it."

"But if you hadn't been upset with me, you wouldn't have been surfing and—"

"Have you met me?" Felicity interrupted. "I surf when I'm happy, when I'm sad, angry. I surf whenever I can because it's my favorite thing to do, no matter what my mood is. I would've been there whether you were or not, and even if you had been on that beach, your weak human eyes couldn't have seen the shark. Oh damn."

"What?"

"My board. I had to ditch it in the water. That was my second favorite board," Felicity said with dismay.

"Felicity, you got bit by a shark! You shouldn't be worried about your board!"

"Lost flesh will replace itself in time, but a surfboard, thats truly priceless," she said solemnly.

Cara laughed and Felicity smiled.

"So," Felicity asked nonchalantly, "how was the rest of your night?"

"It was fine," Cara said, dodging the question.

"Come on, you got the details of my night. Spill."

"Is this some kind of trick? Are you still mad at me for ditching you?" Cara asked suspiciously.

Felicity sighed. "I'm ninety-seven years old, Cara. I don't hold petty grudges against my friends. I understand that you're young, you make mistakes, you're impulsive. Seriously, I'm past it, alright?"

"Alright, well, if I'm honest I had a pretty good time the rest of the night. I drank and danced, but I didn't get too drunk. Some weird kid got kicked out right after you for putting on that song you were dancing to. Umm… hmm… let's see, I had like three guys hitting on me all night. I did make out with that guy Andrew."

"Oh did you?" Felicity asked, sounding completely innocent.

"Yes. Are you judging me?" Cara asked.

"Wow," Felicity said, rolling onto her back, relieved that the pressure didn't aggravate her injury. "The girl goes off to college and suddenly thinks her best friend is some judgy, prudish, Puritan."

Cara turned bright red. "Well, to be fair, you do hate parties, and drinking, and anything resembling physical contact with the opposite sex, and drugs."

"Yes, I hate an excess of hedonism. You drank a moderate amount, and made out, which I believe is just this generation's way of saying you kissed for a while?"

"More or less, yeah." Cara nodded.

"I have no problem with that. You're entitled to your fun, and the fun of your time. And Cara, I will never judge you, alright? You're my best friend."

Cara and Felicity sat in silence. Cara could see Felicity was troubled by something, but she couldn't tell what. In her nineteen years of knowing Felicity, Cara had never once seen her lie about her feelings. She sometimes, often even, kept things to herself. Cara knew it wasn't her actions last night that bothered Felicity, but what was it? Cara opened her mouth to ask but Felicity beat her to it.

"I was born here on this island."

"Uh, what?" Cara had no idea where Felicity was going with this conversation.

"I was born here in the roaring twenties almost a hundred years ago and in that time, there has not been a single shark attack."

"That's what's bothering you?"

"It's been bothering me," Felicity said, standing up and beginning to pace, the movement uncomfortable but not painful. "The paper wouldn't have anything yet. Text your friends; ask if they've heard about anything. I know you young people always get the news first."

Cara stood up and crossed the room, picking up her phone and scrolling through it for a few minutes. Felicity watched her with an unblinking stare that most would find unsettling.

"Nothing," Cara said eventually.

"Nothing," Felicity repeated, her brow furrowing.

"Are you OK?" Cara asked sounding concerned.

"Hush child," Felicity said with a dismissive wave of her hand. She was lost in thought, dots weren't connecting. She needed more information. "Go to work. Ask around. See if you can find anything out."

"Will you be OK while I'm gone?"

"I'll be fine. I'll take it easy for now, but as soon as the sun begins to set, I'm going out. I have some suspicions I have to confirm."

Cara got ready for work and, even though her shift didn't start for another hour, left for the beach. Felicity's wound was still healing, so she was stuck in her bikini until it closed up more. This meant she had to stay out of the kitchen or any staff who walked in might ask questions. Questions were the enemy of a vampire trying to keep a low profile. Felicity pulled up the local online news blogs, nothing about a shark attack, or about a body being found. She started researching sharks, shark attacks, historic shark attacks, shark attacks in the area. Search after search yielded nothing to sway the feeling in her gut that she couldn't shake. Maybe it was a seashell lodged in her guts somewhere from last night? She kneaded her thin torso with her hands just to be sure. Nothing felt out of the ordinary. Hours passed and eventually Cara came home. Felicity paced anxiously around the small dining room as Cara ate dinner with her family.

Sarah looked at her in concern. "Are you OK, Felicity?"

"Sarah, I'm a vampire," Felicity said, turning to show her side which was now almost completely regenerated although there were still clear divots and depressions, and the skin looked sensitive and raw, like the layers of tissue hadn't quite regrown yet.

"You seem agitated," Helen noted.

"I just want the sun to go down far enough for me to go out."

"You'll attract attention looking like that," John said, gesturing to her side with his fork.

"You're right, hold on." Felicity bolted up the stairs, her wound no longer troubling her enough to hinder her supernatural agility. She came back less than a minute later in a loose-fitting white top with puffy sleeves, a pair of light blue jeans, and Converse sneakers. She ran her hands through her long black hair a few times fluffing it up and tossing it behind her.

"Alright, I'm ready," she declared.

"Fel, you've got another half hour at least before you can leave," Cara informed her.

She waited impatiently while Cara finished her meal and got ready. Cara came out of her room looking cute with a gray tank top, black shorts, and sandals. She had also thrown on a little bit of eyeliner and mascara, because she never knew who she might run into out on the island.

"Let's boogie," Felicity said, throwing on a pair of sunglasses and pulling Cara by the arm out of the house.

The sky was lit up in a dazzling display of orange and red and the air was warm and a little more humid than it had been the past few days, but there was a pleasant breeze. Felicity took off in a fast walk and Cara had to practically jog to keep up. They arrived at the beach, and Felicity could detect no signs of her struggle the previous night, which was to be expected—the beach had had a full day of people going about their activities. The blood was nowhere to be found, which was also to be expected.

"What exactly are you looking for?" Cara asked, not sure what her friend was scouring the beach for.

"A body," Felicity answered flatly.

"Maybe no one else was attacked?" Cara offered optimistically.

"No, someone definitely died last night. There was blood in the water. It's what made the shark attack me."

"Maybe it was from a fish or something?"

"No. I'm a vampire. I can survive off fish blood but I'm meant to drink human blood, every part of me is designed for that one food source. I know human blood. That was human blood."

"You also dumped a corpse in the water the night before. Maybe that's where it came from," Cara countered.

"Again, Cara, I drink human blood. The amount that was in the water was way more than would have been left in the corpse I threw in the water. I was extremely thirsty that night. Besides, I threw the body out very far off shore. No, someone else had been bleeding out in the water, which again leads me to my assertion that there haven't been any shark attacks here in at least a hundred years."

"Hey!" a familiar voice called.

They both turned and Felicity's heart dropped. It was the three boys from the night before. She noticed their appearance today. One of them – the one whom she had saved – was about her height with a buzz cut, large nose, and cocky smile. He had the kind of build one gets when a naturally skinny person lifts weights every day. The other boy, the one whose phone she had swatted, appeared to be the younger brother of the first boy. He had a similar haircut but a smaller nose, and an annoyingly sparse mustache. He was built like how she imagined his brother would be if he stopped working out. The third boy, wearing a wife beater tank and cargo shorts, is taller, tanned, and lean, with a blowout. She also noted a bruise peeking out near his armpit from under his wife beater.

"Aren't you the girl from last night?" the brother with the annoying mustache asked, his voice somewhat monotone and deeper than she expected.

"Excuse me?" she asked in an outraged voice. There was no way these boys had gotten a good enough look at her to remember her.

"How are you walking around after that?!" the boy with the bruise asked her.

"I have no idea what you're talking about," she said, beginning to walk away.

"You were bit by a shark. I saw your face, I remember," the older brother called to her. "I even remember your voice."

She kept walking, Cara hot on her heels. The boys ran after them.

"You look pretty creepy chasing after a couple of girls on the beach like this," Cara pointed out.

The boy with the bruise and the boy with the mustache stepped back, but the boy Felicity had saved stayed, although he did put both of his hands up in a "calm down," gesture.

"Look, we're not trying to cause any trouble. We just, well, we saw a shark attack last night." He told them, "I almost got bit and a girl got a huge chunk taken out of her. Honestly, I thought she had died but then we saw you walking around and..." He looked her up and down, his memory telling him it was Felicity but logic telling him there's no way she would be walking around.

“As you can see,” Felicity told him calmly, “I am not her as I am very clearly a living, breathing human being.”

Cara gave her a look that said she was over doing it a little.

“Sorry if we scared you,” the one with the bruise said. “He’s been thinking about that girl all day so it’s no wonder he thought you were her.”

“She saved my life,” he said quietly.

“Yeah,” the one with the bruise said with a laugh, pulling back his wife beater to reveal a fist-shaped bruise. “Then she rocked my shit and ran off.”

Cara doubled over laughing and even Felicity couldn’t help but smile. The boys all joined in laughing.

“I’m Gio,” the boy Felicity had saved said. “This is my brother Vito and the one with the ridiculous hairstyle is Joey.”

Cara shook his hand. “I’m Cara, and this is Fel.”

Joey began to sing, “Fel, Fel fell down a well, the well went deep right down to—”

“You can call me Felicity.”

“So what brings you two to the beach?” Joey asked flirtatiously.

“It’s the summer. We live here. Why wouldn’t we be here?” Felicity replied flatly.

“No one should be here,” Gio said, his voice dark. “We told the police there had been a shark attack and they didn’t do anything about it. No one knows.”

“No one was attacked today though,” Cara reminded him.

“It wasn’t even in the newspapers. It’s like they’re hiding it,” Vito droned.

“Why don’t you do something about it then? Go down there and ask what’s going on,” Felicity challenged.

Vito and Joey exchanged nervous looks. Gio looked like he was having a mental debate but after a moment looked squarely at her. “Fine.”

He was the bold one. She could tell whenever there was a challenge, he was the one who stepped up. The night before, he had dove in the water while his friends watched, and today, he continued to speak to them after Cara had called them out for looking creepy. She couldn’t help but respect someone who wasn’t afraid to put himself out there.

He began to walk off the beach and seemed surprised that Felicity and Cara were following.

“Are you coming with us?” he asked.

“Obviously. We’re from here. If our police are covering up shark attacks, we deserve to know,” Cara boldly declared.

“You guys drive here?” Joey asked them, his eyes looking them up and down, no doubt deciding who he thought was prettier.

Cara sighed dramatically. “No, sadly I don’t even own a car.”

“You really don’t need one on the island,” Felicity told Joey.

Gio reached into his pocket and pulled out some keys, unlocking the door to a white Cadillac SUV. “May not need one, but this one’s mine.”

They drove to the police station and Gio parked across the street. The police station for the island was small. The entire force consisted of ten people, including the dispatchers. There was one police car, which usually patrolled around the island and two officers who rode bicycles. During the summer months, they had an extra guy ride around on a bicycle. The chief usually stayed in the station. Being a police officer on the island was the easiest job, good pay, and no real work. The worst these men had seen was when someone accidentally killed his friend by pushing him into the railing of a deck, which broke off. The man had turned himself in immediately. This was a safe island. The group walked into the station and Gio walked up to the dispatcher’s desk.

"May I help you?" asked the dispatcher, a slightly overweight woman in her late forties with frizzy hair and a name tag that said "Judy" on it.

"Yes, I came here to follow up with the chief about a report I made last night," Gio informed her.

"Well, the chief is busy right now. You'll have to take a seat."

They all sat down on a bench. The faint sound of voices came through the wall, faint that is, for anyone with human hearing. Felicity rested her head against the wall and it was like she was in the room. From what she could tell there were four men, none of whom she had ever spoken to.

"You can't just censor the media like this!" voice number one said angrily.

"And your article will cause a panic," said voice number two, silky smooth.

"People should be panicking if there are sharks! Sharks are terrifying, scary, scary creatures!" voice number one argued.

"Normally I'd agree with you," voice number four – a calm, strong-sounding voice – told him. "But this may not be a simple shark attack. This may be a murder and you reporting it as a shark attack could hinder our investigation,"

"A murder? Don't be ridiculous," voice number two scoffed.

"There hasn't been a confirmed murder on this island in, in, ever!" voice number four chimed in ineloquently.

Felicity could hear the sounds of paper being moved and spread around a table.

"Leah Rayal, age eighteen, non-islander, came here for senior weekend, never found. Our shark attack victim, Bill Henson, age fifty, local. Surfboard of an unknown surfer was found washed up on shore, supposedly a shark attack victim but no body has been located and no one has been admitted to any hospital in a fifty mile radius with shark attack wounds," voice number three informed them.

"Oh please, this means nothing," voice number two assures everyone. "The girl who vanished was reportedly doing drugs. She probably drowned somewhere, happens every year. As for the surfboard, with no body, there's really nothing to report. For all we know it was a prank – someone threw a board in the water. As for the locals, well, there were no attacks today. Why drive the property value down and ruin the local shop owners' profits, have there been any shark sightings today?"

"None," said voice number four.

"There you have it, no need to report anything if there's nothing to report. No murders, one flukey shark attack."

"Maybe," voice number three conceded.

Felicity stood and knocked on the door to the chief's office. No one made any moves and she knocked again

"Hey!" Judy exclaimed, standing up.

The door opened and Felicity was faced with the chief, a broad-shouldered man with a weathered face, obviously the owner of the third voice.

"I'm in a meeting right now, if you wouldn't mind wait—" he began.

"He was a local and that's where the problem is," she interrupted.

"Excuse me?" he said, taken aback.

Felicity stepped inside the office. She looked at the other occupants: A wormy looking man with dark hair and close set eyes was the owner of the first voice, the fourth voice had come from a police officer who looked like he had at one point been an athlete but a few years of island living had made him soft, of course seeing the owner of the silky smooth voice number two, she recognized him immediately, his face was plastered all over the island. Archie Smith was the number one real estate agent on the island. Like his daughter he had platinum hair, green eyes, and a mouth full of perfect teeth. "Looks like we had an eavesdropper," he said with a dazzling grin and just the tiniest hint of annoyance in his voice.

"Couldn't help myself," she replied flatly. "But let's cut to the chase, you," she said pointing to Archie Smith, "don't want anything to drive away tourists. You"—she pointed to the wormy looking man—"are a reporter."

"For *The Sandpaper*," he declared proudly. "Hershel Meyer at your service. These men have been trying to censor me."

"We just don't want you causing a panic," the police officer said.

"Miss, I'm going to have to ask you to leave," the chief told her.

"Just help me hash this out first because it's been bugging me all day," Felicity said approaching the case files on the desk

"Ma'am, this is not a civilian zone," the police officer said, about to grab her.

She moved her arm just as he was about to grab her and snatched up the picture of her surfboard and then the one of Leah. The officer managed to get a hold of her but the chief held up a hand.

"Why did you take those?"

"This Leah girl is a benny. She probably did just get too high and drown. Hell, for all we know she hopped in a dude's car and drove off to Vegas to get married, not our problem. This surfboard is mine, and as you can see, I'm not dead."

"And the shark attack victim?" Hershel asked.

"Chief, have you ever covered up a shark attack? Or have any of your predecessors? Be honest, because I have never heard of one."

"No, I swear, this is the first time in the history of this police station that a shark has ever attacked someone."

"OK, that's what I thought. And that's the problem. I find it hard to believe that a shark would just come and attack someone like that randomly, and then leave. Usually sharks attack people thinking they're seals or turtles, or if the people get too close to them when they're feeding, which they don't do this close to the island. Now, if Bill Henson had been swimming by the rocks and say, cracked his head open, the blood would certainly attract a shark, which would then eat his body, making it look like a shark attack. But Bill was a local; he wouldn't have been night swimming by the rocks. Every local knows better. That's what's been bothering me, and I think even though you couldn't quite put your finger on it, that's what was bothering you, Chief. On top of that"—she looked further at his file—"he had a prosthetic leg, fine for walking but not for swimming. This man wouldn't have voluntarily gone in the water at night, and a shark wouldn't have been there to bite him. It doesn't add up."

Judy rushed into the office. "Chief, we, uh, we have a problem."

The chief answered the phone and a few moments later hung up. He looked around the room. "You youngsters are not to tell a soul about what I'm about to say, you either, Mr. Meyer. We may have a killer on our hands."

"What? No, that, that's impossible!" Hershel said shakily.

"We haven't confirmed it, but this is a suspicious death. A boy was found frozen under the shredded ice at a seafood restaurant."

"I have to report this! The people need to know!" Hershel exclaimed.

"Give us twenty-four hours to get the facts straight," the chief told him. "If it turns out to be just two unfortunate events happening around the same time, you can report that since it won't cause any panic, and if it is a killer, we may be able to catch him before the public finds out, and again, there will be no need to panic. I have to make some calls."

Hershel Meyer left quickly, looking shaken. The police officer had left to help the chief, leaving the group there with Archie Smith.

"No need to worry, children. I'm sure this is all a big misunderstanding," he said suavely. Felicity resisted the urge to hit him; she hated being treated like a child.

Gio turned to them. "Maybe we should step outside guys?"

They went outside and as soon as the door shut behind them Gio jabbed Felicity in the side with his hand causing her to yelp and recoil.

"What are you doing?" she demanded.

"You're a liar," he told her smugly.

She crossed her arms and shot daggers with her eyes. "I don't appreciate being called a liar."

"Then don't lie to people," he retorted. "The surfboard, it was yours. You said so in there. You're the girl who saved me, aren't you?"

Damn, I should've just let this guy get eaten, she thought to herself. She looked to Cara who just stared like a deer in headlights.

"That's none of your business," Felicity told him after a moment of thought. Weak response, she knew, but she was backed into a corner.

"Gio, back up," Vito told his brother. "I don't think she's human." All eyes turned to Vito.

"She was surfing in the dark, which already tells us she has better night vision than normal. She's walking around just fine after a shark bite that should have killed her, and she was able to hear everything they were saying in the chief's office. She can also punch harder than most guys out there. She's not human; look at her."

Gio looked at Felicity, his eyes slowly widening as he realized there was something just slightly off about her. The lack of color in her skin, the way she spoke, all of it. She could see fear settle in his eyes.

Cara looked at Felicity. "This is not good."

"You guys are being weird. Of course I'm a human. The shark bite just wasn't as bad as it looked."

"Show us," Vito challenged. He was smart, far smarter than she had expected.

"OK, how about we go back to the car," she said, hoping maybe a distraction would present itself.

She got her wish, although not in the way she expected. A silver BMW pulled up and out came the blue-haired twins. Out of the driver's seat came none other than Penelope Smith. She directed a look of disgust at Felicity as she walked past. A moment later, the police officer from before came out and asked Cara and Felicity to step back inside. When they entered they saw Penelope next to her father, looking smug. The chief walked over to Felicity and Cara.

"This girl says you would have reason to murder Josh Warrick," the police chief told them grimly.

"Josh is dead?" Cara exclaimed sounding dismayed, "He was from the mainland on one of the shore towns. He came every year to be a lifeguard here. I worked with him," she said to Felicity in response to her questioning look.

"Why would either of us have had any reason to kill him?" Felicity asked.

"According to Miss. Smith over there, you were asked to leave a party. You got violent after Mr. Warrick tried to escort you out," the police chief told her.

"I'm sorry, are you saying that because I pushed a man off of me after he grabbed me, you think I killed him?"

"You or your creepy boyfriend," Penelope chimed in.

"My what?" Felicity said, completely lost. She had never had a boyfriend in her life, much less a creepy one.

"He got kicked out too, for putting on some awful like 1950s music or something," Penelope informed the room.

"It was actually from the forties," Felicity corrected. "He wasn't my boyfriend. I met him that night for the first time. I mentioned that the music sucked and that I wished there was some swing music. He put it on. He and I were kicked out, that's it. We didn't even leave together," Felicity said in a tone that left no room for dispute.

"And what did you do after leaving the party? Come back and kill that boy for ruining your night?" the police officer asked in a tone that made her think he was trying to play bad cop. He was certainly doing a good job at being a bad cop, she thought.

"I went for a surf," she told the chief.

"In the middle of the night?" the chief said incredulously.

Cara nodded. "I can confirm she does that every night."

"I'm the island's surf champion, as was my mother, and grandmother, and great-grandmother," Felicity said in an ever-so-slightly haughty voice.

"Oh! I'm sorry, I've watched you surf before, but well with the, erm, suit I never knew what you looked like!" the police chief said apologetically. Felicity was somewhat of a legend on the island. Every few years she would fake her death and pretend to be the daughter of herself. People eventually started assuming her family just had very strong genes. She had been winning the island's surf competition since 1957 when it first began, although no one knew it was her since she was covered from head to toe to hide from the deadly sun.

"Wait a minute, can you prove you were night surfing?" the police officer demanded.

"You found my surfboard. I surfed for a while by myself and then those boys outside saw me," Felicity said as she gestured toward the door.

The police officer walked out and after a minute or so came back in looking put out. "They said they saw her last night," he said, sounding embarrassed. "But wait a minute! Miss Smith, what time did that boy leave the party?"

"I have no idea. Do you guys know?" Penelope asked the twins.

"He tried to get me to take a rum shot with him while Stacy was throwing up," the boy twin said, his voice soft and slightly breathy.

"Oscar! Don't tell them that!" Stacy screeched.

Penelope silenced her with a wave of her hand, "She was vomiting around one, maybe one fifteen."

"And you were still surfing then?" the chief asked Felicity.

"I think I was home by then," Felicity said. "Cara was with me the rest of the night, we both slept in the TV room by the couch."

"Can confirm." Cara nodded. "What happened to Josh?"

"So what do we know about this boy who was kicked out?" the chief inquired.

"I know he works at that German place, the one on the little island. I don't know its name," Penelope said smugly.

"May we leave?" Felicity asked, trying to sound as polite as possible.

"Yes, your story seems to check out. Remember, keep this to yourselves, alright?" the chief reminded them.

"Of course!" Felicity said as she ushered the others out of the station. "Oh, by the way, the boy's name is Basil." She hurried out and hopped into the white SUV.

"What do you think you're doing?" Joey protested.

"I think we're going to the German place. It's open late since it has a bar in it. Let's go, Gio. Drive. Drive!"

Gio started the car and they began driving. "Where are we going?" Gio asked.

"Go like you're going toward the mainland; I'll let you know when to turn," Cara told him.

"So are we going to address the elephant in the room or what?" Vito asked.

"Are you calling me fat?" Cara said, trying her best to sound offended.

"How are you not still injured? Explain yourself."

Felicity would normally berate them until they dropped the subject, but in this case she needed them to get her to the restaurant before the police got there. She knew she had a small window while the police conducted interviews of Penelope and the twins and got their facts together, but she also knew they would be moving as quickly as they could. She needed to be quicker.

"Prove to me I can trust you guys, and I'll explain everything." She wondered if they would call her out for trying to dodge the question.

"Deal," Gio said.

"Hold on now," Vito argued. "She needs us to get where she's going before the police do. I say we make her walk if she won't tell us. What's to stop her from just ditching us after?"

Felicity grimaced. That had been what she was planning. This boy was irritating, no doubt about it. *I could kill him*, she thought to herself. *I could probably kill them all and just take the car.* Of course, with the police out looking for a murderer, killing three boys when she was the last one seen with them would be a misstep. She began to go through the odds of being able to take out the whole police force. No, no. She shook her head.

"What's to stop you from posting what I tell you all over the internet?" she asked. Maybe she could still push this trust angle.

"What's to stop us from doing it now?" Vito said smugly.

"You have no proof," she retorted.

"I don't need proof, just speculation and a name. People will ask questions. I'm guessing you want to keep a low profile."

Ugh. He was right. He had her. Of course the last person to look too closely into her had been a reporter back in the day. She had made him disappear. No one had ever looked into her again.

"See, you're blackmailing me. I don't trust you."

"Turn down this little bridge," Cara yelled.

They went down a small bridge, which took them to an island with a few houses and a large German restaurant up on top of large wooden pylons. There was a dock where people could drive up on boats to eat.

"Alright, I'm going to go in alone. Basil is a shy guy so we don't want to overwhelm him," Felicity said as she exited the SUV and walked into the restaurant.

"Guten Tag," the host, a young man in Lederhosen greeted her as she entered. "Table for one?"

"Oh, no thank you. I'm actually looking for a boy named Basil. He works here."

"Basil the dishwasher? Yes, he's in the kitchen."

"Could you please get him for me?" she asked with as sweet a smile as she could muster.

"Oh alright. Wait here."

The host hurried off to the kitchen and came back with a confused looking Basil.

"Felicity, uh hi! Um, what are you doing here?" he asked her nervously.

"Where did you go last night?"

"Why? You weren't looking for me were you?" he asked, sounding afraid that she might think he had stood her up.

She held out her hands, trying to calm him down. "Hey, breathe, it's fine, I wasn't looking for you. I just want to know where you went."

"I went home, watched anime until three a.m.," he said, sounding slightly embarrassed.

"Can you prove that?" she asked earnestly.

"I mean, I guess. I have the search history on my computer," he told her, a note of suspicion in his voice. "Why?"

"Because—" Flashing lights caught her eye. "Meet me at Lorraine's Tavern as soon as you can. Don't tell anyone that I was here, please." She strode toward the back door. Just as the police were approaching the front door, she walked out the back and around the patio that surrounded the entirety of the restaurant. She peered out into the parking lot and saw no sign of other officers, so she walked casually to the SUV, which Gio had cleverly moved to the other side of the parking lot. She hopped in and he began to drive away.

"Where to now?"

"I need to talk to Penelope," Felicity informed them.

"Why would you want to talk to that stuck up little rich girl?" Cara asked as she wrinkled her nose in disgust.

"It's not a question of desire, Cara. It's a question of necessity. Penelope's dad apparently knows all the secret goings on of this island. I'm guessing she stayed and listened as the police told him all the details of this maybe murder. I need to know what the police know," Felicity explained.

"Because you killed him?" Joey said accusingly.

"What?" Felicity asked, sounding only slightly less irritated than she felt.

"You're what? Like, some kind of weird government super mutant, right?" Joey said as if she should already have known that.

"You're insane," she said.

"Listen Felicity, I'm not driving you anywhere if you aren't going to be honest with us," Gio said.

Cara looked at her. "Maybe you should just tell them."

Felicity gave her a wide-eyed, almost scared look. She'd never told anyone outside of Connie's family that she was a vampire. Why should she start with these boys she barely knew?

"So you admit there is something to tell," Vito said knowingly.

"Can I trust you to keep it?"

"Of course!" Joey declared boldly.

"You can," Gio said in a gentler tone.

"And you, Vito?" she asked after a moment of silence.

"I wouldn't say you can trust me, but I won't tell your secret."

"I'm a vampire," she told them.

She didn't know what reaction she had been expecting, but silence was not it.

"A vampire," Gio said finally, phrasing it somewhere between a statement and a question.

"Yes."

"Do you drink blood?" Joey asked her skeptically.

"Yes, that's the literal definition of a vampire," Vito said condescendingly. "And by the way, she didn't kill this guy. She killed the girl who went missing, the mainlander."

Felicity felt her heart drop, the icy tendrils of fear sinking into her. He knew. This perceptive little punk knew. She was going to have to kill him. She just hoped Cara would understand.

"Hold on now," Cara argued. "You have no evidence she killed that girl."

"She dismissed it as the girl being a mainlander too quickly. She really thinks a killer is on the loose who may have made a shark attack look like an accident. It's bad detective work to dismiss a mysterious disappearance as just a drugged-up party girl drowning. The police wouldn't have questioned her motives for it because they don't have all the facts."

She should kill him. It would be the safe thing to do. But he was smart. Brilliant even. She might need that, so for now, against her better judgement, this boy to live.

"You can't tell anyone any of this," she said finally, an almost plaintive note in her voice. "I only kill to survive."

"And you need to catch this killer quickly because if the public finds out, they'll be on guard, which will make hunting harder for you," Gio said, his eyes going wide as his brain worked the information out. He was perceptive as well, although she found him significantly more pleasant than Vito. "So where is Penelope?" Gio asked.

"That I can't tell you, because I myself do not know," Felicity told him

"She's at a party on Cherokee street," Cara chimed in.

"How would you know that?" Felicity asked, impressed.

"Andrew invited me to it. If he's going, odds are she'll be there with the twins at some point," Cara explained.

"Alright boys, are you up for a party?" Felicity asked. She knew Basil would be with the police for quite a while so she knew she didn't have to worry about missing their meeting.

They pulled up to a blue two family house on Cherokee Street.

“Andrew’s not from the island,” Cara explained, “but his family owns this house. They use the bottom part for themselves whenever they want a vacation and they rent the top part out to guests. Andrew convinced them to rent to a bunch of frat guys from Pennsylvania and now they’re having a sort of combined house party.”

“Genius!” Joey said with admiration.

“Is it open house? I know some frats charge a cover fee for their parties,” Gio said.

“Only one way to find out,” Felicity said, steeling herself for what she knew was about to be a very loud and crowded experience for her.

Gio parked on the street and they walked up to the house where two boys who looked to be about Cara’s age stood outside the door, one with a large plastic jar of cash and the other with a baseball bat.

“Cara, do you know them?” Felicity asked.

“Not well. They’re both mainlanders who frequent the island. The one with the jar of money is Tony. He’s always out to make cash and he doesn’t care how he does it. The one with the bat is Kev. He’s got bad anger issues,” Cara told her.

“Ten dollars for girls, twenty for guys,” Tony told them in a bored tone.

“Andrew told me to come. He didn’t tell me I had to pay,” Cara told him, doing her best to sound angry.

“Doesn’t matter. Everybody pays,” Tony told her, clearly he’d heard this from every girl tonight.

“And what’s to stop us from going to someone else’s party?” Gio asked, trying to sound like he couldn’t care less where he went.

“Because anyone who would throw a party worth going to is already coming here. Now you can either go get drunk in some nobody’s basement for free, or you can pay the cover and get into a real party. But you can’t stay here,” he told them with only a small amount of derision in his voice, although Kev had taken a step closer, which gave everything a slightly more menacing feel.

"At least tell us this before we pay: Is Penelope Smith here?" Felicity asked them, her patience wearing as thin as theirs.

"What are you deaf? I told you, everyone who's anyone. You think the richest chick on the island isn't gonna be here?" Tony said, contempt dripping from his voice.

Felicity knew she should just pay the fee. It really wasn't much in the grand scheme of things. They could get in and out without causing a scene. But she was annoyed. These punks needed to learn how to respect their elders. She turned to Kev.

"How about a bet?" she asked him.

"What kind of bet?" he asked, eyeing her up and down.

"You seem like a strong guy, yes?" she asked. He was larger than Tony, fatter but definitely also stronger.

"Oh yeah, I'm the strongest guy here, no doubt, no doubt," he said, flexing his pectorals to prove his point.

"Mhm. I'm sure, but I bet that means you're really slow too. Probably couldn't even hit someone if you tried," she said with a sly smile.

"Oh yeah? Ask anyone! I've won every fight I've ever been in," he said angrily.

"Well, that's the bet. I want you to hit me as hard as you can. I'll give you two tries. If you can do it, me and my friends will not only pay double cover, but I'll let you do whatever you want to me. You miss both times, we get that whole jar," she told him matter-of-factly.

"No way!" Tony exclaimed.

"Wow, your friend doesn't think you're fast enough," Vito mocked.

Kev turned bright red. "I'm not gonna hit a girl."

At least he's not a complete piece of garbage, she thought to herself. She slapped him in the face and saw anger cross his features.

"What's wrong, big guy? Afraid?" she mocked.

"Maybe you should be the one sipping beer in a basement and she should be the one with the bat," Joey said with a mocking laugh.

"Fine, but you'd better keep your end of the deal. Anything I want after," Kev said, putting down his bat and taking a step closer so he was in front of her. He threw what Felicity guessed was a half strength punch and she easily moved out of the way. She took the opportunity to slap him in the face again, harder this time. Everyone laughed and pointed at him, even Tony. Kev's cheek hurt but not as much as his pride did. *Fine,* he thought. She wanted his all, she was gonna get his all. Without a word, he took a small step and threw his strongest punch right at her face. If Felicity had been a normal girl, she would have been seriously injured by this punch. *I guess he's not the gentleman I thought he was,* she mused to herself as she dodged easily to the side. Her plan had worked perfectly. Kev's fist collided with Tony's face and knocked him to the ground, spilling his cash everywhere. Gio, Joey, and Vito scrambled to pick it up.

"I guess we win," she told him with a grin.

Kev was madder than ever now. He didn't care about any stupid bet. This girl was going down. He threw another punch just as hard as the first, but a little quicker. It still wasn't quick enough to catch a vampire off guard. Especially not a vampire who had been expecting it. She had already picked up the bat and as the boy's fist came at her gut full force, she simply moved the bat in front of it. Holding it with her deceptively strong vampiric hands, she felt his bones crack and split as his fist collided with the bat. He howled in pain and doubled over, clutching his hand. Felicity, Gio, Cara, Vito, and Joey entered the party, leaving the two boys to bleed and cry on the front porch. Cara stuffed the cash into her purse. They could divide it later.

The party itself looked amazing. There were two decks on the back of the house, both with incredible views and connected by a wooden staircase on each side. The front door guys had been right, this party had everyone worth knowing.

“Spread out,” Felicity commanded. “See if anyone knows anything else, but be discreet. We don’t want to cause a panic”

The group split up. Joey went to flirt with some girls and Gio went to the cooler and cracked open a beer, while Vito just leaned against a wall near a group of people having a conversation. Cara walked over to Andrew and slid under his arm, giving him a hug from the side.

“Hey beautiful, you made it,” he said with a lazy smile.

“How could I miss the party of the summer?” she teased.

“The first of many, don’t you worry. Can I get you anything to drink?” he offered.

“Yeah, that would be great. What do you have?”

“You name it, I have it babe,” he told her as he gestured around them.

“Oh yeah? Can you make me a French seventy-five?” she challenged.

“What is this, amateur hour? Of course I can.” He left and came back a few moments later holding two fancy stemmed glasses. He handed one to her. “A toast,” he said as he raised his glass. “To me, for throwing such a great party!”

“Here here!” two very drunk boys shouted as they knocked their glasses together.

“I’ll drink to that,” Cara told him, clinking her glass carefully against his and taking a sip. “So you know everyone there is to know around here right?” she asked him.

“Of course I do. Everyone worth knowing, at least.”

“Do you know a guy named Josh?”

"Josh T?"

"No, Warrick."

"Ohhh that Josh. Yeah, I know him. He lifeguards here every year. Not a bad guy, always gets too turnt. Why? You're not into him are you?" he asked in a tone that made it clear he thought that would be a mistake.

"No, no, no, but uh, I was wondering if you saw him last night?" she asked, unable to think of an excuse for why.

"I did. I saw a lot of people. Why do you want to know?" Andrew was clearly curious. She would have to think of something quick.

"I'm testing you," she said. *Brilliant, Cara,* she thought to herself. *Now he's going to want to know what you're testing him for.*

"What are you testing me for?" he asked, exactly as she had predicted.

"Well, you claim to know everyone. Do you know who he left with?" she said, challenging him once more. She knew enough about him to know that he was confident, cocky even. He wouldn't miss a chance to prove he was the best to her.

"I'm sure I would if I had seen him leave," he said defiantly.

"Well, no prize for you if you don't tell me their name," she said flirtatiously.

"Prize?" he asked, his eyes moving so quickly down her body that had she not been watching his reaction so closely she wouldn't have noticed.

"Yeah, but you don't get anything until I get a name," she told him, crossing her arms.

He grinned at her. "Let me ask around." He downed his drink and walked off to go hunt down a name for her.

Felicity had located Penelope. The only problem was, Penelope hated her. Penelope apparently hated her enough to accuse her of murder, so she was going to need to be tactful about this. She walked up to Penelope, who was dressed in designer jeans, a white crop top and a pink leather jacket. She had tied the whole outfit together with large hoop earrings. *I could threaten to rip them out,* Felicity thought to herself. Of course, that would draw quite a bit of attention to herself.

"Ew what are you doing here?" Penelope said, interrupting Felicity's thoughts.

"Actually, I wanted to talk to you," she replied. Maybe honesty was the best policy.

"Sorry, I don't talk to albino freaks from the forties," Penelope said in disgust.

Albino is a bit far, Felicity thought, *but the forties thing is spot on.* If only she knew. Felicity smiled at the thought and Penelope scowled. "Why don't you go practice surfing or something?" Penelope sneered.

"I'd love to. In fact, I would love to leave this whole noisy, booze-soaked house, but first I need to talk to you," Felicity said, growing irritated.

"And I told you," Penelope said, sounding just as irritated, "that I don't talk to freaks. So why don't you go flapper dance yourself out of here before I get you kicked out again." There was a hint of a challenge in her voice now. She believed she'd won and Felicity would walk away with her tail between her legs as so many others had done.

"A flapper never would have done that dance; it was from the forties. Flappers are from the twenties," Felicity informed her. "And I will gladly go. However, if I do, I'm going to tell everyone about what I learned tonight, and I'm going to tell them that you told me. We'll see how Daddy feels when he finds out his daughter has been hurting his business."

Penelope blanched. "You wouldn't! You'd get arrested!"

“Yes, but so would you. We’d probably both get put under house arrest for a few weeks. No parties, no mall trips. Which is fine with me. I hate the mall, and I hate parties. What about you?”

“Ugh, fine.” She turned to the two girls she had been talking to. “Could you guys give us a minute?” When the two girls were out of earshot, she turned back to Felicity, and asked, “What,”

“Tell me what the police told you about Josh Warrick. I’m sure you and your dad waited and learned what the police know,” Felicity said, getting straight to the point.

“If I tell you, will you promise to leave the party?” Penelope asked.

“Yes, deal, now tell me what you know,” Felicity said impatiently.

“Alright but keep it to yourself. Josh was super drunk. He had passed out in the display case where they keep the fresh fish at a restaurant. They empty it every night so there was room for him. Someone had filled it with ice covering him and he froze to death. The door had been unlocked with Josh’s own keys. No one had noticed he was in there until they emptied the case tonight. That’s all I know. Now go,” Penelope demanded.

Felicity took a step back, her head reeling. She had been suspicious before, but she was certain now. There was a killer on the island.

CHAPTER 3

Felicity didn't say anything the entire ride back to the tavern. The others watched her with concern. She had pulled them all brusquely out of the party. She was too deep in her own mind to explain to them what was going on. There was a killer at the beach. A killer. At her beach. Someone had the audacity to come to her beach, her island, her *home* and start killing her people. She wouldn't stand for it.

"I won't stand for it," she said menacingly. Everyone in the car was startled.

"Won't stand for what?" Joey asked.

"I won't let someone come into my home and kill people. I'm going to find them," she told him in a low growl.

"And then turn them into the police?" Gio asked from behind the wheel.

"No. I'm going to eliminate them. If I tell the police, then there's a chance they can get off. The police could botch the evidence. Plus, I'd have to go to court which would make me fairly well known. I like keeping a low profile."

"Besides," Vito added, "if she turns him in to the police, they'll tell everyone there was a killer. She's hoping if she kills the killer, then no one will panic and she can keep on being a killer. Am I right?"

"Yes," she admitted.

Vito nodded. “The wolf must protect the sheep from the cougar so it can continue to hunt the sheep.”

Felicity scowled. She didn’t need his stupid metaphors.

They arrived at the tavern and found a booth in the back. The bouncer didn’t give them any trouble for being underage since Cara and Felicity partially owned the place.

“Alright,” Felicity said as she looked around the booth like she was conducting a business meeting, “what did you all find out?”

“Andrew doesn’t know who Josh left with but he’s going to try to find out for me,” Cara said.

“The two guys at the drink table didn’t even know who Josh was,” Gio said with a shrug.

“The girl I was talking to said she hadn’t been at the party, but had a friend who was. I got the girl’s number,” Joey said, sticking his tongue out and nodding with a big grin.

“Wipe that stupid look off your face,” Felicity snapped. “Did you get the number of the girl who saw Josh, or the number of the girl you were talking to?”

“The number of the girl I was talking to. She was cute. I wasn’t going to ask too much about her friend, that would give her the wrong impression,” Joey said.

Gio smacked him on his bruise.

“Ow!” Joey cried, rubbing his chest.

Cara turned to Vito. “What about you?”

Vito shook his head. “I eavesdropped on a few conversations; no one mentioned him.”

Gio looked at Felicity. “What did you find out, you seem a lot more… edgy.”

"I spoke to Penelope. She's as annoying as ever, but as I guessed, she knew enough. Basically, the guy went to the seafood restaurant he worked at, used his keys to unlock the door, then laid down in the fresh fish display."

"The one with all the ice?" Joey asked.

"That's the one, they drain it every night, so he laid down in it and then someone buried him in ice. He died from freezing to death and no one noticed until tonight. Which means someone killed him. Since that shark attack seemed fishy to me to begin with, I'm now sure there's some kind of killer on the island," Felicity said.

"So how do we find them?" Cara asked.

"Felicity will find them with her super vampire powers!" Joey declared earning him a swift kick from Felicity.

"Do not *ever* mention me being a you-know-what in public again. Ever," she told him angrily.

"You do have su— uh, I mean, what exactly can you do?" Gio asked her.

Felicity gave a deep and prolonged sigh before answering. "I can see in the dark, all of my senses are heightened greater than those of a human, I'm stronger than someone of my build should be, I'm inhumanly quick, I heal a hundred times faster than a normal person, I don't ever get tired, and with a few exceptions, I cannot die or be killed. Cara, am I forgetting anything?"

Cara thought for a moment. "Mosquitoes never bite you."

"Yeah and that. Super detective work, however, is not on my list of skills."

"So what do we do?" Joey asked.

"Why are you asking me? I just said I have no idea what I'm doing," Felicity said as she looked around at the expectant expressions on their faces.

"Well, you are the oldest," Cara reminded her.

"Wait, how old are you?" Gio asked her.

"Older than I look," she replied cryptically. She opened her mouth to say more but her eye was caught by the bearded bartender walking toward her.

"Felicity, call for you," he said. "Someone named Basil, he says he's not allowed out of the house and can't meet with you tonight."

"Thank you, Felix," she told him.

He gave a small nod and went back to the bar. He had been working there as a bartender for about seven years now, and Felicity considered him fairly reliable.

"I guess there's nothing to do but wait now," Cara said. "Maybe Andrew will come through with a name of someone we can talk to."

"I guess we should head home then," Gio said.

"We'll be in touch," Felicity told him.

"Please be safe, guys," Cara said, her eyebrows drawn together in concern.

Joey gave her a grin and flexed his arms. "Don't you worry, I'll take care of any bad guys that come our way."

Cara laughed at this and even Felicity couldn't stop a small smile from coming to her lips.

Cara brushed her teeth while Felicity leaned against the bathroom wall. She had no need for brushing her teeth as she was immune to the effects of decay. She did enjoy the smell of mint that wafted from the toothpaste to her sensitive vampiric nose, however.

"Good night, Cara," Felicity said once Cara had completed her bedtime rituals.

Felicity turned and began walking toward the stairs.

"Wait, Fel," Cara called to her. Felicity stopped on the stairs and turned toward Cara, arching one brow.

"Yes?"

"Could you sleep in my bed tonight?" Cara asked her, sounding embarrassed.

Felicity chuckled and walked back toward Cara's room.

"It's just, you know, with the killer on the loose, I'd rather have a vampire watching over me, making sure no one, like, breaks in or anything. You know?" Cara explained.

Felicity just patted her on the head and crawled into bed, going as close to the wall as possible. Cara crawled into bed next to her, maneuvering herself so there was a little bit of space between them. Sleeping with Felicity was always an odd experience for Cara as Felicity's body gave off no heat, so Cara never had the sensation of cuddling with a living human. They had worked out years ago that if Felicity moved to the bed's edge and slept leaning against the wall, Cara would have enough room to comfortably lay in bed without actually contacting Felicity's cold undead flesh. Felicity also made no sound as she lay there, since she had no need to breathe. Cara was grateful for her presence nonetheless as Felicity always made her feel safe. As a child, Cara had never feared monsters under her bed or in the dark because she knew her friend would spot them and protect her. Cara smiled as she settled into her bed, the memories of her childhood lulling her to sleep.

Felicity lay there awake and agitated. She had revealed herself as a vampire for the first time in her life to people outside of the family. Would they tell others about her? No one would believe them, of course, but if they put the idea out there, people might start to connect dots and eventually she would be exposed. That was a problem she may need to address later. For now, she had a killer to contend with. Maybe, if she was lucky, the killer would simply leave the island and go somewhere else. That would be fine with her. Cara's phone lit up in the dark room. *Kids these days are always texting,* she thought. Hopefully it was Andrew texting her with the name of the last person to see Josh alive.

Felicity could tell the sun was rising, even with the blackout curtains. She got up without disturbing Cara and began preparing the kitchen for the day's cooking. There was an edge to her movements. She was anxious for the sun to go down and to get searching for the killer again. *Maybe this was how normal vampires feel during the day,* she mused to herself. She had only ever met one vampire – the one who had turned her. She had no idea if there were others or not, but she always pictured them as gothic predators waiting for the sun to go down so they could hunt their human prey.

Cara got up around noon to go to work. She put on her the blue tank top and gold short shorts that all the badge check girls wore as a uniform. She brushed out her chestnut hair and sat down at the kitchen table. Felicity had laid out her brunch like she did every day. Two eggs sunny side up and a piece of rye toast. Cara ate it all and left for work. She was almost to the beach when she heard screams. She was used to screams at the beach; children always shrieked when they played and women often screamed as their boyfriends dunked them in the water. But this was different. This was a scream of terror. She rushed to the beach and saw a group of people gathered around an arm sticking out of the sand. Two children cried as they clutched shovels and were held by their mother.

"What's going on here?" she demanded.

Chuck, the brawny lifeguard with the frizzy hair, answered, "These kids were digging and found what I'm assuming is a dead body. Tiff already called the police. For now I'm just trying to get the crowd to break up. We've radioed in for back up from the next chair."

Within minutes, lifeguards and badge checkers were pushing back an ever-growing crowd. Four reporters started taking pictures.

"Lifeguard, lifeguard, who was it that found the body?" a young woman in a blue pantsuit asked Chuck.

"Ma'am, I'm not answering any questions. Please step back," Chuck told her.

"You don't think they were buried alive do you?" Hershel Meyer asked nervously. "That's always been a big fear of mine."

"Someone must've killed them then," a middle-aged man with a square jaw remarked.

"Alright, alright, everyone, get back!" the police chief said as he arrived with the entire police force. "Officers, take these reporters in for questioning."

"What? This is ridiculous. You can't do that!" the man with the square jaw protested.

"Legally, we can take anyone in for questioning, and I suspect you four may have something to do with the murder. If I have reasonable suspicion, I can keep you for up to twenty-four hours. Take 'em away!" the police chief shouted. "Lifeguards, get these people out of here. I want the beach from that chair to that chair over there shut down. No one gets by, got it?" The lifeguards got to work clearing the beach.

"Cara, you can probably go home," Chuck told her.

Cara nodded and began walking home. Fel was not going to be happy about this. Cara walked nervously into the kitchen.

"Hey, Fel, I—I have some news for you," she said uneasily.

"What is it?"

"You're not going to like this," Cara began, "but there's been another body found."

Felicity gripped the knife handle so tightly she was worried she would split the handle.

"What happened?" Felicity asked, her voice struggling to remain calm.

"Well, everything seemed normal until someone was digging in the sand and they found, well, an arm. The lifeguards called the police, and they asked all the beach staff to get everyone out of there. There were a bunch of reporters and the police took them in for questioning. They said they could keep them for twenty-four hours."

"Smart," Felicity mused. "The reporters can't report anything if they're stuck in the police station. The police just bought themselves twenty-four hours. Bad news is, after that twenty-four hours, there's going to be panic like this island has never seen."

"Which means we have twenty-four hours to solve this?" Cara said, more a statement than a question.

"Call the boys," Felicity commanded. "Ask them what time they're off work."

"Can't I just text them?" Cara asked as she took out her phone. "Oh good news Fel, Andrew texted me, he knows who drove Josh home."

"What!? Why didn't you say so sooner!?" Felicity was practically shouting.

"Chill, I haven't checked my phone this morning," Cara told her.

Normally, now would be the time people would take a deep breath to calm themselves. Felicity had long ago lost that instinct, since breathing really didn't do anything for her. She instead opted to pace anxiously around the kitchen. Cara observed her for a moment. Felicity wasn't usually one to get worked up and Cara was a little unnerved watching her friend. Felicity moved with the deadly grace of a jungle cat and something deep inside of Cara recognized that she was in an enclosed space with a deadly predator. Felicity stopped and turned to face Cara.

"Sorry, just a little antsy. Who is it that we'll be visiting tonight?" Felicity asked, her voice chillingly calm.

"Gully," Cara told her, bracing herself for a reaction.

"Gully?" Felicity asked, the tension in her breaking at the familiar name.

"Yeah, you know," Cara said, grinning despite the severity of the situation, "your boyfriend."

Felicity narrowed her eyes at Cara, who burst out laughing.

Gio pulled up with Vito and Joey in his SUV five minutes before sunset. Felicity wrapped herself in a blanket to protect herself from the sun, and hopped into the car. The sun was just about to dip fully under the horizon as they pulled up to a restaurant on a white and green boat.

Gulliver "Gully" McMahon was a stocky boy with a nose ring and a perpetual five o'clock shadow. His father had always dreamed of leaving his office job and becoming an adventurer. When Gully was thirteen, his father had sold their house and bought their boat, the "Traveler." He and Gully lived on it year round and every summer parked it at their own private dock to use as a restaurant. The Traveler had been a long-time sponsor of Felicity's and every year they invited her and Cara's family to eat after she won the surfing competition. It had been love at first sight for Gully from the moment he met her.

Felicity and her crew walked into the Traveler and when Gully saw them he almost dropped the tray of drinks he was carrying. He hastily put the tray down and walked up to them, a shy smile on his face.

"Hey Felicity, do you need a table?" he asked her, not quite making eye contact.

Neither Joey nor Cara could contain their laughter while Gio covered his mouth in an attempt to keep the grin off his face.

"No thanks, Gully. Could I get a word with you though?" she asked him, ignoring the others.

Gully looked like he was about to faint from excitement. "Of course you can! You can always have a word, whenever you want!" he told her, nodding enthusiastically and following them to a quieter corner of the bustling restaurant.

“You were at the party at the twin’s house the other night?” Felicity asked him.

“I was! Did you go? I didn’t see you there,” he said.

“She got kicked out early,” Cara informed him.

“No way! I’m sorry. I didn’t realize. When I throw a party, I promise I’ll invite you and kick out anyone you don’t like,” he told her, barely stopping for breath.

“Hey, buddy, focus,” Joey told him gesturing with two fingers to Gully’s eyes and then back to his own.

“Sorry, so what’s up?” Gully asked, gaining some composure.

“What’s up is that you drove Josh home that night didn’t you?” Cara asked him.

“Yeah, he was waaaay drunk,” Gully told her.

“So you drove him where?” Gio asked suspiciously.

“Home, like, to his house,” Gully said, sounding a little confused. “Why?”

“So you dropped him off at home and then what?” Cara said, ignoring the question.

“And then I grabbed my scooter out of the back, locked the car, put the keys in his pocket and went home. Why are you asking me this?” Gully asked again, this time sounding concerned.

Vito spoke up. “Did he say anything to you on the way home?”

“Nothing unusual, just kept going on and on about how hot Penelope was and how he was going to get with her,” Gully said. “Why, has something happened?”

"I will answer your question. I just need you to answer mine first, OK?" Felicity told him, putting a hand on his arm.

Gully's whole faced flushed red at this. "O-OK," he stammered.

Vito rolled his eyes, "Do you remember what else he said?"

"No, that's it, he was really hung up on the idea of hooking up with Penelope. Kept saying she was going to meet up with him and they were going to hook up. I swear that's all he talked about the whole ride home," Gully told them. Felicity believed him; he seemed sincere.

"Thanks, Gully," she said and hugged him. He practically melted. The group hurried back to the car while he stood there, star-struck.

"Wow, way to use your feminine wiles to distract that guy," Joey said, nudging Felicity.

"Hush," she told him brusquely.

"I keep telling her they'd make a cute couple," Cara teased.

"Yeah, you could live out on his boat," Vito said mockingly.

"Cara, where does Penelope live?" Gio asked.

Felicity shot him a grateful look and he nodded as he started up the car. He followed Cara's instructions and soon they were outside of Penelope Smith's three-story aqua mansion, the largest private home on the island.

"So what's the plan?" Vito asked.

"Simple," Felicity said as she opened the car door, "I sneak in and interrogate her."

Gio grabbed her arm as she tried to leave. She closed the door and looked at him.

"What?" she demanded.

"You're very cold," he said, letting go of her and looking at his hand.

"She's always like that. It's because she's technically dead," Cara informed him.

"Neat!" Joey exclaimed. Everyone took a moment to glare at him.

"I think we need another plan," Gio said.

"Why's that?" Felicity asked him, slightly irate.

"Because if she calls the police and they bring you in for questioning, chances are they're going to let you go tomorrow, which means you'll have to either explain why you're refusing to leave the station until nightfall, or burn to ash," Gio told her in an only slightly patronizing tone.

Felicity crossed her arms. "OK, so what's your plan?"

Gio smiled. "We knock on the door."

The group walked up to the front door and rang the bell. When no one answered, they rang again.

"Maybe it's broken?" Cara offered.

"No, shhh," Felicity said, motioning for them to be quiet. She could make out the faintest sound of swimming. Felicity walked around to the other side of the mansion and inhaled through her nose – chlorine. She came upon a pair of glass doors and peered through. As she suspected, there was a pool and in it, she could make out the small platinum blonde figure of Penelope swimming laps in the pool. She was surprisingly fast. Felicity had known she was decent at surfing since she competed in the big island surf competition each year, but she was an amazing swimmer. Felicity waited until Penelope grabbed the edge of the pool and stopped a timer lying nearby before she rapped on the glass door. Penelope let out a yelp of surprise and almost dropped her timer. Felicity gave a small unenthusiastic wave when Penelope looked at the door.

Penelope stormed up to the door and unlocked it. "What are you doing here, creep?" she demanded as she threw the door open.

“It’s about Josh,” Felicity said, her tone and face completely neutral.

“Ugh, again with Josh. I’ve already told you everything I know!” Penelope said irritably, attempting to shut the door in Felicity’s face.

Felicity caught the door and held it with one hand. Penelope pushed harder but the door wouldn’t budge.

“Josh kept saying he was going to meet you that night,” Felicity told her, a hint of menace rising into her voice. Her predatory instincts were beginning to kick in. If Penelope was responsible for the killings on the island, Felicity would drain her right here and leave her face down in the pool.

“Wait, what?” Penelope said dumbly. Her attempts to shut the door halted as her mind tried to process the information.

“Apparently, Gully was the last person to see Josh alive. He drove him home. The entire ride back all he was talking about was how he had to meet you to hook up,” Felicity said, eyes scrutinizing every inch of Penelope’s face for a sign of deceit.

“That is so not true!” Penelope exclaimed, outraged. “I didn’t hook up with anyone that night! You can ask the twins. I stayed the night there!”

“They were both drunk; they may not remember,” Felicity said.

“Oscar doesn’t drink. He remembers the whole thing. I can call him right now if you don’t believe me,” Penelope challenged. The problem was, Felicity did believe her.

“Yes, do that. Can my friends and I come in?” Felicity asked.

Penelope looked at her warily; she still clearly disliked Felicity. “Fine, I’ll let you all in through the front.”

Felicity walked back around the house and found the group awkwardly loitering around the front door. “We’re in.”

The door opened a moment later and Penelope, now wrapped in a towel with another around her hair, ushered them in. She pulled out her phone, tapped the speaker button, and a moment later Oscar was speaking to them.

"Penelope, what's happening?" Oscar asked.

"Where was I after the party at your house?" Penelope asked.

"You stayed over, why?"

"Just had to prove a point. Would I ever hook up with Josh?"

"No, definitely not your type," Oscar confirmed.

"Thank you Oscar," Penelope said sweetly. She ended the call and turned to Felicity. "There, happy?"

"Not particularly," Felicity said in a troubled voice.

Vito spoke up, "Where is your father, Penelope?"

"Police station. He's got a lot riding on the idea that this is a safe neighborhood. He's doing everything he can to stay connected and keep it under wraps that people are being killed," she told them.

"Can you ask him for the details on the body found buried in the sand?" Vito asked.

"I could," Penelope told him obstinately.

"Will you?" Vito asked impatiently.

"No. Now if you don't mind, I'm going to text Gully and tell him to stop telling people I was going to hook up with Josh. See yourselves out," Penelope said with a gesture at the door.

As the group walked toward the door, Cara turned back to Penelope. "When your dad comes home, please ask him for details on the most recent body."

Penelope made eye contact with Cara and looked like she wanted to say something snarky. She settled instead for a curt nod. Cara smiled at her and the group piled back into Gio's SUV.

"What should we do now?" Joey asked.

"Give me a minute to think," Felicity told him.

"I say we go pay Gully another visit. Maybe he'll remember more if we press him harder," said Vito.

"Why don't we go back to my uncle's?" Gio suggested. "I feel like maybe we can examine the evidence or something and figure this out. There's been what? Three murders? Maybe we can figure out a pattern or something."

"That could work," Cara said.

Gio drove to his uncle's house. It was large, and a block from the boardwalk, where Gio's uncle owned a store that he, Vito, and Joey all worked at in the summer.

"Their uncle's probably asleep in his room with the TV on. He won't bother us," Joey assured Cara and Felicity.

"Do you guys want anything to drink?" Gio offered.

"I don't drink anything but blood," Felicity said unenthusiastically.

"I'll take a water if you have any," Cara told him.

Gio tossed her a bottle, which she managed to catch clumsily.

"Hey, so uh, Felicity," Joey began.

She turned her sharp eyes toward him, already sure she wasn't going to like whatever it was he was about to ask her. "What?"

"You're a you-know-what, right?" he asked, seemingly oblivious to her impending irritation.

"Yes, what about it?"

"So do you have like, you know, fangs and all that?" he asked, gesturing toward her mouth with his hand.

Cara turned away. She knew what was about to happen and didn't want to see. Felicity opened her mouth into a sort of half-snarl, half-grimace, revealing her massive, sinister canines.

"Woah," Gio breathed.

"Holy shit," Joey said in awe.

"That's actually terrifying," Vito said.

Felicity closed her mouth and smiled smugly. "Alright boys, any other questions before we get started?"

They all shook their heads, stunned.

"So what do we know about the victims? What do they have in common?" Felicity wondered.

"All of them were killed on the island!" Joey ejaculated.

"Very helpful thanks," Felicity said sarcastically.

"Well, could it be completely random? Like anyone just walking on the street gets knifed?" Gio suggested.

"So far we don't know if any of them were knifed," Felicity reminded him.

"OK so, what? We've got froze to death, shark attack, and buried alive?" Cara said listing them off on her fingers.

"We also don't know if the first one was a shark attack or if they were killed and then dumped in the ocean. We also don't know if this most recent person was buried alive or just buried in the sand after they were killed," Vito pointed out.

"OK, so what you're saying is we don't know anything?" Cara asked.

"Socrates would argue that means we're the smartest people on the island," Vito joked.

Gio chuckled at this and Felicity shot him a look.

Joey spoke up first. "They love jokes about Greek philosophers."

"I can't help it," Gio grumbled.

Felicity rolled her eyes. She was frustrated. She needed more information. But each new piece of information cost someone's life. *Think,* she told herself. She couldn't wait around for other people to die.

"OK guys, I have an idea" she began. They weren't going to like this, she knew already. "I need you guys to take Cara home."

"What? Right now? We just got here," Joey protested.

"Yeah, and where are you going to go?" Cara asked indignantly.

"I'm going for a walk," she declared.

"A walk? In the middle of the night?" Gio asked, clearly not grasping the concept of vampirism.

"Are you all really that stupid?" Vito chastised. "The only thing the killings have in common, other than location, is time. All the deaths happened at night. She's bait."

"No way! You can't use yourself as bait!" Gio protested.

"Have you ever heard of an alligator snapping turtle?" she asked him, slowly standing up. Physically, she may look like an eighteen-year-old girl, but something about her demeanor had shifted—the way her body moved. There was a menacing presence about her now. She held her hands in front of her with her thumbs together forming a sort of crude mouth shape "The alligator snapping turtle lies on the bottom of a lake. It wiggles its tongue like a worm." She wiggled her thumbs for emphasis. "When a fish comes over, thinking itself the top predator, the one who's about to get a meal..." She clapped her hands together loudly and they heard a snort from the other room where Gio and Vito's uncle stirred in his sleep. She waited a moment and then turned back to the group. "I am the top predator on this island, no, I am the *only* predator on this island. Take Cara home. Cara, don't wait up for me. I'll see you all tomorrow." She strode across the room and opened the door, walking out into the night. She got about three steps out of the driveway before Gio's voice stopped her.

"Felicity, wait!" he called. She didn't turn to look at him. "I—" he began before stopping to catch his breath. *He needs to do more cardiovascular training*, she thought to herself.

"Are you here to tell me to stay?" she asked him out loud.

"No way. I've seen you get bit by a shark and be fine the next day. I'm sure you'll be fine," he told her.

"Smart boy. Then what is it?"

"Oh, sorry, no, I just haven't been able to get you alone at all and well, I uh, wanted to thank you," he said awkwardly.

"Thank me?"

"Yeah, for, ya know, saving my life. That shark was going to kill me," he explained.

"Oh, right. Well you caught me on a good night I guess," she said, only half-joking.

"Well, thank you. Don't worry by the way; we'll all keep your secret. I swear," he told her seriously.

"Good lad. You boys are growing on me. It would be a shame to have to put an end to you," she told him with a smile, although there was an unsettling quality to it. She softened a little and gave him a small nod. "Make sure Cara gets home safely." With that, she walked away. She had no real idea of where she was going, but eventually found herself back home. She changed into a bathing suit and carried her surfboard off into the night. She would try a stretch of beach farther south on the island than her usual spot. She walked across the wooden slats that ran parallel to the dunes, separating the sandy beach from the street. She thought this would be a nice compromise between the sidewalk and the beach. The perfect location to murder someone, or so she hoped the killer would think at least.

She walked for a few minutes before her ears detected footsteps. She pretended to stretch her neck and on the last movement used her peripheral vision to confirm there was indeed a person behind her, walking a distance away, but close enough that she could just make out their footsteps. This didn't mean they were the killer, of course. It was late enough that most families were at home, but not so late that it was bizarre to have a person out for a late night stroll. She would have to test them. She turned onto the beach, casting a quick side glance at them as she did so and noticed that they were male, and he had an object tucked in his waistband. She hurried forward onto the beach and stuck her surfboard into the ground. With any luck, on the dark beach, the killer would think she was next to it. Felicity crouched down next to the dune. She wasn't sure what kind of weapon they had, but if they turned onto the same stretch of beach that she had, she would know they were following her, and that she had her killer.

She heard him hit the sand before she saw him. Her eyes immediately went to his waist, where she saw he hadn't pulled the weapon yet. She moved so swiftly that he hadn't even registered he was being hit before she was holding the weapon, a hammer, and he was face-down on the ground. He tried to stand but she pinned him with a knee to the back and leaned over, her fangs mere inches from his neck. She always tried to say something clever before a kill.

"Never bring a hammer to a gun fight," she said smugly.

"Felicity, it's me," Basil said frantically.

"What?" She stepped off of him, stunned.

Basil turned over and stood up. Felicity raised the hammer threateningly and he held up his hands for her to wait and took a step back.

"I can explain," he said slowly.

“Explain why you were following me in the middle of the night with a hammer? I know you weren’t just on a late night stroll, since you live on the other side of the island,” she told him accusingly.

“I know there’s a killer on the loose,” he told her slowly, “and I know the police are covering it up. But people are dying and someone needs to do something about it.”

“So what, you’re out here with a hammer trying to bring vigilante justice?” she asked incredulously.

“Yeah, that was the plan, and then I saw you walking and I thought it was dangerous for you to be walking alone.”

“So you followed me to protect me?”

“I know it sounds hard to believe—” he began, but she punched him in the stomach, doubling him over and making him throw up—some kind of breaded chicken and cabbage by the looks of it.

She grabbed him and dragged him to the street.

“I swear I’m telling the truth!” he said, nearly in tears now.

“Do you have a phone?” she asked him flatly.

“Y-yes,” he said as he pulled out the phone and tried to hand it to her.

“Call the police,” she ordered.

“But—”

“No buts!”

He dialed the police and she snatched the phone from him.

“Hello, yes, I caught a suspicious boy walking the streets. Can you send someone down with a car to take him and make sure his alibis for the nights of each of the past killings— Yes, please, Officer, I know about the killings. I was in the police station when you got the call about Josh. Just come get him and check his alibis.” She handed the phone back to Basil. “Give them a few minutes to track the call. They'll be here and if you're really not the killer, your alibis should check out."

He sat up but didn't try to stand. She waited with him, both of them silent until a police car arrived.

"Hello again, Officer," Felicity said sweetly.

"Hello. Is this the boy?" the police officer asked, looking at Basil like he couldn't quite place him.

"Hello again," Basil said miserably.

"You! I remember now!" the officer said, eyes going wide. "You're the video game player!"

"Yes, that's me," Basil confirmed.

"So now you're out here doing what? Stalking this poor girl?" the officer asked.

"No! I just saw her and thought that if someone's out here killing people, I should make sure she's safe!" Basil exclaimed, clearly frustrated.

"What exactly are you doing out here by yourself, miss?" the officer asked her.

"I came to practice surfing. Have to stay on top. We have some impressive competitors this year," she told him.

"You surf at night? Isn't that dangerous?" he asked.

"For most people yes, but I am the island's champion. How else do you think I got so good?"

"So that's your secret, eh? Well, I won't tell anyone. I'll be rooting for you this year," the officer told her. "Don't worry about this one. We'll bring him in and grill him again, just to be sure he's not our killer." The officer read Basil his rights and cuffed him, putting him in the back of his squad car. Felicity walked back to the beach and laid down next to her surfboard, placing the hammer next to her. This was a strange twist. She looked up at the sky. The crashing ocean waves were the only noise now. She didn't know whether to believe Basil was the killer or not, but she did know she wouldn't know anything more about it until tomorrow. She smiled to herself. *I guess that makes me Socrates for the night,* she thought. She stood up and, grabbing her board, hit the waves. All thoughts of murderers and Basil left her head. It was just her and the waves now.

Cara was not going to just go home. She had received a text from Penelope after Felicity left with the details of the most recent murder victim.

"So, she was in her early thirties, not from the island, and was staying in the Swashbuckler Motel with her two older sisters. They had gone out drinking the night before and she hadn't wanted to leave the bar so they left her there, assuming she would just come back later that night," Cara told the boys.

"Does Penelope know how she died?" Vito asked.

"Hold on," Cara said, typing away on her phone.

"She would've had to walk over two miles to get from the bars by the Swashbuckler to the part of beach she was found on," Gio said.

"Unless she drove," Joey suggested.

"Why would she drunk drive to the beach past where she was staying?" Vito said condescendingly. "Even if she wanted to swim, there were plenty of beaches to go to before the one she was buried at. Not to mention the fact that there's a pool at the Motel."

"Oh! Guys! Penelope says the girl was buried alive!" Cara exclaimed.

"Creepy, just like that guy who was buried in ice at the restaurant," Gio said with a shudder.

"Guys, I hate to be the one to bring it up but, like, are we totally sure it wasn't Felicity?" Joey asked.

"It wasn't Felicity!" Cara exclaimed.

"Well, she is a vampire. She showed us the teeth, ya know? It didn't feel really real until then for me but, like. Damn, ya know? Vampire," he said.

"Eloquent as always Joey," Vito said sarcastically.

"Look, I can promise you Felicity didn't do it," Cara assured them.

"Do you ever get worried living with her?" Joey asked.

"No! Never. She's my best friend. She would never hurt us," Cara told them.

"She seems kind of scary, even if she wasn't a vampire," Joey said quietly.

Cara had to laugh at this, "That's just her way. Apparently she's always been like that, even when my grandma was a kid. But she really is a sweetheart once she warms up to you. She likes you guys, believe it or not."

"Does she?" Vito asked surprised.

"She does." Cara nodded. "I can tell. She's under a lot of stress though."

"How can we help?" Gio wondered.

"By helping her catch whoever this killer is," Cara said.

"Well why don't we go press that guy Gully for more information?" Joey suggested, slamming his fist into his palm.

"I actually agree with Joey," Vito said. "Gully was the last person to see this drunk guy and he gave us bad information on Penelope. So not only do I doubt anything he says now, but he himself admits to having the means to kill this guy. He would just need to drive him to the restaurant and get him into the ice bar."

"Agreed. Let's go do some recon," Gio said as he grabbed his keys.

They got in the SUV and pulled into the street. Soon they were parked out by the Traveler. The restaurant itself was closed but there was a light on in one of the windows – Gully's room, they presumed.

"OK, so what do we do?" Cara asked, voicing the thoughts of everyone in the car.

"To be fair, I didn't really think it through. You got me so hyped up to help Felicity," Gio admitted.

"Let's just go in there and demand he tell us more!" Joey exclaimed enthusiastically.

"Guys wait," Cara said, pointing out the window. They all crowded to her side of the SUV and peered out.

"What am I supposed to be see—" The words died in Gio's mouth as he saw what Cara was referring to. A black BMW had pulled up across the street and Penelope had gotten out, dressed in black boots, high-waisted shorts, a white floral scarf and the leather jacket from the other night. She walked toward the Traveler's private dock.

"A secret meeting between Gully and Penelope?" Cara said scandalously.

"Let's go interrupt. Maybe we can catch them discussing their big murder plans," Joey said excitedly as he rushed out of the car just as Penelope disappeared into the boat's shadow.

The others followed quickly and they heard a scream that was soon subdued into a muffled gurgle.

They arrived on the dock to see a masked figure with a filleting knife in his belt, strangling Penelope with her own scarf. Gio, Vito and Joey all charged the figure at once. He shoved Penelope toward them. She collided with Joey and the two of them fell to the dock. The masked killer pulled his knife out just as Gio and Vito got to him, but they didn't even slow down. In a motion so fluid it almost looked practiced, the two of them slammed into their knife-wielding assailant and the three of them hit the dock's railing hard enough to smash through the wood, plunging the trio into the inky black waters. Under the water, the killer kicked the two of them off and swam under the dock. The killer gasped for air and ripped the mask off before diving back down, just as the brothers surfaced for air. They began swimming after him but he was nowhere to be found. Penelope clutched Cara's arm, crying hysterically as she gasped for air. As Vito and Gio approached, now soaking wet but out of the water, Penelope began to scream and kick.

"Hey, hey, hey, it's just us," Gio said soothingly.

"He tried to kill me," Penelope whimpered as she settled down.

"Come on," Vito said as he grabbed one of her arms, helping her up.

"Wh-where are we going?" Penelope asked, resisting his pull.

"Somewhere where we can keep you safe. You can trust us," he told her.

Joey took her other arm and they lead her to the SUV. They sat on either side of her in the backseat and she clutched their arms in terror the entire time, her long sharp nails digging into their skin. Her green eyes were glazed over, as if asleep. When they pulled into the pebbly driveway of Cara's house, she jolted and let out a terrified gasp.

"Come on Penelope," Cara coaxed as they lead her out of the car and into the house.

"What am I doing here?" Penelope asked in confusion.

"You don't remember? We brought you here," Cara told her soothingly.

"Yes, but why?" Penelope asked angrily.

"Why not?" Joey asked.

"Why am I not at the police station? Or even home? Why would you take me, here?!" Penelope shouted.

"If you want to go, then let's go," Gio said. Vito shook his head subtly, but Gio put out a hand for him to wait. "Come on, let's go back. We can even get your car from the dock."

Penelope took a step toward the door and then stopped, a mental battle raging inside her skull. She let out one deep rattling breath.

“Or if you want, you can crash here and we can all take you back tomorrow,” Cara suggested.

“Like, fine, I guess. Do you at least have some other clothes I can change into?”

“Sure, come on, I’ll grab you some pajamas,” Cara said trying to bring Penelope into her bedroom, but Penelope stopped just outside the doorway.

“Look, uh, could one of the guys go in first. I— Never mind, no, I’m sorry, this is stupid. I should just go.” Penelope took a few steps toward the front door.

“Joey, go check out Cara’s room,” Vito ordered. Joey walked into Cara’s room and looked in the closet and under the bed.

“I’m not a child!” Penelope said, the anger coming back into her voice.

“Sorry,” Joey said, quickly hopping to his feet.

Penelope shooed Joey and Cara out of the room and changed quickly, coming back out of the room wearing a long pink shirt with a shooting star on it. The shirt was large on Cara and on Penelope it hung down off her right shoulder.

“Are you even wearing pants?” Joey teased.

Penelope shot him a glare and lifted the bottom of the shirt to reveal a pair of pastel green shorts.

Cara put a blanket on the couch and Penelope quickly fell asleep curled tightly in a ball.

“She’s actually kinda cute when she’s asleep,” Gio admitted. The others all looked at him like he was crazy.

“So are we really all staying here tonight?” Joey asked with a yawn. The adrenaline from before was beginning to take its toll on him.

“I was hoping you would, at least until Fel gets back,” Cara said hopefully.

"Can you at least set us up with like a sleeping bag or something?" Gio asked.

Cara thought for a moment and then went upstairs, coming down with a pillow, a sheet, and a comforter. She laid the comforter on the floor and put the pillow and sheet on top.

"One of you can sleep here in this nest. Someone can sleep in my dad's favorite chair; it's actually pretty comfy. He always falls asleep watching TV in it." The boys all snickered at this.

"That's such a dad thing to do," Gio said as the other two nodded in agreement. "I'll take the chair," Gio said

"Give me the damn nest I guess," Vito said with a sigh.

"So do I get to sleep with you then?" Joey asked, a provocative note in his voice.

"OK, just for that you get the nest. Vito you get to sleep in Fel's bed," Cara said.

"Why does Felicity have a bed if she doesn't sleep?" Gio asked.

They all jumped as the door opened and Felicity entered. "Sometimes I like to rest my eyes," she said, "Why is anyone talking about sleeping in anyone's bed?" Confusion riddled her features as she surveyed the nest on the floor. Had her jaw not been connected to her face, it would have been on the ground when her eyes came to rest on Penelope curled up asleep on the couch.

"We have news," Cara told her seriously.

"You don't say," Felicity replied sarcastically.

"We saw the killer," Vito informed her.

"What!" Felicity shouted. Penelope yelped and sat up on the couch, her head darting from side to side.

"It's just Felicity. Go back to sleep," Vito told her.

Penelope took a few deep breaths and then settled back down into the pillow. She gave one last deep sighing breath that almost sounded like a sob before her breathing settled and she fell back to sleep.

"OK," Felicity said in a quieter voice, "what the Hell happened?" They all looked at each other, none of them daring to speak first.

"We wanted to help," Gio began.

"Help find the killer, that is," Cara interjected.

"So we figured we'd put the ol' screws to your pal Gully," Joey added.

Felicity looked at Vito, expecting him to add more but he said nothing.

"Anyway, we were sort of parked across the street from the Traveler trying to figure out what to do. I saw Penelope's car pull up and we decided to follow her," Cara explained.

"We ended up finding the killer trying to strangle her to death with her scarf," Vito said, finally adding to the story. "We all went after him, but he threw Penelope at Joey, and then Gio and I ended up falling in the water with him."

"He had a knife," Gio said, as if he needed to make them seem braver, "but I think he dropped it in the water.

"OK," Felicity said, processing the information in stride. "What did he look like?" She was met with only blank stares. "Seriously guys? None of you remember?"

"I was taking care of Penelope!" Cara protested.

"I was getting tripped by Penelope!" Joey said nodding and pointing at Cara.

Felicity massaged her eyes with her fingertips briefly, before looking at Vito. "And you?"

"He had a mask. I didn't see his face," Vito told her with a small shrug.

"I was focused on the knife," Gio said before she could even ask.

“Plus it was dark!” Joey told her defensively.

“So you four are telling me that you not only cornered the killer on a dock, but had actual, physical contact with him, and he still got away?” she asked, the annoyance in her voice slowly being replaced with anger. If she had been there, she would’ve had him. Instead she was out playing bait and getting Basil sent to jail.

“Hey, give us some credit,” Vito told her, gesturing to Penelope. “We got her here. She must have been at the dock for a reason right? We find out what she knows and maybe that’ll give us some kind of clue as to who we’re after. It’ll give us a leg up on the police, and on the killer. Besides, you wanted bait, maybe he’ll come and try to finish the job.”

Felicity had to think about this for a moment. “OK, so add Penelope to the list of victims. The killer failed but he was dead set on killing her, right?”

“Definitely,” Gio said with a nod.

“OK, so what do the victims all have in common now?” Felicity asked thoughtfully.

Joey was the first to answer what they were all thinking. “Nothing! They’re still all different ages, and all different sexes.”

“Hopefully Penelope can clear some of this up in the morning. If my knowledge of the criminal justice system is correct, which it very well may not be, the police can keep the reporters locked up for twenty-four hours, since they likely don’t have any evidence to keep them longer. Then, the reporters will be out with a vengeance. They’ll write tell-alls about what’s been going on and release it the next morning. We have roughly twenty-seven hours to locate the killer, and then kill him,” Felicity told them, surveying the room like a general commanding troops.

“I hate to be that guy,” Joey said, “but the three of us have work tomorrow morning, eight-thirty a.m.”

In that moment, Joey was lucky vampires couldn't kill just by looking at someone, because if they could, he would surely have been dead five times over. Felicity looked as if she might hit him and Gio felt the need to come to the aid of his friend. "I can take Penelope to the police if you want. Joey and Vito can cover for me."

"Glad someone is somewhat helpful," Felicity said reproachfully.

"Come on, Fel, ease up," Cara said, crossing the room and standing next to Felicity. "They did a lot today. It's not their fault they have work and you can't go into the sun."

Felicity grunted and crossed her arms.

Cara turned to the boys. "You should all get some sleep. Don't worry about taking Penelope to the police; I'm sure we'll figure something out. We can plan something tomorrow after we know more."

Cara led Vito up to the closet that Felicity called her bedroom. Joey was asleep before Cara even got back downstairs. Cara put on pajamas of her own and brushed her teeth. She hugged Gio and Felicity before retiring to her own room. Gio sat in the large armchair and observed Felicity silently.

"Can I help you?"

He shook his head. "No, no. I just, I don't know… Are you just going to stand there all night?"

"That was my plan. Someone has to keep watch."

"Don't you get tired?" he asked her.

"No."

"Being a vampire must be awesome then. I'm exhausted," he said with a small laugh.

"Sleep," she told him flatly.

"I want to keep you company," he told her, a small smile playing at his lips.

"You really don't have to. You should sleep. I really will need you tomorrow."

"Alright captain, if you insist," he said as he settled into the admittedly very comfy chair. "Hey, Felicity?"

"Mm?"

"How did you become a vampire?" he asked her sleepily.

"I don't know," she told him as she put out the light. He was asleep within minutes. She grabbed a piece of paper and started to write down everything she knew. Nothing made sense. The killer had no discernible pattern, no consistent method or motive she could pick out. Even she herself had a preferred victim type-partiers. This person had such a diverse spread of people, such a diverse spread of methods. She crumpled up the paper and threw it in the trash. She didn't even have any real suspects. All she knew was that it couldn't have been Basil, Penelope, or any of the reporters since Penelope was almost killed, and Basil and the reporters were all in the police station. *Great,* she thought to herself. *I've eliminated six suspects. Now I just have another hundred thousand people on the island it could be.* "I guess I know it's not Vito, Joey, or Gio either," she said out loud to herself.

When the sun began to show its first light, she went into the kitchen and began breakfast. She was sure the boys would eat a lot—that was something she remembered from her days as a human. Her brother and his friends always had insatiable appetites. Her mother had always baked an extra loaf of bread just for them. Felicity smiled at the memory. She brought the plates into the dining room of the house. Onion and pepperoni omelets with a side of bacon and buttered rye toast. She poured glasses of orange juice for everyone and then turned on the coffeemaker. She was sure the boys would need it. Probably Penelope too. Felicity walked up the stairs to her room and woke Vito, who sat up and rubbed his eyes with a yawn.

"I need you to wake the others. The window in the television room isn't covered and I don't feel like burning down to ash today.

Vito did as he was told.

"This smells amazing. Did you make this?" Gio asked her as they all sat down at the table.

"Of course she did! Felicity makes all the food the tavern serves," Cara bragged.

"I also put on some coffee. How do you guys take it?" Felicity asked as she grabbed some mugs.

"Black for me," Joey told her.

"Give me four sugars and some cream," Vito said.

"Might as well just give you coffee ice cream at that point," Cara teased.

"Hey, it tastes good," he said defensively.

"No need to get cranky," Gio said. "I don't drink coffee. But I'll take a tea if you have it."

Penelope looked up at this. "I'll also take a tea. With honey. My throat hurts."

Felicity's eyes darted quickly to Penelope's still-red neck. She hated the little brat, but her experience did seem to have left her shaken. Felicity obliged their requests and soon hot drinks were served.

"Penelope, tell me what happened last night," Felicity said bluntly.

Penelope blanched. "I don't want to talk about it."

"I don't care!"

"Fel," Cara warned.

Felicity slammed her hands on the table, making everyone jump. "Listen here Penelope, that killer is out there, and we have absolutely no idea who he is. The police have no leads, and bodies are piling up. This island is my home, has been my whole life. I'm not going to let anyone ruin that and this killer, this *killer* is Hell-bent on ruining that. So I'm going to need you to tell me what happened. Start with why were you at the Traveler."

Penelope looked for a moment like she might start to yell, or possibly just leave. Eventually she took a deep breath. "Fine." She took a long sip of her tea and closed her eyes for a moment, then opened them again. "I had texted Gully as you guys left. I was mad that he was going around telling people I had told Josh I'd hook up with him. I really hadn't. Josh and I had barely said anything to one another that night. He ended up telling me to come over so he could give me an apology gift. Gully always has the hottest stuff from taking the boat around in the winter so I figured hey, I could go for some exotic liquor or whatever he was going to offer me so I went down there. He told me to meet him on the dock. I walked up to him and he turned around, and before I could ask why he was wearing a ski mask he had grabbed me by the scarf and was choking me. I—" She took another deep rattling breath and sipped her tea, twice this time. "I couldn't breathe. I don't even think my feet were on the ground. Everything was going dark and then next thing I knew, I was on the ground crying next to Cara and, whoever that is." She pointed at Joey.

"Wait, so Gully called you and told you to come over?" Felicity asked.

"No," Penelope said as if Felicity had asked the dumbest question in the world. "It was all through text,"

"You don't think…" Cara said, trailing off.

"Don't think what? That Gully is the killer?" Felicity asked. Her mind thought back to the boy who could barely look her in the eyes when he spoke to her.

"He was the last person to see Josh alive," Vito pointed out.

"And starting the rumor that Josh was going to hook up with Penelope would throw people off his trail. Make it seem like he wasn't the last person to see Josh," Gio added.

"Then it makes sense that he would try to kill her after she called him out for lying. Maybe he was trying to make sure she couldn't deny it to anyone else," Joey said as he stroked his chin.

"Dammit," Felicity swore. "So Gully is the killer."

Now they just needed to catch him.

Chapter 4

Penelope's father came to pick her up. When he saw her, he threw his arms around her and the two embraced for a long time. He ran his hands gently over the angry red marks on her neck. "Who did this?" he asked, his voice dark.

"It was Gully, Gully McMahon," Penelope said.

"What happened?" Mr. Smith asked.

"Gully invited me over. I went, and he tried to kill me. These guys showed up and tackled him off the dock then let me stay here," Penelope told him, listing the events off without emotion.

"If there's any way I can thank you, please let me know," Mr. Smith told them. "Come on Penelope, we're going to the police."

Penelope looked at him in dismay. "Can I at least change into some nicer clothes? I'm still in pajamas!"

"Hmm, alright, bring the clothes you were attacked in, maybe they can get some evidence off them," he told her.

Penelope and her father left the house, and once the door was shut, Felicity addressed the group. "Alright guys, what are we going to do?"

John and Sarah walked into the kitchen just as she was asking this and the two looked around in surprise. "Do about what? And who are your friends?"

"This is Gio, his brother Vito, and their friend Joey," Cara said, pointing to each boy as she named them. "Guys, these are my parents."

"It's nice to meet you," Sarah said, giving them all a warm smile.

"I see Felicity's been taking care of you," John added with a smile of his own.

"I'm so sorry! I totally forgot to make breakfast for you guys," Felicity cried in dismay.

"It's fine, Felicity. You were taking care of your friends," John told her.

"I didn't even know you had other friends," Sarah teased.

Felicity gave a small laugh. "Jealous?"

"Oh totally," Sarah said with a grin.

"Here, I'll be right back. I can whip something up for you guys lickety-split," Felicity said starting back toward the kitchen.

"No, no. Stay. Entertain your friends," Sarah said.

"We actually have to get going. We have work soon," Gio said, picking up his plate.

Felicity took it and brought it to the sink and then began clearing Penelope's plate and mug.

"Alright, see you guys after sundown?" Cara asked.

"Ugh, we've got a long day ahead of us," Joey whined.

"With any luck the police will catch Gully before nightfall. I'll let you guys nap if that's the case," Felicity told them.

"Which one of you has an actual working phone again?" Cara asked.

Gio groaned.

"Yeah." Vito laughed. "I was wondering when you'd realize you had your phone on you when we tackled that guy."

"You can text me with the deets tonight," Joey told her, sounding a little smug that he still had his phone in working order.

The boys left and Sarah turned to Felicity. "Do they know?"

Felicity grimaced. "Unfortunately. Gio was the boy I saved from the shark."

"Let me guess, they ran into you somewhere and wondered how you were walking around?" John guessed.

"Very astute," Felicity responded glumly.

Cara nudged her. "Come on, Fel, you like them. Don't lie."

"They're useful for the time being," Felicity grumbled. "Not useful enough to actually catch the killer when he was right there, but hey, who am I to judge, right?"

"Don't be such a grump," Sarah told her, giving her a small nudge to match Cara's.

Felicity did her best to hide her smile but she couldn't quite manage it. Sarah and Cara were two of her favorite people in the world. She went to the kitchen and pulled together a quick breakfast for John and Sarah. She put a plate out for Helen, who she guessed would be up shortly, and then set to work making food for the customers. She had a surprisingly large amount of orders for so early in the morning. She guessed that there was a large family of tourists who had heard about her tavern. She was happy to be getting the business so she set to work quickly and, as always, her food was done perfectly.

When Cara went to work that afternoon, Chuck ran up to her. "Hey Cara," he said, flexing his bulging arms as was his habit whenever he spoke to anyone. "So the police called, asking if anyone sees this guy," Chuck reached into his pocket and pulled out a phone, illuminating the screen to reveal a picture of Gully, "we call the police immediately. Got it? He's apparently a super wanted criminal and they're trying to keep it quiet so no one gets scared"

"Got it. Thanks Chuck," Cara said as she grabbed her clipboard from the lifeguard stand and began her rounds, checking people's beach badges. If they didn't have one, they had to either buy a day pass from her or leave the beach. Most people were nice about it but occasionally she had one or two nasty comments from people. She agreed with them in all honesty; the beach should be free. Of course, she would be out of a job if it was, so she also disagreed. She shrugged at the thought. If Gully wasn't caught before the public found out there was a killer, then beach badges may become a non-issue since no one was going to want to come to an island where the police couldn't keep people from getting murdered.

Gio, Vito, and Joey were moving merchandise like it was their job, which it was. Gio and Vito's uncle's T-shirt shop was the second most popular T-shirt shop on the island. Gio was wrapping up a keychain shaped like a shark-bitten surfboard with the name 'Mikayla' printed on it when a police officer walked in and started looking around.

"Have a good day!" he told the woman, who he assumed was named Mikayla, then stepped out from behind the counter, "Excuse me, officer?"

"Can I help you?" the police officer said, not sounding like he was in the mood to be helpful at all.

"Are you looking for Gully?" Gio asked him casually.

The police officer's eyes almost bulged out of his head. "Have you seen him? Wait, how do you even know about—?"

Gio held up a hand to stop him. "I tackled him last night. I was one of the boys who saved Penelope Smith from being killed."

"Keep your voice down!" the officer hissed.

"Sorry, sorry, I just wanted to ask how the investigation is going."

The police officer looked to each side to make sure they wouldn't be overheard. "We put out an APB so if he's within a sixty-mile radius of the island we should catch him. Apparently the suspect has no car so we believe he's stuck on the island somewhere. We have every officer on the force called in doing a sweep of the island. I'm on boardwalk patrol, obviously."

"Can you track his phone?"

"Unfortunately, no. I'm guessing you destroyed it when you knocked him in the water," the officer told him.

"I wish he hadn't gotten away," Gio said regretfully.

"Hey, don't beat yerself up, kid. You took on an armed assailant and saved a girl's life. You've done enough. We'll find him."

"Thanks. Good luck, officer. I'll let you know if I spot him."

"Atta boy, kid," the officer said pointing a finger at Gio as he walked out of the shop.

"What did the cop want?" Joey asked, coming from the back of the store.

"Oh, he was just telling me to tell you guys that we're not getting any sleep tonight," Gio said ruefully.

"Great, just great," Joey said glumly.

Cara finished up her shift and walked home. She checked her phone and found a text from Joey saying the police were searching for Gully but hadn't found him yet. She sighed and walked into her house where Felicity, right on cue, put out a perfectly grilled burger with onion and lettuce, but no tomato. There was a side of parmesan potato wedges that Felicity had crisped to perfection in the oven and a glass of lemonade.

"How was work?" Felicity asked her as she set out plates for John, Helen, and Sarah. Helen didn't put any vegetables on her burgers, Sarah had cheese on hers, and John had one cheese and one hamburger, both with lettuce, tomato, and onion.

"Work was fine, they had us all keep a look out for Gully," Cara sighed again. She might as well just tell Felicity and get it over with. "Joey texted and said the police haven't caught him yet."

"Lovely. Just lovely," Felicity said, trying to keep her voice under control.

"Tell you what, Felicity," John said as she began to pace anxiously around the room, "if you get a map of the island, I can help you plot out where I think the best places to hide out are. I'll even help you search them if you want."

"That's a good idea," Felicity said as she stopped in her tracks and turned to face him.

"Yeah, just let me finish eating."

"Of course," she said, as she stared at him, patiently waiting.

John was fairly used to Felicity. He had been married to Sarah for twenty-one great years and had dated her for another four before that. The one thing he never got used to was Felicity's lack of a need to blink. Normally she blinked anyway, simply because it was a familiar habit and it made her look a little more human. When she was waiting for something or someone, however, she usually stared. While Helen, Sarah, and Cara had learned to just ignore it, John found it very unsettling.

"Come on, Felicity, I'm hungry," he complained.

"I said you could eat," she told him, cocking her head slightly to the side.

"You're creeping me out. Stop staring."

"Such a child," she said, the smallest of smiles playing at her lips. She did as he asked and went into the kitchen to make sure the chefs who replaced her every night were doing adequate work.

"That girl," he said shaking his head.

"Respect your elders, John," Helen teased.

"It's hard to when they look the same age as my teenage daughter." He laughed with a shrug.

"Hey! I'm only a teenager for another year," Cara protested.

"Our girl's growing up," Sarah said.

"I know. How do I make it stop?" John groaned.

Helen pointed a bony finger him. "Time waits for no one. And you, young lady," she said, pointing now at Cara, "shouldn't be in such a rush to grow up. Enjoy your time as a teenager. Go to the beach, see a film! Have some fun."

"Maybe I can get Gio to drive to the Wing 'n' Egg," Cara suggested. "They're open twenty-four/seven so we can go after the big hunt for Gully."

Felicity walked back into the room. Cara didn't bother telling her the plan; she had likely heard it all from the kitchen anyway. Felicity looked impatiently at John, who held up a finger as he finished his burger. Once he was done, he stood up and cleared his plate. This gave the rest of the family an extra minute to finish their food.

"Alright, now that everyone's done, I'll look for my map," John said at a slightly slower pace of speaking then normal. Felicity groaned in dismay. John found his map of the island and spread it out on the table. "Alright, so we need to consider a few things. Number one is that the police have had every lifeguard and badge checker on the lookout." John used some paper towels to cover up the beach and bay sides of the map. "Number two is that the police have been, and likely will continue, patrolling high traffic areas." He ripped some pieces of napkin and used them to cover up the places on the island like the amusement park, boardwalk, mall, and Island Village, which was a popular tourist spot full of shops, restaurants, and a parking garage where people could park and walk to the island's other popular tourist spots.

Felicity examined the map, trying to think where she would hide. "We need to pay Penelope Smith's father a visit," she said finally. "If I was hiding out on the island, I would be trying to find a house that no one was staying in and lay low there."

Cara walked over and looked at the map. "For someone who claims she hates Penelope, you certainly have been seeing a lot of her the last few days," she teased.

"It's not my fault this whole thing keeps bringing her back into my…" Felicity trailed off. Cara could tell she was deep in thought. Felicity crossed one arm over her body and the other she rested on her lips as she examined the map. Finally, after a few moments, Felicity looked at Cara. "Tell Gio we're coming to him." She turned to John. "Grab the map, we're going." Her tone left no room for argument and John did as he was told. Felicity may have looked the same age as his daughter, but in times like these, he could feel the weight of her age behind her words. He was a child compared to her.

Felicity threw on her black crop top hoodie, black yoga pants, and sturdiest pair of running shoes. She was going into stealth mode tonight. She also grabbed a comforter as the sun had not gotten low enough for her to safely be in its rays. John unlocked the car and she ran in, the comforter shielding her from the sun. John grabbed a golf club from his golf bag, just in case. Cara hopped in next to Felicity, who was still in the comforter. A few minutes later they were pulling up to Gio's uncle's house. Felicity left the comforter in the car as the sun was now about to dip below the horizon. She leapt out of the car, walking quickly up the path to the front door. She rang the bell and heard a groan inside. The door opened and Joey stood in the doorway.

"Oh come on, Felicity, you promised we could nap!" he whined.

Felicity pushed past him into the house. "No time," she said brusquely. John gave Joey a small shrug as he entered and Cara smiled apologetically.

"Can we at least finish eating?" Gio complained as he ate a plate of spaghetti and meatballs.

John laughed. "She hates waiting for people to eat, but yes, I suggest you do. We have a big night ahead of us."

Felicity took the map from John and gave it back, now spread open. "Look and listen, boys, here's the plan. I realized that Penelope seems to, for some reason, be at the epicenter of all this. My guess is that Gully is going to come back for her. She's the first failed attempt so far, so either they faked it together and she's involved or he's coming back to end her. Either way, keeping an eye on her may lead us to Gully."

"Oh, I'll totally keep an eye on Penelope," Joey said suggestively.

"Perfect. Vito you can keep an eye on Penelope," Cara said.

"Not fair," Joey complained.

Felicity rolled her eyes. This boy's priorities were clearly not in order. "How about you focus on catching the killer before you focus on meeting women? How does that sound?" she asked, sounding angrier than she had intended. In a calmer tone, she continued, "Anyway, don't be too upset. You get to spend the night with Gio and Cara."

He perked up at this and asked, "So what are we going to do?"

"Simple. You three will check out every house on the list that Mr. Smith gives us. Look for houses that should be empty but aren't," Felicity instructed.

"We should check out the Swashbuckler. If that's where the woman was staying when she was killed, maybe Gully has a room there or something," Gio added.

Felicity smiled. She liked Gio the best of the three of them; he was smart but not obnoxious about it. "Very good. Meanwhile, John will be checking out the playgrounds around the island. Maybe he's sleeping in one of them. John, if you have time, you can check a few boats that are docked by people's houses. Maybe he snuck on one."

"And what about you?" Vito asked.

Felicity pointed to a big green area on the map at the bottom of the island. "The nature reserve is a perfect place to hide: no one lives there, plenty of animals to eat, lots of land to hide in, and a few tiny islands off to the side in case the police do a sweep of the reserves. I'll be scouring them."

"Alone?" Gio asked, concern in his voice. Felicity looked a little taken aback. Cara laughed and John hid a grin behind his hand. Joey shook his head sadly and Vito looked smugly at his brother who was turning bright red.

"When I was still alive, it never took me this long to eat!" Felicity snapped, breaking the tension.

The boys quickly stuffed the remainder of their dinners into their mouths and got ready.

John hopped into his own car and started it; he rolled down the window as Felicity approached.

"Let Cara know when you finish. If you see him, call the police. I don't need you dying trying to be a hero, OK?" Felicity said with an atypical softness to her voice.

John flashed her one of the charming smiles that had won Sarah's heart all those years ago. "Oh, don't you worry Felicity, I'm in no mood to get stabbed to death tonight."

She rolled her eyes as he backed his car out of the driveway. Cara and the boys were already in Gio's SUV. Felicity joined them and soon they were on the road.

Vito seemed nervous. "So what exactly are you going to say to Penelope? Like 'Hey, we think the killer might come back for you so I'm here to protect you' sounds a little foolish, wouldn't you agree?"

"Just let me do all the talking," Joey said smoothly.

Felicity doubted his ability to charm Penelope and her father but she wasn't going to argue about it. They pulled up to Penelope's mansion soon after and knocked on the door. To no one's surprise, Oscar answered the door.

"What do you want?" Oscar asked lightly.

"Is Mr. Smith home?" Joey asked.

"Oscar!" Stacy screeched from within the house. "Who is it?"

"Come in," he said with a sigh.

The group entered to find Stacy and Penelope on her couch watching some rom com. Fury lit up Penelope's eyes when she saw them. "What are you doing here?" she demanded.

"We came to speak to your father," Felicity said flatly.

"Why?" Penelope asked, still sounding irate.

"Because we want to ask him about renting a house," Felicity said, her irritation finally giving way.

Mr. Smith walked out from one of the halls. Apparently the argument had been loud enough for him to hear in the other room. "What in the world is going on here?"

"They just showed up at our door and say they need to talk to you about house rentals," Penelope informed him.

"You're in luck. It's still early in the year so houses are still available. Another two weeks and every house on this island will be booked up."

"Can you give me the addresses of all available houses?" Felicity asked.

Mr. Smith narrowed his eyes suspiciously, "Why?"

"Because Gully likely hasn't left the island, and as far as I know, the police haven't spotted him all day. Now if I was going to hide somewhere, it would be in an empty house," Felicity said, voice full of ice. Mr. Smith studied them for a moment and then walked away down the hall. A few moments later he came back and handed them a list.

"Thank you, Mr. Smith," Felicity said. "One more thing, I'd like to leave Vito here. Just in case Gully returns to finish the job."

Penelope went pale. Stacy stood up and glared at Felicity. "You bitch! You shouldn't go around saying things like that to people!"

Felicity said nothing and instead turned and gently pushed Joey and Gio backward, indicating it was time for them to leave. She followed them and Cara went too. Vito stayed put and Mr. Smith didn't protest.

"Ugh does he have to stay?" Penelope protested.

"Yes, I'm heading out to help the police try to navigate the media minefield we're about to go through tomorrow. I'd feel better having a little extra muscle around, no offense Oscar," said Mr. Smith.

"None taken," Oscar said with a wave of his hand.

"Wait!" Penelope exclaimed as she looked Vito up and down. "Can we at least get the one with the hair?"

Joey turned around and Felicity caught him by the back of the shirt. "No," she said without emotion.

Mr. Smith walked over to Gio and handed him a ten dollar bill. "You look like you work out. Ten dollars to stay and protect my daughter."

Gio sighed and tossed his keys to Vito.

Felicity, Cara, Vito and Joey left the Smith mansion and drove off. Felicity gripped the handle inside the car tightly; Vito drove like a mad man. Soon, they were at their destination—the nature reserve at the south end of the island. Felicity opened the door and stepped out. Before she shut the door, she turned to look at Joey and Vito. "If anything happens to her, there is not a place on this Earth that the two of you can hide from me, do you understand?"

Vito nodded solemnly and Joey gulped. Felicity shut the door and ran into the reserve. Vito drove away, putting the first address into Cara's GPS as he did so.

"So what are the odds of us actually finding this guy?" Joey asked. "I mean do you think he's really just chilling in some house that no one rented?"

Vito looked at him in the rearview mirror. "I'd say our chances of finding him in one of these houses is as good as Felicity's chances of finding him in the reserve, or Cara's dad finding him hiding in some tube slide," Vito stopped at a red light. The group was about half a mile away from the first house on the list and despite what Vito had just said, they were all starting to feel nervous.

"Not gonna lie guys, I'm a little worried," Cara said.

Joey held out a hand, "Hey if you need to hold my hand I totally get it."

She elbowed him in the side. "Do we have a plan on how we're going to check if he's actually in these houses?"

"Sort of," Vito said making an abrupt turn that threw everyone to the side. "First, we see if any lights are on. If not, then we check the doors and windows to make sure they're still locked. If everything seems normal, we leave. If not, we call the police and have them take care of it."

He stopped the car and they all got out. The house had no lights on.

"Alright, we check the doors first, then windows," Vito instructed. "Cara and I will do the front; you do the back."

"Why do I have to go alone?" Joey whined.

"Because all the gel in your hair probably acts like a helmet giving you extra protection. Now go!" Vito commanded.

The pebbly driveway crunched under Joey's feet as he ran around to the other side of the house. Vito walked up the three stairs to the front door and pulled, but it was locked. Cara tugged on the windows but they, too, appeared to be locked. She cupped her hands to the side of her face and peered through, half expecting to see a face pop up in front of her. She could just barely make out the outline of a couch and television.

"Anything?" Vito asked from behind her, making her jump.

"No," she gasped. "Nothing I could see."

"I didn't find anything either," Joey said as he walked back around to the front of the house.

"On to the next one then," Vito said as he pulled out the list of houses and crossed that one off.

Gio wasn't thrilled to be stuck with Penelope, Stacy, and Oscar. Mr. Smith had left to speak to the police and the four of them had the house to themselves.

"I hope you don't feel like a hero," Stacy said, her speaking voice somehow simultaneously piercingly shrill and raspy. It reminded Gio of a high-pitched parrot. "And you'd better not be thinking Penelope owes you anything just because you saved her life."

"I'm literally just here to guard the house. I don't want anything else from anyone. I just want the killer caught," Gio told her.

"You'll have to excuse my sister," Oscar said softly. "Personally, I'm glad to have such a strong man around."

Penelope stood up. "I absolutely cannot relax right now. You guys are all putting me on edge." She walked away. Gio hurried after her, grateful to have an excuse to get away from the twins.

"What do you think you're doing?" Penelope asked him as he followed her to her room.

"I, uh, I don't know, just trying to keep you safe," he fumbled awkwardly.

She gestured to the inside of her room. "Fine, give it a sweep if you must, then get out. I'm getting changed."

Gio walked into her room, which wasn't as big as he had expected but did have a walk in closet complete with shoe rack. The furniture was all painted white and the bedsheets had little flowers on them. On the desk there was a dog calendar. A small wooden shelf contained three trophies and had hooks with medals hanging off of them. The medals were all for swimming and the trophies were for soccer and track.

Penelope cleared her throat. "So, can I put on my swimsuit now?" She held up a pink one-piece to emphasize her point.

Gio hastily left the room and a few moments later Penelope came out wearing the suit. "I'm going for a swim. If you want to grab one of my dad's suits you can join me," she told him, gesturing toward a door. Gio hesitated for a moment but entered the room. This was more like the grandeur he had been expecting. King-sized bed, watch holder full of fancy looking watches, and a number of framed photos. There was one of a younger looking Mr. Smith and an elegant blonde woman—a wedding photo. Gio opened up a few drawers in the large dresser until he found a bathing suit and slipped it on. He felt sort of gross wearing a bathing suit someone else had worn but figured it had probably been washed. He walked back into the hallway to find Penelope waiting for him. She led him down to the basement, past a sauna, through a room with a pool table and shuffleboard, and into the pool area. He noted there was also a small hot tub in the corner. Penelope threw a towel from a towel rack to him and took one for herself. She began to stretch.

"You know how to swim?" she asked.

"Of course I do! I'm a great swimmer," he bragged.

"Mhm, we'll see," she said and jumped into the pool.

Gio laughed. The deepest part of the pool was only five feet and she had to tread to keep her mouth above the water.

"Yes, I'm short, I know. Get in," she ordered.

He jumped in next to her. "What stroke are we doing?" he asked.

"Butterfly, backstroke, breaststroke, freestyle. In that order. Got it?"

"Got it," he said. He was fairly confident he could outswim her through sheer muscle power alone. His height would help too since he knew professional swimmers were always tall.

"Ready? Go!" she called.

Butterfly was his worst stroke; he always found the movement to be unnatural. Penelope pulled ahead and he began to wonder if he would catch up after she began doing her backstroke. He kept getting water in his mouth during the backstroke and she pulled farther ahead on the breaststroke. She completed her freestyle as he began his. When he finished, he gasped for air.

"How. Did. You. Do that?" he asked between gasps.

She laughed at him. "I practice. And you're a very slow swimmer."

"I am not," he argued.

"When was the last time you did a cardio workout?" she asked.

"Senior year of high school. I used to be a varsity distance runner," he told her.

"Why'd you stop?"

"Well I had the energy to run, or to lift weights. I chose weights because I figured I'd impress more girls that way," he said, flexing his arms.

She laughed so hard that she slipped under the water, popping up a few moments later somehow still laughing.

Gio turned bright red. "What? I'm strong. I can put up over two hundred pounds on the bench press," he told her, feeling the need to defend himself.

"Oh don't get so defensive," she said, pulling herself out of the pool. "Hot tub?"

He pulled himself out of the pool the same way she had and joined her in the hot tub.

"Are your friends OK with just being left alone in your house?" he asked.

She waved her hand at him dismissively. "They're fine. We grew up together and I love them to death but they can get on my nerves; they know that. They'll probably crack open a bottle of wine and throw on another movie." She paused for a moment and looked at him. "Thank you, by the way. You saved my life and I don't think I ever actually thanked you."

"Oh, you're welcome. I'm just glad we were there to help."

She studied him curiously. "Why were you there?"

"In the spirit of full disclosure, we were staking out the place. Something about Gully's story wasn't adding up," he told her.

"You guys seem Hell-bent on solving this. Why don't you just let the police take care of it?" she asked, sounding genuinely curious.

"Well, Felicity is Hell-bent on solving it; we're just sort of in it for the ride," he said with a chuckle.

She grimaced. "I know she's your friend and all but I can't stand that girl."

"Hey come on, she's awesome. You just don't know her well," Gio said defensively. "She cares a lot about her friends, and she's super selfless. I trust her to catch Gully way more than I trust the police, to be honest."

Felicity dropped to all fours, sniffing the ground like a dog. Her acute sense of smell would pick up Gully's scent if he had been here recently. She stood up again and ran. This late at night she didn't expect to hear or see any humans, save for Gully. If he wasn't camped out in an empty house, the reserve was the most likely place to find him. Three square miles of land to hide in and plenty of animals to eat. Felicity stopped dead in her tracks and sniffed the air. The wind had shifted and she was getting a whiff of something, or more accurately someone, familiar. She turned her head left and right to get a better bearing of the direction it was coming from. She turned a few degrees to her left and broke into a sprint. She had caught Gully's scent. She was in full predator mode now. Nothing was going to stop her from sinking her fangs into the neck of the boy who for so long had had a crush on her. She wondered if he had planned on killing her at some point. She wished he had tried so she could have ended him before he had hurt anyone else. No matter. She would be putting the final word into this ugly chapter of her island's history. Hopefully, before the papers managed to cause widespread panic.

She followed the scent to shoreline and looked across the dark waters. There were a few small islands off the coast of the reserve, birds used them for nesting and people weren't allowed on them. With her vampiric vision, she could see them clear as day, about a quarter of a mile away from the reserve. She ran into the water, fully clothed and swam the distance easily. She could tell Gully was on that island. She crouched down as she walked through the tall vegetation of the island. Her keen eyes spotted an egret and a few seagulls, but no sign of a human. She crept along. It didn't make any sense. The scent was strongest here, but there was no sign of him. Something metallic caught her eye. The scooter. It was lying partially buried in a patch of sand. She walked toward it and realized why she hadn't seen Gully. *He* was buried, in the sand. She ran over and examined the area. Someone had come here at low tide and buried Gully. The water had come in and washed away some of the sand, partially exposing the body. She threw back her head and screamed, the sound echoing across the water.

"Dammit!" she swore. "Dammit, dammit, dammit!" she screamed again and then ran into the water, swimming to the nearest dock. Not needing air made swimming an easy task for her. She heaved herself off the dock and hurried to the nearest house, ringing its doorbell until a tired and angry woman opened the door.

"Do you have any idea what time it—" the woman began before Felicity, still soaking wet, pushed past her and into the house, grateful that the bit about vampires needing to be invited into a house was just a myth.

"I'm calling the police!" the woman shouted.

"I'm already calling them!" Felicity shouted back as she picked up the phone. They answered before the second ring. "Hello, yes, I know where Gully McMahon is. Yes, he's on the first island off the coast of the reserve. He's buried in the sand next to a scooter, right by where the tide comes in. He'll probably be under water when you get there." She hung up the phone and dialed Cara's cell. "Cara? Yes, it's Felicity. Come get me. I'll be on the main road on the way to the reserve. You can stop looking in houses. I found Gully."

Chapter 5

Felicity read the morning paper. The police had apparently gotten to the newspapers in time for them to report that Gully was not only the killer, but also dead. Her mission had been accomplished. The police took full credit for the "solving" of the crime and the people felt safe knowing they were in the "capable" hands of the island's police force. The killer had been stopped and everyone could go about their lives. Everyone, that is, with the exception of Felicity. She knew that the real killer was still out there. She felt some guilt over dragging an innocent boy's name through the mud. Gully had been the sweet boy she had thought he was all along, merely another victim of whatever sick game the killer had been playing. She was glad that the police and newspapers had managed to avoid panic, even if it was by misleading the masses. She wondered if the killer would strike again. They had had their chance to leave the island, all of the blame was on Gully. There was even a chance Gully was actually the killer and some vigilante had caught him first. That's what Joey had suggested last night when she told them what she had found. She ran through the list of victims in her head, unsure of whether or not Gully himself counted as a victim, and still found no pattern, nothing to help her determine what was happening.

"Good news?" Sarah asked as she entered the room to eat the breakfast Felicity had prepared.

"Honestly, I'm not sure Sarah," Felicity said.

Sarah hugged Felicity. "You worry too much."

She opened her mouth to reply but John beat her to it: "I worry the perfect amount."

She glared at him and he winked at her.

Sarah laughed. "Worry less, it'll cause wrinkles."

Felicity turned the glare on her. Felicity wouldn't give her the satisfaction of pointing out that she couldn't get wrinkles. Sarah and John both laughed and Sarah hugged her again.

Maybe Sarah was right. The police had all the information that she had. If there was still a killer out there, they would handle it. If not, she had nothing to worry about. She went about her day, hoping everything would be back to normal. She cooked Cara's breakfast, which, as usual, doubled as a lunch because she slept so late. Cara had never been one for mornings, which was fine with Felicity since it meant Cara could stay up late with her.

"Morning," Cara said sleepily, sitting down and taking a bite of the omelet Felicity had made her.

"Do you have any plans for tonight?" Felicity asked.

Cara shook her head and yawned loudly, stretching as she did so. "Should I call the guys? We never did make it to the Wing 'n' Egg."

"No, they wake up earlier than you. I've been keeping them up too late, and they need to rest. Tomorrow we can go out with them if you want."

"So what do you want to do? We could rent a movie," Cara said, putting a thoughtful hand to her mouth.

Felicity smiled. "We can go to O'Flannigan's and see if they have any good movies to rent. We can even get you some snacks if you want."

Cara gave Felicity a rueful look. "Do you actually have any money or is this 'we' that you keep talking about actually just me?"

"To be fair, I do the work of an entire kitchen staff by myself, every day, for free," Felicity retorted. "I see your point, however, and I will be acquiring some money soon, hopefully. I have to go down to Island Village to ask around for sponsors for the surf competition."

"Alright, after work, why don't we go and do that, then hit O'Flannigan's and get a movie and some snacks. It'll be great to have a girl's night."

After they had dinner, they did just that. John let Cara take his car to Island Village. She wasn't a particularly good driver but she at least had a license, unlike Felicity who had never gotten hers. Cara found a spot to park fairly easily and the two girls stepped out into the cool night air.

"Rain's coming," Felicity said, looking up at the dark, starless sky.

"Alright then, let's hurry up and get you some sponsors before it comes down," Cara said, also looking up at the sky.

They hurried into the Chowder Coddage, the island's most famous chowder restaurant. They walked through the wooden saloon style doors and had to sidestep a father and his two children walking out with chowder in bread bowls. The restaurant itself was tiny, with just six barstools around the edge of the interior where people could sit and eat their chowder. They walked up to the counter and were greeted by a teenage boy with horrible acne and a friendly smile.

"How may I help you fine ladies tonight?" he asked them.

"Hello, I was wondering if the manager was in tonight. I have to talk to him," Felicity said in a neutral tone. She wasn't one for pleasantries but she also tried to avoid being needlessly rude.

"Sure thing," the boy said as he hurried out of sight into the small kitchen. He came back a moment later with the owner of the Chowder Coddage, an overweight balding man by the name of Greg.

"Felicity!" he said jovially. "I had a feeling I'd be seeing you soon. Here for another sponsorship?"

"Yes I am. The prices are the same as last year," she told him.

"Deal, but I want a better spot than last year. My logo could barely be seen that far down your arm," he complained.

"You're the one who picked the location," she reminded him. She wasn't upset that he was trying to barter for better real estate on her wetsuit. Everyone always did. It was just good business, but she hadn't been born yesterday. The people who'd experienced business with her found her to be intelligent and fair, yet indomitable.

"Tell you what, do you think you'll be winning again this year?" Greg asked her. She knew she was about to strike a deal.

"Of course. I've won every year. As has every member of my family before me," she said, sounding uncharacteristically cocky. She knew this was a man who liked confidence.

"Excellent! Then here," he pulled out a wad of cash and leafed through it, giving her a stack of large bills. "Put me right across your back, so everyone knows that the Chowder Coddage *backs* the champ." He shot finger guns at her and Cara doubled over with laughter.

"Consider it done," Felicity said with a small nod.

"Pleasure doin' business with ya, as always," he said grandly.

"Likewise," she said as she turned and walked out through the doors, turning her body to avoid a group of high schoolers walking in.

"Wow!" Cara said as Felicity handed her the stack of money. "I didn't think you'd be making this much!"

"Arms and legs cost less, the thighs and upper arms cost more than the calves and lower arms. Feet and hands are the same as the calves and lower arms. Torso is the priciest. Center of the chest is reserved for the woman who makes the wetsuits," Felicity explained.

"And you make this much every single year?" Cara asked. She had never actually seen Felicity make the transactions.

"Correct. Always in cash, since I don't have a bank account," Felicity said as she walked past the fudge girl giving out free samples. Cara stopped and grabbed a piece of the chili dark chocolate flavor.

"Hey, Cara! Hey, Felicity!" Julia, a pretty girl with dark hair and bright blue eyes, welcomed them as they entered. She was a former high school classmate of Cara's and had been working at the fudge store since she was fourteen; her mother was the owner.

"Hey, Julia! How are you?" Cara asked her brightly.

Julia tossed a sample of the maple walnut fudge to Cara. "I'm great! Just got invited to a party by Andrew. He is so hot," she said, practically swooning.

"Be careful with him," Felicity warned. "He's not boyfriend material."

"Wait a minute, don't you have a boyfriend already?" Cara asked her.

"Oh here we go again," another girl spoke up as she finished boxing up a customer's fudge. Andrea was a heavy set blonde girl who came from the mainland to work every summer.

"He and I are no longer seeing one another," Julia said in a tone that screamed 'Ask me what happened.'

"What happened?" Cara obliged.

"Well, he thought making out with another girl wouldn't count as cheating as long as I'm not around to see," she told them.

Felicity shook her head. "Disgusting. Absolutely disgraceful."

"Agreed," Andrea chimed in. "You're just the third person she's told today."

"It's part of the process!" Julia cried in dismay.

"Julia, you're a lovely girl and need to raise your standards," Felicity chastised.

Andrea laughed. “I take it you’re the mom friend?”

Cara elbowed Felicity. “More like the great-grandma friend.”

Felicity rolled her eyes but didn’t disagree.

Julia handed her a paper bag. “Mom left this for you. She said same arm as last year.”

“Thank you. Give her my best,” Felicity said calmly but sincerely.

“Hey, will I see you guy’s at Andrew’s party?” It’s at Penelope’s house” Julia asked.

“I wouldn’t count on it,” Felicity told her just before walking out the door into the rain that had just begun to fall.

“See ya later!” Cara called as she followed.

Felicity and Cara hurried to the car. They managed to make it inside just before the rain began pouring in earnest.

“It’s like someone’s tossing buckets on the windshield,” Cara noted.

“We should hurry and get to O’Flannigan’s before the streets flood,” Felicity told her. Cara nodded. She knew just as well as Felicity that during big rainstorms, parts of the island flooded bad enough to come up to a person’s knees. They had good luck with the traffic lights and made it to O’Flannigan’s Grocery Store quickly. They hurried inside and Cara grabbed a basket.

“I should get pizza rolls!” she told Felicity.

“Get whatever you’d like. I don’t eat, remember?”

“Ugh, can’t you just like get excited about food with me though?” Cara whined.

“No.”

Cara shook her head and hurried to the frozen food section. As she rounded the corner of the aisle, she walked straight into a tall figure in a green T-shirt.

"I'm so sor—" she began as she looked up and realized it was Andrew. "Hey! What are you doing here?"

"Hmmm," he said pretending to think long and hard. "I'm not sure. What could I possibly have come to a grocery store for?"

"Oh wow, you're hilarious," she said sarcastically.

He grinned at her. "I know, I know. I'll be here all week. Speaking of the week, are you going to the big party at Penelope's this weekend?"

"I thought you were throwing a big party?" Cara countered, remembering what Julia had said.

He looked pleased. "Are my parties that famous that you've heard already?"

"I just came from the fudge shop," she explained.

"Ah, Julia, of course. She's a cutie but she loves to talk," he said, nodding sagely. "My party is at Penelope's. It's a sort of a 'congrats on not dying' party."

"I don't know if I'm going. Penelope and I aren't exactly friends," Cara said.

"You have to! You owe me remember?" Andrew reminded her, "I found out who the last person to see Josh was."

"Oh yeah, what exactly had our deal been again?" Cara asked, trying and failing at not blushing.

"You said I get a prize. It was very non-specific, but I'm cashing in said prize. Come to the party," he said.

"Fine, but then we're even," she said.

Meanwhile, Felicity had run into a familiar face as well. Basil walked up to her as she was picking out a movie. He stood there awkwardly, looking like he wanted to say something.

Felicity broke the silence first. "Hey."

"Hi," he said, emotions swirling in his voice.

"I'm sorry about the other night," she told him. "Sincerely. It's noble of you to have wanted to protect the island from danger. And I appreciate you wanting to protect me."

He blushed and ran a hand through his dark hair. "It's fine I guess. At least it proved I'm not the killer right?"

"Very true. Anyway, can I make it up to you?" Normally Felicity wouldn't care much about this sort of thing but Basil seemed to be a rare holdover of decency in an indecent age.

"Well, uhh." His eyes darted downward. Normally, she would think he was checking her out, but she could tell he was just nervous and avoiding eye contact. His eyes looked around the room and eventually found their way back to her face. "I don't know. What do you want to do?"

Cara finished her conversation with Andrew and made her way over to Felicity. "Fel, we needed to go to a party at Penelope's and I know you're going to say no but—"

"Yeah OK," Felicity said, cutting her off.

"We— Wait, what?" Cara asked, flabbergasted.

"Yeah, let's go. Basil, I'll make it up to you by bringing you to a party at that dumb bitch Penelope Smith's mansion. Sound fair?"

"Yeah! Sounds great!" he exclaimed enthusiastically.

"Lovely. I'll see you there this weekend then?"

He nodded vigorously and walked, still facing them, toward the exit. He tripped over the corner of the doorway and scurried out the door.

"Why'd you invite him?" Cara asked.

"I owed him. Besides, he's a nice guy," Felicity explained. "Where is your food?" she asked, gesturing toward the empty basket in Cara's hands.

Cara blushed and hurried back to the frozen food section. While she was gone, Andrew paid for his groceries and walked past Felicity, then stopped and turned to her.

"You're Cara's friend right?"

"Felicity," she said icily.

"Right, Felicity. You're coming to Penelope's party, right? You of all people should appreciate surviving Gully trying to kill her."

"What?"

"Well, he had a huge crush on you right? If you had gone on a date with him, he might've gotten you alone and, well..." He brought his finger across his throat.

"So you definitely think Gully was the killer?" she asked him.

His eyes went wide with fear, but he did a good job of keeping it out of his voice. "That's what the paper said. You don't think the killer's still out there do you?"

Oh great, she thought to herself. *He's the gossiping type, if he thinks the killer might not have been Gully he'll definitely tell someone, and people will listen. Great move Felicity, you're going to cause a panic.* "No! No!" she said, waving her hands. "The police said it was him so it must be. I'm just so shocked, you know? Like it's scary. It could've been me. You're right, what if he had gotten me alone? I guess I'm just in denial. But Penelope said she saw him right? She's awful but she's not blind. She knows Gully when she sees him." She was really banking on him not knowing exactly what Penelope had said.

"Yeah, I know what you mean," he said nodding. "He could've gotten any one of us. But hey, he's dead now so why worry about it anymore? Let's party!"

Felicity forced a smile. "Yeah, I'll be there."

He left and Cara arrived with the snacks soon after. Felicity held up the movie she had rented, a thriller about sharks. Cara laughed. "Are you sure you're ready for that, Fel?"

Felicity laughed and put on a fancy voice. "Quite the contrary, my dear Cara, I love sharks, having been acquainted so closely with one simply makes the experience of the movie all the more thrilling." She punctuated her sentence with a grand sweeping gesture of her hand.

Cara laughed even harder. "Wow, someone's in a good mood."

"I'll be in an even better one when we get home and away from this rain. Ready?"

Cara gave a quick nod before the two of them sprinted through the rain and into the car. The roads were beginning to get bad but not so bad that the water came over the bumper of the car, as both girls knew it would in an hour or so. They parked in the pebbly driveway and ran into the house.

"Did you girls have a nice swim?" John teased.

"Hey, at least I don't need to shower now." Cara laughed.

Felicity and Cara both changed into T-shirts and fluffy sweatpants. Cara opened up all of the snacks: pizza rolls, popcorn, and sodas. The pair looked for all the world like typical nineteen-year-olds.

The movie was actually decent, although the fake-out ending was disappointing. Cara stretched and yawned. Felicity thought she was going to bed but instead she pulled out a checkerboard.

"You sure you want to lose a game of checkers this late at night?" Felicity asked patronizingly.

Cara scoffed, "Oh please, I could beat you in checkers in my actual sleep." This was their typical pre-checkers banter. They set up the game board and Cara looked at Felicity. "This is your last chance to give up before the absolute domination begins."

"So you admit I'm about to absolutely dominate?" Felicity countered.

The game began. Piece after piece was moved. Cara was good, very good in fact, but Felicity had decades of experience on her. She double-hopped Cara's pieces. "King me." Felicity had this match in the bag, or so she thought. Cara got two of her pieces kinged in the next two turns. On and on the game raged, each girl determined. In the end, Felicity won. She extended a cordial hand. "Good game."

"As always," Cara said, shaking her hand. Cara brushed her teeth and washed her face. She was tired and ready for bed.

The rest of the week went fairly quickly. The boys would come by and they'd play a board game or go for a beach walk, sometimes they would grab an ice cream. Everyone seemed to have forgotten about the murders and about Gully. Everyone with the exception of Felicity. She sat perched on a kitchen chair like a gargoyle, deep in thought, wearing a black crop top, black yoga pants, and a pair of light sneakers. The boys had let themselves in. Vito had on blue jeans and a crisp gray button-down shirt. Gio was wearing a tight-fitting black V-neck and black basketball shorts. Joey had a purple striped tank top and cargo shorts. Everyone was waiting for Cara. Eventually she came out dressed in a white tank top with black stripes and black jeans.

"Did you guys bring bathing suits?" Cara asked the boys.

"You think I'm bringing this hair anywhere near a pool?" Joey asked, running his hand gently over his blow out.

Cara rolled her eyes. "Such a diva. What about you two?"

"I wouldn't miss a chance to show off these guns in a pool now would I?" Gio asked as he flexed his entire body at once. She wanted to make fun of him but she had to admit, he was pretty ripped, although he lacked the mass that Joey had.

"Alright! Then, let's go!" Cara said enthusiastically.

They began to walk toward Gio's car but Vito stopped Felicity before she walked through the door.

"You think the killer is still out there," he told her. "And that he'll be there tonight."

"How would you know that?" She asked him, stunned.

He sighed, "Because I think the killer is out there still, and I know you're smart enough to come to the same conclusion as me. Gully dying was written off by the police as an accident. Most people are happy to believe that's the truth, but I think you and I both know that's a little suspicious."

"Yeah, OK, but how did you know that I thought the real killer would be at the party?" she asked, trying to follow his train of thought the way he seemed to be able to do with her.

"Because you're wearing what you were wearing when you went to the reserve. I assume this outfit makes it easy to move around and fight, and probably hides blood since it's black?"

"Annoyingly perceptive as usual," she said flatly.

He shrugged. "What I don't know is why you've been relaxed all week and tonight you're suddenly on edge. What makes you so sure tonight is the night?"

Gio answered from in the doorway. "Because the killer has unfinished business. Whoever it is would be happy everything got pinned on Gully. They got away with it, but they'd be bothered by the fact that one got away. Penelope was literally in their hands and she got away. This is the perfect opportunity to kill her."

Vito didn't look convinced. "There's so many witnesses. Why wouldn't you do it when there's no one else around?"

Felicity chimed in, "There's so many witnesses that no one will see. If a strange car pulled up to Penelope's house on a normal night, it might be noted but no one will question a car being parked outside her house when there's a dozen other cars. If she vanished tonight at the party, everyone would assume she had left with someone else. There would be tons of confusion and no one would be able to straighten out the story, not to mention the fact that with alcohol involved, people's memories will be fuzzy. That's how I do most of my killing, if I'm honest."

Gio looked at her. "Aren't you going to tell me how impressed you are with my deduction skills?"

"Congrats, the two of you combined were able to figure out what I already knew," she said, pushing past him and walking to the car. Gio and Vito got in a moment later.

"What took you guys so long?" Cara asked.

"Just discussing some things with the Hardy Boys over here," Felicity told her.

"Hardy Boys?" Joey asked.

"How do you not know the Hardy Boys!?" Gio exclaimed, outraged. "Brother detectives? Team up with Nancy Drew sometimes?"

"Glad someone reads," Felicity said quietly.

"Are you kidding? He used to love those stories," Vito said. "Those and Nancy Drew. He and his friends used to go around the elementary school solving quote-unquote mysteries."

Felicity looked at Gio, amused. "Did you guys have a name for your detective agency?"

Gio turned bright red. "The Mystery Team," he said under his breath.

"I'm sorry," Cara said, grinning, "I didn't quite catch that."

He sighed. "The Mystery Team! OK?"

"Hell yeah," Joey exclaimed. "I was a member of the Mystery Team, ya know."

"So did you guys ever actually solve any mysteries?" Cara asked.

“Sort of,” Joey said cryptically.

“Explain,” Felicity demanded, intrigued.

“Well, we think we solved a few but the principal said since we couldn’t actually prove any of it without searching someone’s house, and since we couldn’t search their house, we ended up not ever bringing the suspects to justice,” Gio explained.

“You sound like you’re still bitter about it,” Felicity pointed out.

“I am still bitter about it!” Gio said.

She reached forward and patted his shoulder, careful not to jostle him too much as he drove.

“Everyone be ready tonight, OK? We think the killer might strike tonight, and before you ask,” Vito said as Joey opened his mouth to ask a question, “no, we don’t think Gully was the killer. So just be on your guard, guys.”

Gio parked a block from Penelope’s. Her house was packed. People were in the basement, in the yard, on the first and second floors, but Penelope’s and Mr. Smith’s bedrooms were off limits along with the third floor. Vito went off to explore the snacks while Cara and Joey went to pour some drinks for themselves. Felicity casually made her way through the jostling crowd. She stopped and turned around, giving a questioning look to Gio who was following her.

“What?” he asked.

“You’re following me,” she said, sounding like it should be obvious.

“Yeah? What’s the problem?” he asked, genuinely confused.

“No problem, I’m just wondering why. Wouldn’t it be better to split up and cover more ground?” she pointed out.

He looked a little embarrassed. “Yeah, I guess. I, uh, well, never mind.” He hurried toward the staircase to move up to the second floor. Felicity pushed him from her mind and continued to make her way through the house. She saw a number of people she recognized, although she didn't know them personally. She wasn't even really sure what she was looking for. It wasn't like she had any leads. Anyone in this house could be the killer, or none of them could be. Maybe she was way off base. This was going to be harder than she thought.

Cara and Joey were out on the lawn. They had gotten caught up with some people shot-gunning beers and now Joey was on his knees funneling a beer as someone poured a shot of vodka into the funnel. He took it like a champ.

"Impressed?" he asked Cara.

"Oh please, any guy here could've done that."

"True," he admitted, "but I like to think none of them would look as good doing it."

She laughed and put her hand on his arm.

"Well, well, look who made it," a voice said from behind them.

Cara jerked her hand away from Joey's arm and turned around. "Andrew! Hey!"

Andrew looked as good as ever in designer jeans and a designer T-shirt. "It's good to see you," he said, giving her a hug. "And who's this?"

"Oh, this is Joey. He's just a friend," she said.

"Nice to meet you," Andrew said, shaking Joey's hand.

"Yeah," Joey replied, looking like he did not think it was very nice to meet Andrew.

"We were just funneling some beers, if you'd like to join us," Cara offered.

Andrew gave her a dazzling smile. "I'd love to, but I have to find Penelope. Have you seen her?"

Cara shook her head and Andrew left to find Penelope. Joey seemed a little put out.

Gio walked around, lost for a bit until he saw Penelope. She was wearing leather pants and a black bandeau, along with the scarf from the night she had almost died. She had a drink in each hand and looked distressed.

"Hey," Gio said walking up to her. "What's up?"

She looked at him like she was about to yell at him but then her expression softened. "I can't stop shaking."

"Are you cold?" he asked.

"No! It's like, every time I see this scarf I feel like I can't breathe, and wearing it..." She shuddered. "It's like I'm there again. My heart's pounding."

"Then why don't you take the scarf off?" he asked.

She downed the drink in her left hand, a blue mixture of some kind. "That's exactly why I'm wearing it. If I stop because of what he tried to do, then he's winning. Does that make sense? Like if I let him impact me like that, then even if he didn't kill me, I still lost a part of me to him. A part that loves this scarf." She paused a moment to rub the end of her scarf. "I'm just going to get drunk and hope it goes away. Since I've now had a shot of tequila and that glass of jungle juice, and I'm five-foot-nothing, I'm sure I'll be drunk pretty soon." She began to drink from the other cup, which contained what looked like champagne, and walked away.

Gio watched her go. He felt a mixture of pity and admiration for her. He found a group of people talking and smiled at them, although none of them paid any attention to him. He decided to wait for a chance to join in their conversation.

Vito, meanwhile, was in the basement, playing bartender. This was the perfect way for him to scope out the crowd, listen in on gossip, and not look like a creep by standing on the outskirts of a conversation.

Stacy walked up to him with Oscar. "You again!" she screeched.

"Is that any way to talk to your friendly neighborhood bartender?" he asked.

"Oh yeah? If you're a bartender, how about you make us drinks then? Hmm?" she demanded.

"She likes Bloody Marys. I don't really drink," Oscar told him, looking apologetic for his sister's behavior.

Vito made a Bloody Mary and gave it to Stacy who downed it with frightening speed, and slammed the glass back onto the bar. "Another!" she screeched.

Vito sighed and made another. Oscar took it. "Slowly," he told his sister before handing it to her. She obeyed and he turned to Vito. "Sorry about her. You're one of the guys who saved Penelope, right?" he asked, eyeing Vito up and down.

"I am. What's your take on the whole killer situation?" Vito asked.

Oscar looked around to make sure no one was listening, "Well I think it's a little distasteful that they're having this party. Penelope didn't even want to have it, but Andrew convinced her. She hasn't been herself since the attack, she's been jumpy."

"Understandable."

"Yes, yes, of course. I think she's hoping maybe the party will be the closure she needs to get back to her usual self," Oscar told him.

Felicity was still scoping out the place when she heard rapid footsteps behind her.

“Felicity!” a voice yelled. Felicity whirled around just in time to get a face full of hair as Julia threw her arms around her in a big hug. “Oh wow, you’re really cold,” Julia said, releasing her. “Do you need a sweatshirt or something?”

“I’m fine. How are you, Julia?” Felicity said, not even attempting to match Julia’s pep.

“I’m great! I just got here and I’ve already got two guys hitting on me. I’ll have a new boyfriend in no time,” she said happily.

Felicity opened her mouth when she saw Basil being pushed toward the exit by two boys. One of them was a ‘roided out muscle head while the other looked athletic but not gigantic.

“Julia, could you hold that thought for a second?” she said as she hurried over to Basil.

She grabbed the two boys by the shoulders and whirled them around. “What do you two think you’re doing?” she demanded.

They both seemed surprised that someone was trying to stop them, especially since that someone was an attractive girl.

“We were just throwing this creep out,” the ‘roided out one said, sounding as if she should consider it a great service.

“And why,” she asked, anger rising in her voice, “would you do that?”

“Because he’s not wanted here?” the athletic one said, sounding confused that she would even ask such a thing.

“You’re really going to come to the ‘congrats on not dying’ party of a girl who’s alive because my friends saved her life, and then throw out one of *my* guests that I *personally* invited here? I’d say perhaps I should speak to Penelope and see who is and is not wanted here,” she said with menace. The boys looked at one another and then walked away, unsure of what to say.

“Thanks,” Basil said dismally.

Felicity punched him in the arm.

"OW!" he exclaimed, rubbing his arm. "What was that for?"

"Stop sounding so sad. I brought you here; you're wanted. Are you ready for me to make it up to you that I got you arrested?" she asked him forcefully.

"Why do your words sound so nice but also sound so aggressive?" he asked her, looking a little frightened.

"Because I'm aggressively nice!" she snapped at him. She grabbed his hand and pulled him across the room.

"What's going—" Julia began.

"Julia, stop dating losers who cheat on you. Those guys you met tonight, trash. This is Basil. He's a good friend of mine. He's reliable, courageous, and protected me from the killer."

"What?!" Basil asked, mortified.

"He did?" Julia asked.

"He did. He was patrolling the beach because he wanted to make sure no women were attacked and he saw me and made sure I was safe. He also put on my favorite song at a party even though he knew it would get him kicked out. Even if you don't date him, he's a good guy to have around so do me a favor and give him a chance, OK?" Felicity turned to Basil. "Be yourself, and try not to scare her off, OK? She's a really sweet girl, don't be nervous." She patted him on the back and walked away.

Felicity saw Gio standing awkwardly at the edge of a circle of people, smiling and nodding in an attempt to join the conversation.

"What are you doing?" she demanded.

"What do you mean what am I doing? I'm trying to join this conversation," he told her angrily.

"Well, why are you just standing over here like a weirdo?"

He blushed and looked away. "I don't know how to get into the conversation. I don't know anyone here."

Felicity suddenly felt awful. She hadn't considered the fact that Gio, Vito, and Joey weren't even from the island. Everyone here but Cara, Penelope, and the twins was a complete stranger. That's probably why he had been following her; she was the only person he knew. "Hey, Gio, I'm really sorry. I forgot you didn't know anyone. I sort of threw you to the wolves before when you were following me."

He forced a smile. "Yeah, I figured Vito could handle himself, and Cara and Joey were together, so you and I could check out this place together."

"You're not mad at me, are you?" she asked. Her eyes widened in shock. Why would she ask that? "Oh no."

"Oh no, what?" he asked, looking around nervously.

"I care about you," she said, upset at this fact.

"You do?" he asked, looking both confused and pleased.

"I do. I really don't talk to anyone outside of Cara's family. You're the first real friend I've made since I became, well, you know. I just realized it. I actually care if I hurt your feelings," she told him, the realization startling her. She hadn't realized she was capable of feeling any kind of attachment to anyone outside of her immediate household. Gio surprised her even further by hugging her.

"Wow, you're—"

"Really cold, yes I've been told," she interrupted.

"So, what's the plan?" Gio asked.

"Well I've been trying to figure that out. I have absolutely no idea who the killer is. I mean obviously if he's the only middle-aged man here, then that's our guy, but so far everyone looks like a bunch of twenty-something-year-olds."

"OK, well, what if we stop focusing on the who and focus on the when," Gio suggested.

""The when,"" Felicity repeated thoughtfully. "OK so if I was going to kill someone at a party, I would do it after everyone was too drunk to remember, but not so late that people began to leave, because then people start keeping track of who's going where."

"Why don't we find Cara and Joey, and they can be our sort of drunk guides," Gio said, gesturing toward the window.

"Good thinking," Felicity said.

They made their way through the house to the yard but couldn't find Cara or Joey.

"Hey! We've got a vodka luge! Come luge with us bro!" a shirtless Filipino boy yelled, throwing an arm around Gio.

"Yeah, sure, but I gotta find my friend first. Have you seen him? Dude with the blow out?" Gio said to the boy as he led him to a table surrounded by people, one of whom was Cara.

"Cara!" Gio shouted as he ran up to her, Felicity following.

"Hey guys," she said, swaying a little. "What's up?"

"How much have you had to drink?" Felicity asked, putting her hands on her hips in a maternal fashion.

"Not a clue," Cara said with a drunken giggle.

"Dammit," Felicity said.

"Penelope's drinking really hard tonight. If the killer doesn't act fast, she'll start throwing up and attract a crowd," Gio said, turning to Felicity.

"We need to find Penelope," she said, pushing him toward the doors to the pool while she herself ran back to the front door.

"Gio!" Joey roared from the pool. He was hammered and soaking wet, surrounded by other drunk and soaking partygoers.

“What are you doing?” Gio asked, shocked.

“I’m turning up! I’ve got everything I need—beer, a pool, and all my best friends in the world!” he shouted, gesturing to the pool full of strangers who erupted into cheers.

Gio shook his head and went into the room with the bar and shuffle-board. “Vito, thank God.” He breathed a sigh of relief to see his brother, who, while also being surrounded by drunk strangers, was at least sober himself.

“Did something happen?” Vito asked, immediately handing a shaker cup to a girl and walking out from behind the bar.

“I’m not sure, but have you seen Penelope?” Gio asked hurriedly.

“Not for a while. She and Andrew got a drink from me and then went upstairs. She said she was feeling kind of sick,” Vito told him.

“Dammit,” Gio said, echoing Felicity’s sentiment from before.

Felicity was on the ground floor. She knew she didn’t have much time. *Where would I take someone if I wanted to kill them?* she thought to herself. Third floor or bedroom. Bedrooms could have drunken couples come in hoping to secretly make out. She ran to the second floor, weaving her lithe body through the crowd. The closer she got to the third floor, the more she knew this was the spot. She shoved a boy out of the way and hit the staircase. The third floor had a small dining area and a hallway with four rooms. She braced herself for a fight and threw open the first door, second, third, and finally came to the fourth door. The doorknob didn’t move. She threw herself through the door, smashing through the wood. She saw Penelope standing alone on the balcony and *shck.* Two blades penetrated deep into Felicity’s lower back.

Chapter 6

Minutes *earlier.*

Penelope felt sick. She had drunk way too much way too fast.

"Come on," Andrew said, guiding her through the house.

"I don't want anyone to see me," she whined.

"Hold on a little longer. We're going to the third floor," he said as he moved people out of the way for her, like her own personal security guard.

They made their way to the third floor and she ran to the guest room, grabbed the trash can and threw up into it.

Andrew put on a glove and locked the door. "So, no one comes in," he explained.

Penelope nodded. She didn't need anyone seeing her throw up.

"Why don't you go onto the balcony? Get some fresh air," he suggested.

She shook her head and vomited again into the can. "Can you grab me a glass of water?" she asked weakly.

He went downstairs and came back up with a glass of water and two kitchen knives, which he tucked into his waistband before locking the door behind him. She drank the whole thing and then went out on the balcony, breathing in the fresh air. He slipped on his other glove. It was time. His plan had been perfect. He had told Josh that Penelope wanted to hook up with him and that he just had to go to his job after the party to meet her. Josh had drunk himself into a stupor as he always had. All Andrew had to do was tell him to lay in the display case and wait for Penelope. Josh's intoxication had knocked him out minutes later and Andrew dumped the ice in on top of him. Josh didn't even stir. Cara asked him who was the last to see Josh and of course, everyone thought it was Gully. Penelope had asked Gully if he had been telling people she was going to hook up with Josh. Andrew hadn't planned on texting her from Gully's phone after he had killed him, but he hadn't been able to stop himself. He couldn't resist killing the island's perfect little princess, now could he? Then it was just a matter of making Gully disappear and everyone would think he had done all the killing and escaped, never to be seen again.

But those interlopers had ruined everything. He had had Penelope in his clutches, literally. He breathed heavily at the thought and looked at her out on the balcony. He had lost. He had failed to kill Penelope Smith. Andrew Mannish did not fail, and he certainly did not lose. He was going to right this wrong and finish off Penelope. It would be easy. He would simply toss her over the balcony, and then blend back in with the crowd downstairs. He would even make out with Cara who at this point would be drunk enough to give him an alibi for when Penelope fell. It would all look like a big accident.

As he crept toward her on the balcony, he heard a sound. Someone was in the hallway, opening doors. He hurried backward as the doorknob jiggled, he pressed himself against the wall just as the wood of the door splintered and Felicity came through. He wasted no time in plunging two large, serrated knives into her lower back.

Chapter 7

Felicity felt the blades leave her back, slicing up her organs on their way out and dropping her to her knees.

"I was aiming for your lungs. If I pierced both, you can't talk or scream," Andrew informed her.

Penelope screamed.

"Oh, right. Forgot about her," he said casually. He kicked Felicity in the face and strode toward Penelope.

"You-you're," Penelope said, hyperventilating.

"Yes, yes, yes, I used Gully's phone to get you to come to his boat so I could kill you and frame him."

Tears were falling from Penelope's eyes. "But why?" she asked weakly.

"Why? Why what? Why kill people? Because I wanted to see if I could. I'm the king, Penelope. Everyone on this island is my little pawn and I wanted the challenge of killing someone without getting caught. I didn't lay a finger on Josh. I set up the pieces and then left him buried in ice. I killed him with just my mind, my words, and some crushed ice, Penelope. That's power. Then, of course, I needed to frame someone. Not only did I take his life but I also destroyed his reputation. Of course, that's all down the drain now that I've stabbed Felicity to death. Still, it's worth it to be able to kill you, I think."

He was right in front of Penelope now and she looked up at him, eyes full of hurt. "But why me?"

He looked genuinely perplexed at being asked that. "Are you kidding? You're this island's golden goose—rich, pretty, popular. People consider me to be the guy version of you. Without you, I'm just me, the undisputed cream of the crop. Nothing personal, I promise." He threw one knife to the side, grabbed Penelope's long platinum hair, and yanked her head back, putting the knife to her throat. Her eyes went wide and her hands grasped at his arm.

Felicity moved with a ferocity she hadn't felt in a very long time. She sunk her long fangs into his neck and wrenched her head to the side, ripping a large chunk of Andrew's flesh out. She brought her mouth back to the wound, her fangs digging into his neck and holding there. He struggled as she drank greedily. His eyes grew panicked with the kind fear that only comes from being in the clutches of a predator. He could feel the life draining from him and into Felicity. She was so strong, he couldn't fight back. He punched weakly. With fading breath, he stuck his hand in the knife wound he had put in her back. She released him immediately, letting him drop to the floor as she reared back and let out a choked gurgle.

Penelope, who had been standing there in a state of shock, let out a bloodcurdling shriek. She tried to run past Felicity, who reached out to grab her only to feel a searing pain through her leg. Andrew had picked up his knife and sliced her Achilles tendon, dropping her to the ground. Penelope backed up toward the balcony as Felicity tried to crawl after her.

"Where do you think you're going?" Andrew rasped, taking his shirt off and wrapping it around his neck to stifle the bleeding.

Penelope ran to the balcony and looked over the edge. Would she survive a jump like that? She turned and saw Andrew coming toward her with the knife, the sick joy of a hunter oozing from his being. Penelope climbed onto the balcony railing. She was just able to get her hands on the edge of the gutter jutting out from the roof above her. She jumped and swung her legs around onto the roof, pulling the gutter out of its place as she did so. She crawled up the steep roof, her head spinning. There was a deck on the very top of the roof which led down to another deck on the third floor. If she could get to the roof deck, she could escape through the house.

Andrew ripped the gutter down farther. With his height, he was able to fit between the gutter and the roof and pull himself up. This hadn't been the way he had planned this, but he was in too deep now. He was breathing heavily, his heading spinning just as much as Penelope's. The bite from Felicity had taken a lot out of him. Bitch. She would be dead by now, he was sure of it. He would say she and Penelope were the killers. It made sense. Felicity had been the one to find Gully's body. Once he finished off Penelope, it would be a simple matter of going to the hospital and reporting their attack to the police. Everything else would be considered self-defense. His family could afford a lawyer good enough to make that believable, he was sure of it. He smiled at the thought of getting out of this scot-free.

Gio had rushed into the room just in time to see Andrew pull himself onto the roof. He looked down and saw Felicity on the ground, two holes in her back and a gash through the back of her ankle.

"Felicity!" He yelled as he dropped to her side. She tried to speak but her punctured lungs couldn't produce the air necessary for words. She grabbed him and used him to stand and limp over to the balcony. Even with one leg, she was strong enough to jump from the balcony's railing up to the roof and pull herself up. Her entire body was screaming in pain, but she would never forgive herself if she let Andrew escape. She crawled along the roof. Each movement was agony, and each ounce of pain added to the rage that fueled her in her pursuit.

Penelope was almost to the rooftop deck. Vito was there with his shoes off, tying the laces together as he cheered her on. Just a little farther and this nightmare would be over. Her hopes came crashing down as a hand closed around her ankle and pulled her back down the roof. Andrew straddled her, keeping her pinned under the weight of his legs, breathing heavily. His heart was racing; he couldn't do this much longer, but luckily he wouldn't have to. He took a few more deep breaths before raising his knife. A pair of shoes tied together at the laces caught his knife arm, wrenching it backward and disarming him. Andrew scrambled to grab the knife that was sliding down the roof. Penelope took the opportunity to crawl away and he reached back and grabbed her ankle again. He was prepared to just toss her off the roof when he saw a sight that chilled him to the bone. Felicity, in all her vampiric glory, was crawling toward him, her black hair whipping in the breeze, his blood on her mouth like a neon sign, highlighting the inhuman fangs jutting from her gums. His grip on Penelope slackened and she pulled away. He was going to die, he realized. He could barely keep his head up and this girl, this, this thing was coming toward him. He had stabbed through her, no, *its* lungs, and cut out its Achilles. It should be dead, or at the very least immobile back where he had left it, not crawling toward him with murderous intent.

"I lost. But I never lose," he said sadly as Felicity ripped the shirt from around his neck and sunk her fangs into him. She drank until his body was completely devoid of blood, savoring every last drop. She dragged herself to the rooftop deck and Vito helped her over the railing. She convulsed in pain on the deck, still not able to get enough air to produce words.

"Penelope is with Gio in the SUV. I called the police for a noise violation and spread the word that they're on their way so the crowd is dispersing. Do you want me to show them Andrew?" he asked. Felicity shook her head. "Am I going to have to hide his body?" Vito asked. Felicity nodded and pointed in the direction of the beach. Flashing red and blue lights were coming from down the street. Felicity knew the police would be gone once they realized the party was over. She used Vito to help her stand and he brought her down to the third-floor deck. They went inside and found Gio.

"She passed out. I think from the stress and alcohol," Gio told them. "She's asleep in the SUV. Most of the people are gone already, and the cops are here now from the sound of it. Felicity, are you OK?"

Felicity grabbed a pad of paper and a pen that were lying on the counter and began to write down instructions. *When the cops leave, get my surfboard and bring Andrew to the beach. Put it on his leg and toss them both on the rocks. Make sure NO ONE SEES.* She looked earnestly at them and they both gave her a thumbs up.

"What are you going to do?" Gio asked her.

Felicity laid on the floor and closed her eyes.

"Yeah, that's fair," Vito said.

Gio cautiously went down the stairs, making sure no one was there. All the partygoers had left with the exception of Cara and Joey, who were both belligerently drunk and hiding behind Penelope's couch.

"Alright, both of you, come with me," he ordered. They followed obediently and got in his SUV.

"Penelope!" Cara said happily.

"Shhhhh," Joey said, putting a finger to his lip and swaying from side to side. "She's sleeping."

"Or is she dead? Gio! Penelope's dead!" Cara exclaimed.

Gio sighed. "She's not dead."

"You're lying!" Cara yelled.

"SHHHHHH," Joey hissed. "You're gonna wake her up."

By the end of the short drive back to Cara's house, Gio was about ready to rip his hair out. He carried Penelope inside and put her on the couch, covering her with a blanket. Joey and Cara went to Cara's room. When Gio walked in they were both passed out in her bed, fully clothed, shoes on. Gio rolled his eyes. He walked outside and grabbed one of Felicity's surfboards and managed to get it inside his SUV by leaving the trunk open and bungie-cording it in. He drove back to Penelope's house and Vito brought Andrew's dead body out.

"This is really gross," Vito said in a voice that was far too calm for the situation.

"Yeah, I know, but we're friends with a vampire, so I guess committing felonies is just our thing now," Gio said as he lugged the surfboard to the beach. They strapped the leash of the surfboard around Andrew's ankle and tossed both body and board onto the rocks. A wave crashed over it and jostled the corpse, further damaging it on the jagged edges of the rocks.

"It's kind of scary how Felicity was able to think of this," Vito noted. "The rocks will tear the body up enough that the bite wound won't be noticeable."

"She has been doing this a long time," Gio said, sounding much calmer than he felt.

The brothers went back to Penelope's mansion and filled two large pasta pots with water. They took them to the roof and tossed them out in an attempt to wash the blood from the shingles. They couldn't see if it worked or not since they didn't have the night vision of Felicity, but neither of them wanted to wake her from her slumber. Her wounds looked pretty bad and although they knew she'd heal, she had clearly been in a lot of pain.

They found some hydrogen peroxide and used it to clean the blood from the floor and balcony. "What are we going to do about the gutter?" Gio asked, pointing to what was left of it, now twisted and hanging low.

"That looks like a whole lot of not our problem," Vito said with a shrug.

Gio and Vito went to where Felicity lay; her eyes immediately opened at their approach and they felt their hearts skip a beat in fear.

"Help me up," she said, her voice hoarse.

They did so and brought her to the SUV.

"How do you feel?" Gio asked her.

"Like someone fatally stabbed me twice and then cut out one of my leg tendons," she said irritably.

"Always so grumpy," Vito said with a smirk.

"I will murder you right here," she said angrily.

"See what I mean? Grumpy," he said to Gio.

She crossed her arms and sat back in her seat. He was right; she was grumpy and she knew it. When they walked into her house, she saw Penelope on the couch. She tried to walk toward her but Gio, who she was using as support forced her toward the stairs.

"We can deal with her tomorrow. Tonight, you need to rest," he told her firmly. She protested and tried to move back toward Penelope, but he pulled away and she accidentally put pressure on her hurt leg, causing waves of pain to shoot through her body. She almost fell but he caught her. "Like I said: Bed, now," he told her, helping her up the stairs and into her bed. She closed her eyes and went back to sleep. She knew what she would have to do tomorrow, and she knew the others wouldn't like it.

The next morning, she awoke to screams. She hurried down the stairs, able to put a small amount of weight on her foot, even though her tendon was not fully healed. She found Penelope being comforted by Gio and Vito. When Penelope saw her, all the blood left her face, and she began to flail wildly. It was time, Felicity knew. She bared her fangs and limped toward Penelope. She'd make it quick. Just before she could sink her fangs into Penelope's tender flesh, John grabbed her from behind, lifting her and throwing her onto the couch.

"Felicity, what are you doing?!" Sarah demanded.

Cara and Joey sleepily exited Cara's room, hungover and dazed.

"She knows," Felicity said, struggling aggressively against John's grip, her back screaming in pain.

"Let me go!" Penelope shouted as Gio and Vito restrained her.

"Can we all just take it down a notch? My head is killing me," Joey whined.

"Stop complaining and help me!" John commanded.

Joey seemed to rouse then and rushed over to put his weight on Felicity. Between the two of them, they managed to hold her and she settled down, although her body remained tensed, like an animal ready to thrash free at any time.

"Let me go!" Penelope shrieked. "Help! He--" Her voice was muffled by Gio, who covered her mouth with his hand.

"I need to kill her. You know she'll tell someone," Felicity hissed.

"Fel, you can't just go around killing people!" Cara protested.

"I have to!" Felicity said fiercely.

"Let us talk to her," Gio suggested.

Felicity shook her head. "No, I have to be sure."

Penelope struggled against the brothers' grips but she wasn't nearly strong enough. They brought her into Cara's room and shut the door.

"I'm calling the police! When my dad finds out you kidnapped me—" Penelope began.

"Will you shut up for like two seconds!" Gio said, exasperated.

"What is that girl? She's some kind of monster. She has fangs. She killed Andrew. Oh God, Andrew," Penelope said, her eyes bulged as her mind replayed the events of the night before.

"Andrew tried to kill you. Felicity saved you," Gio said in a soothing voice.

"She's a vampire," Vito said as if that explained the whole ordeal.

"But, but vampires aren't real; they're make believe," Penelope said, trying to convince herself.

"Yeah, you're right, my mistake," Vito said sarcastically.

"No, but I saw the fangs," Penelope said. "She got stabbed and brushed it off like it was nothing." Penelope began breathing heavily and Gio sat down on the bed next to her, taking her hand. She looked pleadingly into his eyes. "Vampires are real?"

"Yes," he said sympathetically.

"Why aren't you freaking out? Unless—" Her eyes went wide with fear and she scooted away from him.

"No, no, I'm not a vampire. Look." He showed her his very human teeth.

"But Felicity is," Penelope said, reality settling into her addled brain. "Oh God, she's going to kill me."

"She would certainly like to," Vito confirmed.

"I need to call the police. Where's my phone?" Penelope asked.

"Yeah, I have your phone," Vito said holding it up, out of her reach, "And that's exactly why she wants to kill you. She thinks you're going to tell people."

"Of course I am! She's a blood-sucking monster! Someone needs to know!" she exclaimed.

"It's just me, let me in," Cara called, knocking on the door.

Vito opened the door and Cara entered. Vito took the opportunity to slip out of the room.

"Heyyy, Penelope," Cara said awkwardly.

"Hey?! Hey?! Is that really the best you can come up with?!" Penelope asked angrily.

"Look, I know this is probably a lot to take in, but—" Cara began.

"A lot to take in?! One of my longtime friends tried to *kill* me last night. I was saved by a vampire—by the way, *those* exist now—and now she also wants to kill me. Not to mention I've been kidnapped by you people. So why don't you come at me with something a little better than 'hey?'" Penelope was feeling many things at the moment, and anger was the emotion taking the front seat.

Cara sighed. "OK, what about please?"

Confusion crept into Penelope's features. "Please?"

Cara took Penelope's hands. "Please don't tell anyone about Felicity. Or Andrew."

Penelope looked down at her hands in Cara's hands and pulled them away, crossing her arms over her chest. "Why?"

"Because Felicity is my best friend and I don't want anything to happen to her," Cara said.

"Plus, you owe her. She saved your life," Gio reminded Penelope. "And before that, I saved your life."

Penelope shuddered at the memory of Andrew's hand around her hair, his sharp blade pressed to her neck, ready to end her life. She sighed. "What are we going to tell the police?"

"Nothing," Gio said simply. "We took care of the body. Made it look like he died surfing. The blood is mostly cleaned from your house, other than the gutter, which you can play off as party damage."

"Apparently someone's been busy," Penelope said wryly.

"Yeah, seriously," Cara said, looking at Gio in surprise.

"You both got super drunk early in the night. It was like eleven o'clock when Andrew tried to kill you," Gio said.

Penelope lay back on the bed. She felt tired. Exhausted really. "Damn," she said with a sigh. Gio and Cara looked at her apprehensively. "I seriously got saved from a serial killer by a vampire," she said, sounding mildly bothered. She sat back up. "Fine. What's the story I'm supposed to tell everyone?"

Cara threw her arms around Penelope. "Thank you so much!"

Penelope pushed Cara off with one hand. "Don't touch. You people aren't my friends. I don't even particularly like most of you."

Gio opened the door and Penelope walked into the living room. "I'll keep your secret. Just tell me the cover story."

"I don't know if we can trust her," Felicity said, looking at Gio.

Penelope rolled her eyes. "Listen, I don't like you. I'd even say I hate you. But Gio's right, I owe you and I owe him. I'll keep your secret. You can count on that."

Vito stepped forward. "The cover story is simple, the gutter got ripped down from some drunk partygoer who climbed onto the roof to watch the stars and slipped. Andrew died in a surfing accident sometime after he left the party. That's it. You don't know anything else."

Penelope shrugged. "Seems easy enough." She looked at Vito. "Can I have my phone back now?"

Vito glanced at Felicity, who looked unhappy but didn't stop him as he handed Penelope's phone back to her.

Penelope opened the door, spilling sunlight into the room—which Felicity had to dive onto the floor to avoid—and slammed it shut behind her. Gio and Joey helped Felicity up.

"Felicity, is there any chance you could make us an omelet or something?" Joey asked her. "I feel like a booze-soaked turd in a dumb and dumber tux."

"Same," Cara agreed.

"I'm sorry, you what now?" John asked in confusion.

Gio rested his face in his palm. "They're hungover."

"I'm sorry, I really can't be moving around the kitchen, my ankle is killing me," Felicity told them apologetically.

"It's OK, Felicity," Sarah assured her. "You caught a killer last night, yes?"

"Yeah, what did happen last night?" Joey asked.

"Turns out Andrew was the killer. He tried to pin it on Gully, couldn't stand that Penelope got away, and planned that whole party just so he could get away with killing her. He stabbed me in the back twice, I bit him, he stabbed me in the leg, Penelope got away, I killed Andrew but Penelope found out I'm a vampire," Felicity told him.

"And they ripped the gutter down from Penelope's house," Vito added.

"Yes, and that," Gio agreed.

"Wooo! We caught him! Well done!" Joey yelled, holding up his hand for Cara to give him a high five, which she did.

"I hate you both," Gio said.

Helen rang a bell from the other room and everyone turned to look at her in surprise. "Breakfast is served everyone," she said.

Everyone but Felicity, who remained seated on the couch, went into the dining room and was amazed; there was French toast, eggs, bacon, sausage, juice and milk. It looked like something out of a catalog.

"Grandma, I didn't know you could cook!" Cara exclaimed.

"All grandmas know how to cook, dear," Helen replied.

The food that Helen had made was delicious. When the boys had had their fill, Gio drove them back to his uncle's. They were all exhausted. Cara went back to bed as well and even Felicity spent the majority of the morning passed out on the couch. In the Sunday paper the next day, Andrew's obituary was posted. The paper made no allegations of foul play. It was believed that he had died night surfing, which the papers claimed was growing in popularity since the island surf champion, Felicity, let slip that she night surfed as part of her training for the island's competition.

The next week was a strange one. Andrew had been a popular figure among the island's young people. People mourned and lit candles for him, and many people attended his wake. Penelope was among the people who went. She wore the scarf that Andrew had not once but twice tried to kill her in. The casket was closed, but Penelope knew that he was in there and that was enough to make the shaking and the panic attacks stop. She was a survivor.

Felicity healed quickly and was back to surfing in no time. She was as spry and athletic as ever, and she decided to go for a run across the bridge to the mainland to the cemetery where people who died on the island were always buried so she could pay a visit to Gully's grave.

"Gully, I'm sorry. You were a sweet kid," she said to the gravestone. She gave it the kiss that Gully had never gotten from her in life. She decided she would put the Traveler logo on her suit for free. She owed at least that much to Gully's father. She walked down the rows of stones and found where Connie was buried. She touched the gravestone and crouched down.

"Good to see you, Connie," she said with a melancholic smile. "I miss you so much." She gave a bitter laugh. "Most people would be crying right now but you know I can't do that. You wouldn't believe the summer I've had. I got bit by a shark, Connie. Isn't that just my rotten luck? Never once has there been a shark attack in this island's history, and the first one ever, it's me who gets bit. First murderer in the island's history, and who gets stabbed? Me. I mean I got better, but come on! Don't worry though, I'm still looking out for your family. Even now. We still run the tavern. Business is booming, bigger and better than ever, believe it or not." She rested her chin on her knees and stared silently at the gravestone of her old friend. "Take care, Connie." She stood up and looked around. Her brother and father weren't buried here or she would visit them too. Her mother, Lorraine, had been cremated after dying from the flu. Her ashes were buried somewhere in the sand on the island as per her last wish. Felicity began her long run back to the island.

Another week passed and other than what Hershel Meyer reported as "Every Diver's Worst Fear," in the paper when a diver's tank had ruptured and she'd drown, there were no more deaths. Things returned to normal: The sun was shining, tourism was booming, the tavern was full of jolly people, and Felicity found that she was actually enjoying herself. Everything would be perfect were it not for a nagging feeling that she could *not* shake.

"Come on, Felicity, you got the guy. Let it go," Joey said when she mentioned it at their late-night visit to the Wing 'n' Egg.

"I hate to say this but I have to agree with Joey on this one," Vito added. "You literally watched Andrew try to kill Penelope. He stabbed you; you saw him."

"But something doesn't feel right," she told them, unable to phrase it any differently.

"No one else has been murdered since. Maybe you're just looking for something that isn't there? Like when you're a kid and you freak yourself out thinking there's someone in your room but it's really just an empty room," Gio suggested.

Felicity shrugged. "Probably. I've always worried too much, even back when I was human."

"Now that you mention it," Joey began as Cara desperately tried to catch his eye and shake her head. "How did you become, ya know, what you are?"

Felicity grimaced. Even Cara hadn't heard the story. It wasn't one she liked to talk about.

Gio kicked Joey under the table. “Come on man, don’t ask her that,” he admonished.

Felicity gave Gio a look of amusement.

“Sor-ry, I didn’t realize it was such a big secret,” Joey said sassily.

“It’s fine. Just, please, can we change the subject?” Felicity asked.

“OK, how excited are you guys for Shark Night?!” Cara asked with enough enthusiasm to overpower the awkward tension that had filled the air.

“I love Shark Night!” Felicity exclaimed, earning her terrified looks from the boys. “What?” she asked, seeing their expressions.

“I have literally never seen you this excited, ever, in all the time I’ve ever known you, ever,” Joey said.

“Sharks are my favorite animal,” she said simply.

“OK, even so, what is this ‘Shark Night’ you speak of?” Vito asked.

“Shark Night is sooo fun,” Cara said. “They put a huge blow-up movie screen in the bay and everyone gets big pool floats and goes out in the water and there’s little food stands on the shore and you can put out a blanket or chair and they play shark movies all night. It’s super fun.”

“It must be if Felicity’s getting this excited about it,” Gio teased.

“Hey! I get excited,” she protested.

They all laughed at her and Joey pointed at her with his fork. “I’d think you’d hate sharks after one took a bite out of you.”

“Oh please, you can’t blame a shark for that. It was just trying to eat. Besides, I take bites out of tons of people so I guess that’s just sort of the universe balancing out right?” she said speculatively. “Either way sharks are definitely the neatest animal out there. I’ll love them no matter how many bites they take out of me.”

“Hopefully they leave that number at one,” Cara said, casting her eyes down to Felicity’s side.

"It would've been zero times if this fool hadn't decided to go swimming in the middle of the night," Felicity said with a gesture toward Gio.

Gio sputtered as he gestured toward Vito and Joey "Hey! They told me to!" This erupted into another round of laughter.

Penelope entered the restaurant and for a brief, tense moment she and the group stared each other down. The tension was broken when the waitress stepped in front of the table and delivered the check. The group paid and left immediately.

"Damn, what are the odds of seeing her here?" Gio asked when they were all in the car.

"Pretty good seeing as this is the only twenty-four-hour restaurant on the island," Cara pointed out.

"OK, true. Have you guys ever been to that amusement park?" Gio asked.

"No, we've lived on this island our entire lives and never once took a trip to the amusement park," Cara said sarcastically.

"Did you know that it's also a waterpark?" Joey added.

"Are you suggesting we go to the waterpark?" Felicity asks.

"I mean yeah, why not?" Joey said, enthusiastically.

"Well, the waterpark closes at six so unless you want to watch my flesh sear off of my bones in a matter of seconds, the waterpark is out," Felicity told him.

"We could skip the waterpark and go to the amusement park part after the sun goes down," Vito suggested.

"That sounds like fun!" Cara exclaimed.

"Yes, it does indeed sound fun," Felicity agreed.

"So, I'll pick you guys up tomorrow after sunset?" Gio asked as he dropped the girls off at their house.

“Sounds good to me. Good night,” Felicity said as she shut the door.

“You going surfing tonight?” Cara asked once they were inside the house.

“I’m not sure,” Felicity admitted. “I need to check a few things out.”

“Alright, good night then. I’ll see you in the morning,” Cara told her as she went into the bathroom to get ready for bed.

Felicity stood awkwardly for a few moments before deciding on a course of action. She sprinted out into the night. There was something she had to confirm before she could rest easy. Aided by the fact that she could run at a full sprint indefinitely, she arrived at the Wing ‘n’ Egg fairly quickly. She walked in and spotted Penelope eating with the twins and two boys she didn’t recognize. She walked over to them, ignoring the hostess asking if she wanted a table.

“What do you want?” Stacy screeched as Felicity approached the table.

“I need to speak to you,” Felicity said to Penelope.

Stacy opened her mouth to protest, but Penelope held up a hand to silence her. “Fine, but make it quick,” Penelope said as she slid over the boy next to her and out of the booth. They walked outside and Penelope leaned against the building. Felicity guessed that it made her feel safe having something solid to hold onto now that she knew Felicity was a vampire. “So? What do you want?” Penelope asked her impatiently.

“Your father would know if there had been any more murders on the island, right?” Felicity asked.

“Yes, definitely,” Penelope confirmed.

“Have there been?”

Penelope shook her head. “Nope, not as far as the police know. Why?”

“I don’t know,” Felicity admitted. “I just can’t shake the feeling that something’s not right. I have no evidence for it. Andrew’s definitely dead. No one else has been killed, but I have this annoying nagging in the back of my head, telling me something's just, I don't know, off, I guess."

Penelope looked at her intently. She was wearing sandals so the difference in their heights was readily apparent. Eventually Penelope spoke. "After Andrew tried to kill me the first time, I kept having flashbacks. I couldn't get a full night's sleep because my body wouldn't relax. It's called hypervigilance. It's basically when your body can't relax because it thinks you're under attack even if you're not. It went away after the funeral. He's dead, you need to remember that, the threats over."

"You're probably right, sorry to bother you," Felicity told her, turning and sprinting off into the night.

Penelope stood and watched her until she was out of sight.

When Felicity arrived back home, she grabbed her board, the only one that was left in pristine condition, and ran to the beach. The waves were breaking just right and her worries were soon forgotten. Penelope was probably right. The threat was over. There was nothing at all to worry about.

Chapter 8

Cara's excitement to go to the amusement park with the boys was contagious and Felicity couldn't help getting excited too, at least as excited as she ever got. Imaginary Island was built in 1985. It wasn't particularly large but it had a few pretty intense rides as well as a large Ferris wheel and an arcade, along with an assortment of carnival games.

"What's taking them so long?" Cara whined, looking at the time on her phone.

"The sun hasn't even set yet," Felicity pointed out.

"I know but still."

"Be patient. I'm sure they'll be here soon. You know, back in my day we didn't have all this instant gratification. When I was your age, we had to wait days to receive a message because it would come on a handwritten piece of paper sent through the mail," Felicity lectured.

Cara rolled her eyes and flopped onto the couch. "Yeah, OK, Grandma"

"Please, I'm not that old, dear," Helen said, as she walked into the room.

Felicity smiled as Helen entered. "How are you feeling?"

"A few aches and pains but otherwise I feel fine. And yourself?" Helen asked her.

Felicity shot her an unamused look. "Very funny."

“Thank you, thank you, I’ll be sure to remember you when I get my own comedy show,” Helen said, giving a small wave to an imaginary crowd.

Someone knocked on the door and Felicity opened it, revealing Gio, Joey, and Vito.

“Finally!” Cara exclaimed, standing up and walking over to hug each of them.

Helen hugged Felicity and Cara goodbye. “Have fun tonight. You boys better take care of these girls!”

“We will, don’t worry,” Gio assured her.

“Does she forget that you’re like a billion years old?” Joey asked Felicity.

She glared at him. “I’m not even a hundred years old yet, and no she didn’t forget. She just wants to make sure you know how to treat a lady with respect.”

“He knows how, whether he does so or not is a different story,” Vito teased. Now it was Joey’s turn to glare.

“Prove him wrong, Joey,” Cara teased. “Buy my wristband.”

“It is what a gentleman would do,” Vito agreed, although his tone made it clear he was goading Joey.

“Fine. Fine! I’ll pay for your wristband, but then I want all of you to admit that I know how to treat a lady,” Joey said, pointing at each member of the group.

“Works for me,” Cara told him.

“Yeah sounds fair,” Vito said smugly.

Gio scoffed. “You guys are all ridiculous.”

They parked in the Island Village parking lot which was shared by both the waterpark and the amusement park. It was crowded, which normally would bother Felicity but she couldn’t help feeling a sense of relief looking at all of the smiling, happy tourists. Her island was safe; people were still coming. Out of the corner of her eye, she caught Gio watching her admiringly. "What?" she asked.

"Oh nothing," he said, blushing and turning away quickly, "You just look, I don't know, different."

"I haven't looked different since 1944," Felicity said unenthusiastically.

"No, he's right, Fel. You look way less tense," Cara told her.

"Do you guys all think I'm just uptight all the time?"

"Sort of," Gio admitted.

"Totally," Joey said.

"Definitely," Vito nodded.

"Not all the time, just like, ninety percent of the time," Cara said soothingly.

"Well, tonight is that ten percent. I am going to let my hair down and kick back," Felicity declared.

Gio bought Felicity's wristband for her and Joey, true to his word, bought Cara's. Vito paid for his own and the group set out to find their first ride to go on.

"Let's go on the Shrimp Dragon!" Cara exclaimed, pulling on Joey's arm and pointing at a rollercoaster that looked like a dragon with two curly, shrimp - like tails.

"Shrimp Dragon it is!" he said loudly, and the two of them began to race toward the line.

"Those two were made for each other," Vito remarked.

Felicity looked at him curiously, "You think so?"

"Yeah, you don't think so?" Gio asked.

"Honestly, I hadn't really considered it. That kind of thing doesn't usually occur to me," she told him truthfully.

"Interesting," was Gio's only response. The line for the rollercoaster was short and the ride itself was simple and quick. There were no corkscrews or loops, it just went around a track and took some sharp turns.

"Is that really the most intense ride here? Come on, I want to really scream!" Joey shouted.

"You may regret that," Felicity told him, pointing to the Sea Serpent. The Sea Serpent was her favorite ride here. It looked like a giant Viking boat with a serpent's head on each side and swung side to side until you were completely sideways.

"Please, all it does is go side to side," Joey said with a cocky sneer.

"I wouldn't be so sure," Cara warned.

"I'm going to sit this one out," Vito said. "I'm actually not a huge rides guy."

"Aw how cute. You're scared of rides?" Cara teased.

"I'm not scared," Vito said crossing his arms and turning his head to the side like a pouting child. "I just don't like the feeling in my stomach when they drop."

"That's my favorite!" Felicity exclaimed.

"That's surprising," Gio told her.

"When you have superhuman reflexes, rollercoasters don't really do it, even if they go really fast. But that feeling in your stomach? I feel that as a vampire just like I would if I was a human. It makes me feel so alive!"

"That actually makes a lot of sense," Gio admitted.

"I like to think I always make sense. Come on." She led them to the end of a line, which was significantly longer than the line for the other rollercoaster. Felicity saw Vito walk over to the equally long line for the merry-go-round.

"Let's go right by the head," Joey told Cara when it was their turn to get on.

Cara shook her head. "No way am I going by the head. The middle goes high enough as it is."

Felicity pushed Joey toward the Sea Serpent's head. "Come on, I'll ride the head with you."

Felicity pulled the lap bar down until it was secure, although she had a lot of wiggle room because Joey's body was a lot bulkier than hers. As the ride began to rise, Joey let out a whoop.

"Ha! This is nothing," he said as the ride rocked back and forth in gradual arcs. She smiled; the fool had no idea what was coming. The ride suddenly lurched up to double the height of the previous swing and Joey let out a gasp. It did it again, rising somehow even higher. At the peak of each swing she took in the sensation of being completely upside-down and vertical with the ground, and then free-falling downward only to swing back the other way. Joey's cries echoed through the night and she wondered if the others could hear him, or if she would have to make fun of him herself. Her question was answered as soon as they got off the ride and found Vito waiting for them.

"So which one of you was shrieking like a woman from a horror movie?" Vito asked with a smug grin. All eyes turned to Joey.

"Hey! That's not fair, at least I rode it," he protested.

"A man who knows his limits is better than a man who exceeds them," Vito retorted.

Gio pointed to the Ferris wheel. "Why don't we ride that? It'll be nice and easy for everyone."

"Sounds good to me, the view is super pretty up there," Cara said. The line for the Ferris wheel moved quickly since six people fit in each car. As the wheel brought them up, Felicity took in the view. Her vampiric vision allowed her to see with a distance and clarity that the others couldn't even dream of.

From the top of the Ferris wheel, she could see the individual golf balls on the mini golf course and the gulls settling down on the roof of a building. Moments like these were when she was most grateful for being a vampire.

"Does anyone want an elephant ear?" Joey asked once they were off the Ferris wheel.

"Ooo yes, I love elephant ears!" Cara said enthusiastically.

"I can go for an elephant ear," Vito said, exchanging a look with Gio.

Gio nodded. "I'll wait here with Felicity, since- ya know, you can't eat."

"Oh thanks," Felicity said flatly.

Vito, Joey, and Cara walked to the elephant ear line while Gio and Felicity stayed where they were.

"Sooooo," Gio began awkwardly.

"So?"

Gio looked into Felicity's eyes and took a deep breath. "OK, so Joey and I made an agreement tonight."

"Oh?"

"Yeah, he's over there right now with Cara. Vito's going to find some excuse to leave them alone, and he's going to ask her out," Gio said, speaking slightly faster than normal.

Her eyes widened in surprise. "Oh, wow, OK, I guess that explains why you and I are waiting here then."

"Well, hmmm," he said, looking like he was grasping for words. "Yeah, see, the agreement was that we would both make a move on the girls we liked."

"You like someone too?" she asked him.

"Yeah, you."

"Oh,"

They both stood there in silence for a moment before Gio spoke again. "So, what do you think?"

Felicity didn't know what to think. This wasn't a situation in which she often found herself. She glanced over toward the elephant ears. "Let's walk," she said at last. She didn't want the others coming back halfway through the talk she was about to have. They walked into the arcade and she sat down against the wall, wrapping her arms around her legs and resting her head against her knees, so she could look at him. He sat down and leaned forward slightly, looking at her expectantly. "Gio, you're the first friend I've ever had outside of Cara's family."

"This is either going to be really good or really bad," he said ruefully.

She gave him an apologetic smile. "I'm sorry."

"Here it is," he said knowingly.

"No, no, look, Gio. You're a great guy. I just… don't date. Like the whole idea of being with someone like that is, I don't know. I just don't like it. Never have, even when I was a human, but now that I'm a vampire, I really don't date," she told him.

"We could always have like a casual thing. We wouldn't need to put a label on it," he tried.

"No, like, I don't even feel attraction to people. Not just you, really. I actually don't feel attraction to anyone. I do like spending time with you, but I don't want this to get… weird."

"You took a shark bite for me and I helped you get rid of a dead body. How much weirder can it really get?" he joked.

She gave him a small smile. "I don't want you to get your hopes up that things are going to change though, alright? I really do want to be your friend, but if you don't think you can handle that, I understand."

"No, I get it. Really, I do. It might take me a few days to switch gears but I'd like to stay your friend at least. You're amazing," Gio told her.

"Am I? How so?" she asked.

"You're beautiful, and athletic, and fierce, and take charge. I love that." He blushed and looked away. She laughed, and then laughed harder. "What's so funny?!" he said, defensively.

"I hate that this is true but you"—her laughter interrupted the words—"you just described Penelope."

"What?!"

"I'm athletic because I'm a vampire. When I was human, other than being decent at throwing a baseball, I was not an athlete at all. Penelope, on the other hand, has been training her whole life and actually is an athlete. She's definitely fierce and takes charge," Felicity told him. "And I promise you this, she's a lot more pleasant to cuddle than me. Ask Cara, I have no body heat." She pressed her hand against his arm for emphasis and he flinched at the touch. "See what I mean? Cold."

"Damn," he leaned his head back against the wall and closed his eyes. "I wonder how things are going for Joey."

"Honestly, I couldn't tell you. But Cara does seem to enjoy being around him. She thinks he's funny at least."

"Here's hoping."

She nodded and they both sat there in silence as the arcade whirred and buzzed and people walked by them, laughing and talking with enthusiasm. Felicity finally broke the silence. "Can I trust you?" she asked softly.

He looked at her, startled. "Of course you can."

"Promise?" she asked, a note of apprehension in her voice.

"Yes, I promise. You can trust me, Felicity," he assured her.

"Alright, then I'm going to tell you something that I haven't told anyone since Cara's great-grandmother. If you're up for it."

He turned to face her. "I'm totally up for it."

"So, remember when you asked me how I became a vampire?"

"Yeah, you said you didn't know and that you don't like to talk about it."

She grimaced. "That's because I don't know how and I don't like to talk about it."

He made a sort of choking noise for a moment. "What?"

"Just, shh. OK, I was born in 1926. I grew up here on this island with an older brother and my best friend Connie. Connie is Cara's great-grand-mother. My father and brother both went off to fight in the Second World War. Neither of them made it home."

"Oh, I'm so sorry," Gio told her. He didn't know what else to say.

"To make matters worse, the flu spread throughout the island. My mom and I got sick and she died. It's fuzzy in the end. I was close to death for a while. The flu really isn't a pleasant way to go. But I remember a man. He had fangs. He's the last thing I remember before everything went black, but when I woke up he had done something to me. I truly don't know what. I never saw him again. He left me two notes. One explaining that my brother had saved his life in Japan and that he was repaying his debt by saving me. It also said that he was a vampire and I was now a vampire. The other note had a list of things to avoid, things to do, basic instructions on how to live as a vampire. I've been here ever since."

Gio's eyes were wide with awe. "So, there are other vampires?"

She gave him that look that meant he had asked her something stupid. "How would I know? I only ever met the one, that one time. He could be dead for all I know, so maybe I'm the only one, maybe I'm not. I am the only one on the island at least."

"Thanks. Thank you for telling me," he said.

"You're welcome."

She stood up in one ridiculously graceful motion, then turned and pulled him to his feet with an ease that startled him.

"One of these days I want to put you on a bench press and see what you can do," he teased.

She rolled her eyes and motioned for him to follow her. "Maybe someday."

They spotted the rest of their group almost immediately because the others were walking around searching for them. Joey waved them over when he spotted them.

"How'd it go?" Gio asked.

Joey held up a half-eaten elephant ear. "Went great. They're amazing. Want one?"

Gio glanced at Vito who began to snicker. "No, no, no, Joey, I swear if you didn't keep up your end of the deal!"

Vito burst into laughter. "I'm guessing things didn't go your way?"

Gio growled and snatched the elephant ear from Joey, taking a large bite as he did so.

"I'm confused, what's happening right now?" Cara asked.

Felicity pat her on the shoulder. "I'll explain later, alright?"

"You guys want to hit the arcade or play some carnival games?" Vito asked.

Joey laughed. "I feel like Felicity is stupidly good at carnival games."

"Felicity *is* stupidly good at carnival games," Cara confirmed.

"I can't deny it," Felicity said with a small shrug.

"Let's play then! Maybe we can clean these guys out of their prizes," Vito said, rubbing his hands together like a cartoon villain.

They walked over to the games and Felicity heard a familiar voice, as well as the pattering of footsteps behind her. She turned around just in time to see Julia coming toward her. Julia threw her arms around Felicity and then did the same to Cara.

"Hey guys! Long time no see!" she said, peppy as ever. "Who are your friends?"

"This is Gio, his brother Vito, and their friend Joey," Cara said, pointing to each in turn.

"It's nice to meet you," Gio told her.

"Nice to meet you!" Julia said.

"Are you here with anyone?" Cara asked.

Julia turned red. "I am. I'm actually on a date right now." She turned around and walked away a few feet before grabbing someone who was skulking in the crowd and pulling them over. Everyone's jaws dropped in shock.

"Basil!" Felicity said in a rare show of excitement.

"Hey, Felicity," he said, awkwardly hugging her.

"So how did you two meet?" Joey asked, looking in disbelief between Basil and Julia.

"Felicity introduced us at Penelope's party!" Julia said brightly.

"Oh, wow, that was really nice of her," Cara said, also sounding stunned.

"Yeah, turns out we get along really well. We were actually supposed to go to the waterpark today cuz it was so hot out, but, like, they were closed," Julia explained.

"That's weird, why were they closed?" Vito asked.

"Apparently someone snuck in last night and fell off the top of one of the slides and well..." Julia began.

"Died," Basil finished.

"Woah, are you serious?" Joey asked.

Basil nodded gravely. "Yeah, that's why I always stick to the lazy river. I'd be afraid I'd slip and fall off or something. I'm terrified of heights."

Felicity grabbed him by the shoulders so quickly that it was almost imperceptible to the human eye. "Say that again," she ordered, her fingers digging into him with frightening strength.

"I-I'm afraid of heights," he said, voice shaking.

She released him. "Terrified of heights," she said quietly to herself.

"Felicity, are you OK?" Julia asked, blue eyes shining with concern.

"I need to go." She turned to the others. "We need to go, now," she told them before walking in quick but controlled steps toward the exit.

"Sorry about that. It was nice seeing you," Cara said, hastily hugging Julia and following Felicity.

"Nice meeting you!" Gio said as he and Vito also followed.

Joey gave Basil a thumbs up as he left. "Well done, my guy!"

When the group got to the car, Felicity was waiting impatiently. "What took you guys so long?" she demanded irritably.

"What's wrong?" Gio asked.

Felicity shook her head as she hopped into the SUV. "I need to see something. Something's definitely not right."

"What are you talking about?" Vito asked but she remained silent, her mind was racing.

After what felt like an eternity, they arrived back at her house. She leapt from the SUV before Gio even put it in park and ran into the house. She grabbed a piece of paper and began to write.

"Felicity, what's going on?" Sarah asked.

Felicity didn't answer, she just continued to write.

Gio, Vito, Joey, Cara, Sarah, and John all crowded into the dining room. Felicity had written the names of everyone who had died over the summer along with their cause of death, with a big line through the middle of the page and then the words *scuba girl* and *waterpark guy* under it.

"Felicity," Vito sighed, "Are you listing all the deaths because you think that these two"—he pointed to *scuba girl* and *waterpark guy* - "were murdered?"

She ignored his question and continued to stare at the paper, as if she was trying to read a foreign language.

"Look, we've been over this," Gio said gently. "Andrew is dead. These were probably both accidents. Accidents do happen."

"How about we all stop talking to me like I'm a child," she snapped. They all took an involuntary step back. She looked back at the paper and wrote Penelope's name. "John, do we still have the paper from the other day? The one about the diver who drowned?"

"Let me check," he told her as he began to rifle through a pile of newspapers for the recycling. "Yes! Here." He handed it to her and she began to read through.

"OK, tell me what the pattern is here," she said as she wrote, *age 33* next to *scuba woman.*

"Um, I don't know?" Cara said.

Felicity began writing the ages of the other people on the list. "How about now?" she asked once she had finished.

"There's no pattern I can see," Vito admitted.

"Right! Exactly!" Felicity shouted. "That's exactly what I thought—all different ages, sexes, and methods. But then check this out." She circled Josh's, Gully's, and Penelope's names. "What's the pattern between these three?"

They all stared at the three circled names silently finally Vito spoke up. "Those three are all our age,"

"Yes! Exactly!" Felicity said, pointing to him.

"Fel, no offense but you sound like a crazy person," Cara told her.

"Hold on a minute," Vito said, holding up a hand to silence Cara. "I want to see where this is going,"

"When Andrew was going to kill Penelope, he said he did it for the challenge. He told her that he killed Josh the way he had because he wanted to see if he could manipulate someone enough to get them somewhere he could kill them without even needing to touch them. Gully, he killed to frame him for killing Josh. Penelope, he did because she was going to talk to Gully and he thought it would help the framing, coupled with the fact that she was his social equal, and he didn't like that. But there's a flow to them. A narrative. The other murders don't make sense. They're random."

"Oh my God," Vito breathed, eyes wide. "You're right, look at the shark attack guy. He died the same day Andrew killed Josh. Either you're wrong about his death being a murder, or someone else killed him."

Felicity punched her fist into her palm triumphantly. "That's exactly what I'm saying, and I think I found the pattern—fear,"

John cocked an eyebrow at her. "Fear?"

"So, these all seem like random deaths right?" Felicity said, tracing her finger over the list of deaths as she spoke. "Shark attack, buried alive, falling, scuba malfunction. They really don't seem to be at all related. All of them could theoretically be ruled out as accidents."

"How is being buried alive an accident?" Joey asked incredulously.

Gio answered before Felicity could. "If you didn't realize that it could kill someone and you buried them for fun, or as a prank. The beach also gets driven on and manicured sometimes. Someone could've fallen asleep in the hole and been buried at night when a beach driver was smoothing the sand."

"OK," John said slowly, like he was measuring his words carefully, "then what makes you think these aren't just a series of unfortunate events you're connecting to one another? We know Andrew killed two people and tried for a third. What makes you so sure you're not assigning bodies to a killer but they really are just random accidents?"

"Like I said before, there's a connecting factor—fear," Felicity said.

"Yeah, still don't know what that means," Joey said snarkily.

"What did Basil say about the waterpark?" Felicity asked him.

Joey thought back, trying to remember. "Something about being afraid of heights."

Felicity nodded and held up the article about the diver, pointing to the headline. "Exactly and this here says what?"

"Every Diver's Worst Nightmare,'" Joey said, sounding like a child being scolded by a teacher.

Felicity nodded. "And that night we were all at the police station, I was eavesdropping, and Hershel Meyer said, 'sharks are terrifying creatures,' which in a sense is right, tons of people are terrified of sharks."

Cara's eyebrows shot up. "On the beach, someone said they had always been afraid of being buried alive."

"I, myself, am actually afraid of being buried alive," Felicity admitted.

"I wasn't until you mentioned it," Vito said with a shudder.

"Let me just make sure I'm getting this right," Gio said. "You think that someone is killing people in ways that encapsulate people's worst fears?"

"That is exactly what I'm saying," Felicity said. She wondered if the others would think she was crazy. She certainly felt crazy, but more than that, she felt certain she was correct.

Vito pulled the paper over and he and Gio stared at it for a long time. She could tell they were both going over the names, the ages, the deaths, trying to find some other pattern. The two boys were ever so perceptive but in such different ways. If they both told her she was crazy, she would believe them.

Gio took a deep breath like he was about to say something but remained silent. Vito crossed his arms and finally looked back up at Felicity, "You might be right."

Gio nodded. "So, what do we do?"

Felicity threw her arms in the air. "How should I know?! I didn't even graduate high school. You should be happy I even managed to figure out this much."

"Gio should tell Penelope," Cara said.

"Why?" he asked.

She shrugged. "I don't know, I just figure if one killer tried to get her, maybe the second one will too, prove he's better or something."

"OK, but why me?" Gio asked.

"You're the only one of us she seems to be able to stand," Cara told him, smiling encouragingly.

"Fine," he conceded.

Vito made a noise of annoyance in the back of his throat. "This means everything we knew, we don't know anymore. Everyone's alibis from before, they don't check out anymore, right? Oh no, alright, Felicity, you need to go; you need to find Basil and Julia. If he's the killer, she could be in danger."

"He's right," Joey agreed. "That guy is majorly creepy."

"Alright, Gio drop me off at Imaginary Island on your way to talk to Penelope, I'll try to track down Basil and Julia. While I'm gone, I want the rest of you to come up with a plan," Felicity instructed.

When she was gone, Vito looked around at Joey, Cara, John, and Sarah. He gave a sigh of dismay. "She really didn't leave me much to work with here."

Sarah shrugged. “Less than you think too, since John and I are going to bed.”

They both kissed Cara good night and went to their room.

“OK,” Vito said, pacing the room as he spoke. “Where do we start?”

“Suspects?” Joey suggested.

Vito shook his head. “It could be someone we don’t even know. Cara, how many people live on the island?”

“Around ten thousand year-round residents,” she said, remembering from her history of the island class in school, “During the summer we have about ten times that at any given time.”

“OK, wait a minute,” Joey said, his brain slowly churning out a thought. “We caught that Andrew guy by figuring out who and where he was going to attack next, right? Well, what if we did that with this guy? We won’t need to know who he is, as long as we know where he’ll be and what he’s going to be doing, right?”

“OK, I take back what I said before about not having much to work with,” Vito admitted.

“See that? I’m smarter than people think,” Joey told Cara with a grin.

“Alright smart guy, so where is the killer going to strike next?” Cara asked.

“Well what else are people afraid of? Ghosts?” Joey suggested.

“I take back my taking back of not having much to work with,” Vito told him.

“Hang on,” Cara said, holding up a hand for them to give her a second to think. “If you’re killing people based on what other people are afraid of, then a horror movie would be the best place to do it right? What about Shark Night? Everyone’s either in the water or on the beach, thinking about how a shark could be in the water, ready to attack at any moment. That's like the best place to do it; make everyone's fear come true."

"That's really smart," Joey told Vito.

"Yes, it is," Vito admitted.

Felicity sniffed the air, like a bear. She smelled cotton candy, zeppole, popcorn, gasoline, and about a thousand people. She walked toward the arcade. It seemed like a place Basil might go. She hoped desperately that he and Julia hadn't left yet. She would never forgive herself if he turned out to be a killer and she had set him up with Julia. She picked up her pace, needing to cover more ground quickly.

As she exited, she saw a car pulling out of the parking lot, and Basil was in the passenger seat. "Thank God for vampire eyes," she said to herself as she began to run toward the car, not so fast that it caught people's attention but fast enough to make it to the exit relatively quickly. Julia had already made her turn and was on the main road. Felicity wanted to swear but she didn't have time for such luxuries. She sprinted across the street, while the walk light was on and ran on the sidewalk, dodging people. She would have to hope Julia stopped at a light somewhere. Three blocks later, she finally caught up. She then ran down the street parallel to the one Julia's car was on. Her vision was good enough to see across the block to the main road and she didn't want Basil to see her.

Eventually the road she was on ran out and she ended up running through a few people's backyards, and then on the beach. How far was Julia going to drive? It turned out she was driving Basil home. They both leaned in, her for a kiss and him for a hug. Felicity cringed with secondhand embarrassment. Basil went inside and Julia drove away. Felicity waited. She couldn't tell exactly how much time passed but it must have been hours. Eventually the light in what she assumed was Basil's room shut off and she made her way back home.

After Felicity had left his car, Gio went to Penelope's house. He rang the doorbell and Mr. Smith answered the door in his pajamas. "I was just about to head to bed for the night. What can I do for you?" Mr. Smith asked Gio, a note of suspicion in his voice.

"I'm just here to see Penelope. Is she around?" Gio asked.

"She's in the pool. You can head on down there if you want, I assume you know how to get there?" Mr. Smith said, ushering him inside.

"Yes, thank you very much," Gio said.

He walked through the mansion into the basement, memories of the party flashing back as he walked through each room, and into the room with the indoor pool. Penelope was swimming laps, as usual. She finished a lap and hit a button on a stopwatch lying by the side of the pool.

"New record?" he asked, causing her to jump with a small yelp.

"Don't do that!" she yelled.

"Sorry, I thought you'd seen me."

She lifted herself from the pool and began to dry off. "So what kind of bad news are you about to give me?"

"What makes you think I didn't just come to say hi and ask how you've been?" he asked indignantly.

"Oh, well, hi. I've been alright. My swimming times have plateaued and it's frustrating because I think I might have hit my limit. What about you?"

"Hi, I've been alright, although I do have some bad news."

She laughed. "There it is."

"You might want to sit down for it," he told her.

"Look, I know you've sort of seen me freak out and cry like twice in the past few weeks but I promise, I'm tougher than I look," she assured him.

"Alright, well, we think there's a second killer," he said in a casual tone, hoping she'd take the news well.

She turned bright red. "Do you think this is funny?!" she said angrily, "I was almost killed twice, and you come into my home in the middle of the night to what? Try to scare me?"

"No, and let's be real here, it's not the middle of the night. It's not even eleven o'clock yet. I came here to warn you, just in case this guy decides to try to finish what Andrew started. Maybe he won't, but maybe he'll want to prove he can do what Andrew couldn't. I don't know. We just figured you deserved to know." He turned and began walking away.

"Wait! Where are you going?" she called.

"I did what I had to do, now I'm going back to Felicity's to see if they've figured anything else out."

Her eyes went wide. Wait a minute, are you being serious? Like this isn't a joke or something?"

"No, of course not! I can even show you the paper that Felicity drew on to illustrate her point," he told her.

She sighed and grabbed onto his arm. Her head was reeling. "You're right. I should have sat down." Once she steadied herself, she looked up at him. "Thanks for letting me know. I'll be over tomorrow to find out what you've learned."

"Are you sure? You don't have to—"

"Of course I have to! You really think I want to go over there? No. I want to know everything you know, so I'll be over there tomorrow. After sunset, I assume?"

He nodded.

"Good. I'll see you then. I'm going to go make sure all my doors and windows are locked."

"OK," he told her, leaving through the glass double doors that led outside. "I'll see you tomorrow. Stay safe."

Chapter 9

Felicity sat in the back of Gio's SUV. She was not happy, not happy at all. Gio could practically feel her glare through the headrest.

"Remind me again why we're going to Penelope's house?" Felicity grumbled.

Gio sighed; she knew exactly why they were going to Penelope's house. "I told you already Felicity, Penelope wants to be involved."

"And she texted me saying we could go to her house to make a plan, which I agreed to since her house is huge," Cara added.

"Someone's cranky from staying up all night watching Basil," Joey teased, something he immediately regretted as Felicity's glare turned on him.

"I don't need sleep. Staying up all night watching Basil's house has nothing to do with it," she hissed.

Cara laughed. "Yeah, she's just always cranky." Felicity's eyebrows shot up and she turned to Cara who quickly threw her arms around her friend. Felicity grunted in annoyance but didn't protest the hug.

"I'm pretty sure I just saved your life Joey," Cara teased, still holding onto Felicity.

"Don't push it," Felicity warned. Cara laughed again and let Felicity go.

When they arrived at Penelope's house everyone got out and walked to the front door which opened as they walked up to it.

"Hey. Come in, make yourselves at home," Penelope said. Her entire demeanor was remarkably similar to Felicity's. Gio laughed and Penelope cocked an eyebrow at him. "What's so funny?"

"Nothing. How are you?" he asked.

The look she gave him wasn't exactly friendly but it was much less unfriendly than the one she had given everyone else. "I'm the same as I was yesterday. It hasn't even been twenty-four hours."

"A lot can happen in less than twenty-four hours," he pointed out.

"True," she conceded. He walked past her into the spacious room and sat down on her massive L-shaped couch. "Do you guys want anything to drink?" she asked.

"Do you have any ginger ale?" Vito asked.

Penelope looked at him with annoyance before opening the fridge and giving a deep exasperated sigh. "I really hate the fact that I actually do," she pulled a box of ginger ale out of the fridge and brought it to the coffee table in front of the couch. Everyone but Felicity took a can.

"Do you not drink soda?" Penelope asked, sounding mildly offended.

Felicity flashed her a dazzling smile, fully exposing her fangs. "No, I only drink blood," she said sweetly.

Penelope let out an involuntary squeak. She quickly recovered and walked to the other side of the couch, sitting down without another word.

"So, what have we come up with?" Felicity asked, doing her best not to let the satisfaction she felt from rattling Penelope show.

"We think whoever this is will kill again on Shark Night," Vito said, addressing the room as if giving a classroom presentation. "We believe that the killer is choosing methods of killing that are related to fears, fear of sharks, fear of scuba equipment malfunctioning, et cetera. The next logical step would be to kill people watching what are essentially shark horror films on a beach."

Felicity nodded. "That does make a lot of sense, although I wonder how they would pull it off. There's people everywhere, I'd be worried that someone would see."

Penelope offered a suggestion. "What if he did it before, and just left the body for the crowd to find?"

Cara shook her head. "No, people swim in the bay all day; they'd find it before Shark Night happened."

"That would ruin the thematic element," Vito added.

"Why does this guy stick to a theme?" Joey asked. Everyone turned and looked at him, mouths poised to give an answer but all that came out was silence. Joey took a sip of his ginger ale and looked around at the baffled faces of his friends. "I'm just saying, if you're gonna do it, why not just do it? Why the, well, ya know." He wiggled his fingers, moving his hands in big circles like he was performing some kind of dance number.

"That's a good question actually," Vito agreed. "Why go through all the trouble of luring sharks over to the island, or getting a woman drunk just to get her to the beach and bury her alive?"

Felicity's eyes lit up. "Wait a minute, say that again."

"Why go through all the trouble of luring sharks over to the island, or getting a woman drunk just to get her to the beach and bury her alive?" Vito repeated with the exact same inflection as the first time.

"Have the papers reported on the person who died at the waterpark?" Felicity asked. Penelope brought over a copy of *The Sandpaper* and handed it to her. She scanned through it silently until she found what she was looking for. "'Authorities say it appears the man had been drinking heavily the night he fell,'" she read aloud.

"And that's significant because?" Vito asked, his voice's natural condescension elevating higher.

"It tells us that he's manipulative. He plans his kills before he does them," Penelope said with a shudder.

Felicity looked at her and saw that in that moment they were reliving the same event. "Andrew killed that first boy by getting him wasted and convincing him to lie down in the display case. He didn't need to use force or anything. This killer probably gets his prey drunk and then convinces them to follow him to wherever."

"What about the first guy, the one the sharks ate?" Cara asked.

"Ok wait a minute, I have a theory," Gio declared.

"Let's hear it," Joey said enthusiastically.

"What if this killer is weak?" Gio proposed. "Think about it, they take out a one-legged man, they get two people drunk and lure them somewhere and don't even really kill them."

"Wait, what do you mean don't even really kill them?" Cara interjected.

"Think about it. When Andrew tried to kill Penelope, he was there, killing her." He shot Penelope an apologetic look. "The first time he strangled her with a scarf, the second time he was going to use a knife, but he was still using his own power. She could fight back and she would lose." He shot her another apologetic look.

"Just get on with it," Penelope snapped.

"OK, OK, sorry," Gio continued, "Anyways this guy, or girl now that I think about it, probably got the first girl drunk and convinced her to let him bury her. Then he'd just have to cover her head with sand and sit on top of her until she suffocated right? The sand really does all the work. Same with waterslide guy. He probably got him drunk and said, 'Hey, let's go to the waterpark at night, no one will be around to stop us.'"

"Yeah, not gonna lie though, we should totally do that," Joey said.

"Right, thanks for proving my point. Then all the killer has to do is lift the drunk guy over the rail, gravity does the rest. There's not really any kind of fight. The scuba woman, the water does all the work killing her. It's the perfect plan" Gio concluded.

Penelope spoke up. "Look, when I think serial killer and weak, I think Basil. That kid's super weird and looks like he hasn't touched a weight in his life."

Cara looked at Felicity. "You followed him to his house yesterday, right? What happened?"

Felicity shrugged. "Julia drove him home. He stayed in his room until four in the morning, then went to bed."

"Woah, hold on there," Penelope said, looking like she needed a minute to process what Felicity just said, "Julia as in fudge shop Julia?"

Cara nodded. "Yeah, they were on a date yesterday at—"

"WHAT?" Penelope said, jaw dropping in disbelief. "Julia is wayyyy out of his league,"

"She right," Joey agreed.

"I introduced them at your party. Basil's a nice guy," Felicity said defensively.

"I'm pretty sure he's the killer," Vito said skeptically.

"OK, he *might* be a nice guy," Felicity said, feeling foolish.

"Wait a minute, guys, why don't we just tell the police there's a second killer?" Penelope asked.

Felicity turned a pair of fiercely intense eyes on Penelope. "Because if the police start investigating the possibility of a second killer, people might start to notice. If they notice, they start taking precautions against the killer. Those precautions will also be making things very difficult for me, as a vampire, to do the things that I need to do. So, what we are going to do, Penelope, is find out who the killer is, and get rid of him. No police, no mess, no fuss. No one needs to know and no one panics, life goes on. Got it?"

"OK, I was just asking, geez," Penelope said, shrinking back into the couch.

Gio leaned forward to diffuse the tension. "Right now, the only person on our list of suspects is Basil. Why doesn't Felicity keep following him the rest of the week? If he doesn't do anything suspicious, we know it's not him and we can move on. Shark Night is next week, right? We have until then to figure out how this creep is going to attack."

"Don't you think it's a waste of time to have me follow Basil around like that for the next week?" Felicity asked.

"If you don't and it turns out he is the killer, Julia's probably going to be the next one he goes after," Penelope said venomously, "and that'll be on you."

Felicity scowled. It was like Penelope could read her worries. Of course, Penelope was a master at finding people's fears and insecurities. It's part of what let her become the island's queen bee.

Cara came to her aid. "Hey, why don't we all calm down, we don't even know where they are right now."

Penelope held out her phone, showing her a text from Julia. "Yes, we do, she's playing mini golf right now with some friends. He's working late tonight but they have a date tomorrow night.

"Ok so tomorrow, why doesn't Felicity follow them?" Vito suggested. "At least until we have some kind of idea as to how the killer is going to strike. As far as I can tell there's no other fear themed ways to kill someone on an island, right?"

"Unless they do something ghost-themed," Joey said quietly.

Vito sneered at him. "Alright genius, what would a ghost theme entail?"

"I don't know, like ya know. Oooo spooky ghost killer," Joey said, waving his arms in a ghostly manner.

"Actually, that's not a bad idea," Felicity said, more to herself than to them. Looking at Gio, she said, "You're going to need to guard Penelope."

"Excuse me?" Penelope asked, sounding offended.

Felicity shrugged. "I mean if you'd rather risk letting someone try to kill you for the third time this summer, be my guest."

All the blood drained from Penelope's face. "What do you mean?"

"It's simple, people know someone tried to kill Penelope at one point this summer, right? But they think the person behind it was Gully, who is dead. If you wanted to strike fear into people, wouldn't the best way to do it be making it look like Gully came back from the dead and finished what he started?" Felicity explained.

"How do we know it's not a vampire killing people?" Penelope countered. "Apparently those exist."

Felicity shook her head, "If there was another vampire, I'd know. Trust me."

"Tell you what, I'll stay with Penelope if you promise to follow Basil tomorrow," Gio asked, extending a hand.

"Deal," she told him.

"Fine," Penelope said reluctantly.

"So, what are we going to do tonight?" Cara asked.

"Gio is staying here," Vito said, standing, "The rest of us are going to the bay."

"Why?" Felicity asked.

"I've never actually been to the bay," Vito admitted. "I can't plan a murder if I don't know the layout, and if I can't plan a murder, I won't be able to figure out what the killer's plan is."

"Alright that actually makes a lot of sense," Felicity admitted. "Can you drop me off somewhere on the way?"

"Why?" Cara asked.

Felicity couldn't quite find the words for her reasoning. "I'm not sure. I want to walk around, maybe something will come to me,"

"Fine," Vito said. "Gio, keys." He held out his hand and Gio reluctantly handed over the keys.

"Can I at least get my overnight bag from the car?" he asked.

Cara looked at him curiously. "Why do you have an overnight bag in the car?"

"With the amount of times I've been sleeping out and pulling all-nighters with you people, I figured it would be smart to pack an overnight bag and leave it in my car," Gio explained.

"True, true," Joey said.

Gio got his bag and the group dropped Felicity off on a random side street.

"Have fun," Joey told her.

Felicity looked at him like he was dumb, but Vito drove off before Joey could react. A few minutes later, the SUV was pulling into the parking lot for the bay. Separating the parking lot from the sand was a lane of grass. To the left was a playground bedded with wood chips. Three high school boys were on the swings, two were sitting on the normal swings and one was standing in one of the baby swings. Vito, Cara, and Joey walked onto the sand. The bay was still, as it always was.

"Usually the only people to swim in the bay are little kids, and their parents, I guess," Cara informed Vito and Joey.

"How deep does it get?" Vito asked, crouching down to get a better view of the water. "It looks like there's a fence out there," he noted.

Cara nodded. "That's right, and it depends on the tide but it gets to be about, oh, I don't know, deep enough that a little kid would have to stand on his tippy toes to breathe but not so deep that a little kid wouldn't be able to breathe if he was on his tippy toes."

"You should become a scientist with those precise measurements," Vito said sarcastically.

Cara put her hands on her hips, "I haven't been to the bay since I was like, I don't know, ten maybe?"

"Yeah, yeah," Vito said waving a dismissive hand at her. "Where do they put the screen?"

"They float it out just behind the fence, and then tie it to the fence so it doesn't float away," Cara said.

"Hmm," Vito said, crossing his arms and staring at the fence the way an interrogator would stare at a suspect. "Does it go down to the bottom or is it just on the top as a marker for where to swim?"

"It goes all the way to the bottom. You can't swim under it if that's what you're wondering," Cara answered.

"Guys," Joey said, "I'm thinking about it, right? And there's like nobody around."

"Oh wow, you're brilliant," Vito sarcastically replied.

"Shh, let him finish," Cara said, elbowing Vito in the side.

Joey smiled. "Thanks, Cara. As I was saying, there's no one here, other than those high schoolers over on the playground. We could really do anything right now and no one would know. The killer doesn't need to do the killing on Shark Night. He's just gotta kill someone and make sure they're not found until Shark Night."

"Problem is, kids play all day in the bay. If you stashed a body there, it would be found way before Shark Night," Cara said.

"Right, but kids only play in the fenced in part. If I put someone outside it, no one would know until they brought the big screen out there. I could even probably swim up behind the screen while the movie was playing and stash a body under it and they wouldn't find it until they moved the screen," Joey said, running a hand gently over his hair.

Vito stomped his foot and gave a guttural yell, causing both Joey and Cara to jump, and the high schoolers to begin shouting expletives.

"What was that about?" Cara asked him.

"Do you know what this means?" Vito asked, his voice taking on an edge that she hadn't heard before. "It means our timetable is ruined. The killer doesn't need to kill on Shark Night. There could be a body down there right now and we wouldn't even know, which means we're more or less back to square one."

Joey's interest was piqued. "Do you think there's a body down there right now?"

"I— What? No, you're missing my point," Vito fumbled.

"Dare you to go check," Cara challenged.

"If I hop in there I'll ruin this hair. What's in it for me?" Joey countered.

"You'll be the bravest guy here," she said sweetly.

"Challenge accepted," he said, throwing off his flip flops and ripping off his shirt as he ran across the beach to where the fence met the land and made his way around. Just outside the fence, Joey was able to keep his hair out of the water but it came up to around his chin giving Vito a better idea of how deep the water was. Joey returned from the water and flexed. "Bravest guy in the bay."

"Any bodies?" Cara asked with a laugh.

"Nope," he said, picking up his shirt and sliding on his flip flops.

"We might as well go home then. Cara, do you want to do the honors of telling Felicity that we have no way of knowing when the killer is going to strike next?" Vito said.

Cara laughed nervously, "Oh wow, thanks guys, way to give me the hard job."

Gio and Penelope were in Penelope's pool, racing once again. When they finished their third race, Gio checked his time on the stopwatch. "How am I getting slower?" he cried when he saw his time. "And how are you getting faster?"

Penelope laughed, "It took me a few laps to warm up. Plus, you don't have the endurance I do. If we raced again, my time would probably stay about the same and yours would go down even more."

"How are you so good?" he asked in dismay.

"I practice every day. I've always been small so other swimmers have always had the physical advantage, which means I had to work that much harder to make up for it," she told him.

"Swimming seems like a tough sport," he admitted.

"Yeah, it is. Half of swimming is mental. You have to be disciplined and you have to push yourself to keep going, even when you're exhausted and your body's screaming for air," she confirmed. He cocked his head to the side, scrutinizing her. "What?" she asked.

"What, what?"

"Why are you looking at me like that?"

"Honestly? I never saw you as tough until now. But you are. You've been through a lot," he admitted.

She rolled her eyes. "Yeah I'm real tough. That's why I have you here as my bodyguard right?" She took a breath and began swimming again. He felt a sense of something well up in his chest. He wasn't sure what it was – pity, admiration? He wasn't sure. When she finished swimming, she looked at him and splashed him in the face. "Stop looking at me like I'm a lost puppy."

He laughed. "Sorry."

"Race me again, while I'm still winded from those laps I just did," she ordered. He obliged and still she outpaced him.

"Again," he said, breathing heavily. He hoped that maybe with the laps on top of the race they had just done, she would be out of stamina. Unfortunately for him, he was also out of stamina from the race before; Penelope on the other hand, was still going strong.

She grinned playfully. "Had enough, or are you thirsty for more?"

"I think I swallowed enough pool water on that last lap to never be thirsty again," he wheezed.

She laughed and pulled herself out of the pool. "Come on, let's get you dried off. I need a shower and a snack." He pulled himself out of the pool as well and caught the towel she tossed his way. "We have a second shower if you want to take one," she offered.

He took her up on that offer and soon they were both on her couch eating pretzel chips and hummus, watching a sitcom from the nineties.

Felicity, meanwhile, was walking the streets of the island. She needed to think. She was a predator, which meant she was the best suited to catch the killer. She reasoned that all she had to do was figure out what she would do, and that's what the killer would do. It made perfect sense to her. Where would she start if she was hunting? She always started with the type of person. She only went for people who did drugs or drank heavily. She and the killer apparently shared that. Maybe the killer was also just trying to protect the island from scum? No, that didn't make sense. The first man killed hadn't been a drug user or drunk, he was a local, and the scuba woman hadn't been a drunk or on drugs, she was just going for a scuba trip. The killer was definitely preying on easy targets. She stopped walking as she came to a realization. She couldn't think like herself. She was strong, an apex predator. The killer was weak. She killed for food. Andrew had killed for the thrill, to prove he could, because it made him feel superior. What did she know about the mystery killer? They were weak, and they chose methods of killing that seemed to be based on things people feared. He or she didn't even make it look like a murder, they all almost looked like accidents. Why? She was stuck. Maybe the others were right, maybe it was Basil who was the one behind all of this and just following him would be enough to prove it.

The next day the group met back up at Felicity's house just before sunset. Cara hadn't told Felicity about what they'd concluded at the bay.

"So how was everyone's night?" Joey asked brightly.

"No one tried to kill me, so that was a plus," Penelope said flatly.

Felicity shared her feelings of doubt. "I realized I can't get inside the killer's head because we don't hunt for the same reason. We don't have the same mindset. Please tell me you figured something out at the bay."

Joey and Vito both looked at Cara who rubbed the back of her head. "Yeah, so you know how we thought we'd at least narrowed down when and where the killer would strike? Well, turns out we were wrong, since they don't actually need to kill someone at or on Shark Night to have the body found there."

Felicity gripped the top of the kitchen table so hard that it was a wonder it didn't snap. "So, what you're telling me is that we actually know less now than when we started yesterday?" she asked through gritted teeth.

"So it would seem," Gio said sympathetically.

Penelope spoke up. "I at least know where Julia and Basil will be. She's working until nine tonight so they're going to walk around Island Village afterwards."

"Hopefully that turns something up," Felicity said ruefully.

Penelope stood up. "If there's nothing left for the rest of us to do, I'm going to go. Oscar and Stacy want me to go to a party with them." Gio opened his mouth to protest but she spoke before he could. "Don't worry, I'm not going to drink. I'll be careful, and they'll both probably end up sleeping at my house. I'll be fine." She left before anyone could say anything.

"You guys up for a game of night mini golf after we drop Felicity off? It's right by Island Village," Cara asked.

"Yeah, I'm in. We can go to Wing 'n' Egg after if you want," Gio said.

Felicity rolled her eyes. Great, they were all planning some fun while she was out stalking people. Her expression softened. They were young; they should be enjoying themselves. She looked at each one of them, melancholy setting in when she realized she had never been their age. Her life had ended when she was eighteen.

"Fel, are you OK?" Cara asked when she saw her face.

Felicity shook her head to clear the thoughts away. "Yeah, I'm fine, Cara, just thinking. Let's go, I don't want to miss them."

When the group got out of the SUV in the Island Village parking lot, Vito, Joey, Gio, and Cara went toward mini golf while Felicity walked toward the fudge store, keeping a careful eye out for Basil. Island Village took up two blocks, with a road leading to the parking lot down the middle. The left-hand side was up a walkway, which was where Felicity went, giving her a bird's eye view of the fudge store. She stopped at an outdoor sunglasses stand and pretended to look at sunglasses. Eventually, she saw Julia and Basil leave the fudge store. Julia looked as pretty as ever in a dark blue top with black jeans. Basil was wearing the exact same basketball shorts and anime T-shirt he had

had on the day Felicity had first met him, when they'd both gotten kicked out of the party.

Felicity followed them as they went into a store that sold little knick-knacks and shore themed objects. This store started at the lower level and had a second entrance on the upper level where Felicity waited for them. With her superior hearing, she could hear Julia laughing about the squid curtain, which Felicity couldn't see but she pictured a curtain shaped like a squid. As she heard their voices come up the stairs, she turned and faced the railing overlooking the street. They didn't notice her as they walked to the right. She waited a moment and then continued. This went on throughout the night. They would enter a store and then exit and she would try to be inconspicuous. They stopped by a candy store and got licorice whips; turns out they were both fans of dark licorice. The night grew dark and they walked across the street and down to the beach. Felicity felt safer following them on the beach. She knew it was cloudy enough to block out the moon and stars which meant they couldn't see much at all. Felicity, however, could see them just fine. Of course, she could have followed them without seeing them; they were certainly loud enough. They began to walk back toward one of the streets a block down from where they had entered. As they got to where the beach and street met, Felicity began to notice Basil acting different. Julia didn't seem to notice but he was looking around apprehensively, almost as if he was trying to see if anyone was around. He seemed nervous. Every muscle in Felicity's body tensed. She crouched down; she was ready. His hand shot out in front of Julia and she sprinted toward them. As she did so, she saw that Basil was not trying to kill Julia but was actually putting himself between her and two large masked figures who had run out from behind a car. One of them had a bat in his hand and Felicity leapt toward them. Landing in front of the figure with the bat, in one fluid motion she punched him in the chest and took his bat. The punch had been strong enough to knock him to the ground. She spun quickly, using the bat to take out the legs of the second figure. Basil and Julia both stood there, stunned as their brains tried to comprehend what had just happened. The entire altercation had taken place in under a second.

"What the Hell?!" the figure whose legs she'd taken out yelled angrily, taking off his mask, revealing himself to be Tony, the boy with the jar from Andrew's party. He rubbed the back of his head to see if he was bleeding, which he was not. "The agreement was no real punches, and you didn't say anything about her being here," he said, gesturing to Felicity.

The other figure stood up and took off his mask, revealing himself to be Kev. "Yeah, what the Hell! That really hurt!" he shouted, rubbing his tailbone and chest simultaneously.

"Can someone please tell me what's going on?" Julia asked, sounding more distressed than Felicity had ever heard her before.

"What's going on," Tony said, "is that this kid paid us to come and pretend to mug you so he could pretend to fight us off and look like a hero in front of blue eyes here."

"Key word, 'pretend,'" Kev said angrily.

"You what?!" Julia said, outraged.

"Julia, I'm sorry, I—" Basil pleaded but Julia began to storm off.

"You can drive yourself home you, you lying creep!" she shouted, not turning around to look at him.

"And you owe us extra for breaking contract," Tony said to Basil.

Basil looked at Felicity for help and she held up her hands to let everyone know she wasn't going to intervene. Basil gave all of the money, exactly eleven dollars, to them.

"And you owe us for pain and suffering," Tony said to Felicity.

Anger flashed in her eyes and they both took a step back. "I owe you nothing," she said fiercely. They had crossed her twice now and she wasn't happy about it. She was also angry at Basil so she would allow them to take the rest of his money, "I suggest the two of you leave before you don't have any hands left to carry that money in," she said, glancing down at Kev's hand that was still wrapped in a cast from last time they'd met.

Kev gulped. The combination of the memory from last time he'd crossed her and the pain coursing through his body from this time told him they should leave.

"You're right, I apologize," Tony said, realizing it was in his and Kev's best interest to quit while they were ahead. They both turned and began to walk toward the car they had come from behind.

"Wait, guys can I have a ride home?" Basil called, but they ignored him. He turned to Felicity. "Could you drive me home? I live pretty far and Julia was my ride."

"I don't have a car and even if I did, I would make you walk," Felicity lectured. "What were you thinking? Julia's the sweetest girl on the island and you, what, hire people to pretend to mug you?"

"I'm sorry," he said, looking like he was about to cry. "I just wanted her to like me."

"You stupid, stupid boy! You dumb child!" Felicity yelled. "She already likes you! It's obvious! Even *I* can see it, and trust me when I tell you, I know absolutely nothing about relationships."

"Wait, Julia likes me?" Basil asked, excitement lighting up his features.

"Well not anymore!" she yelled. "Her ex-boyfriend cheated on her so I introduced her to you, said you were a nice trustworthy boy, and you do this!"

"I'm sorry! I just thought in all the TV shows the guy saves the girl from thugs and she falls in love with him even if she's way out of his league. So, I got those guys to attack us so I could fight them off and—"

"Wait wait, shh shh shh," Felicity ordered, holding up a finger to silence him. "Basil, you're brilliant, you've given me a great idea." She turned and took a step, about to sprint away when she turned around and punched him in the stomach, not hard enough to do any lasting damage, but hard enough that he tasted the licorice coming back up and doubled over. “Apologize to Julia tomorrow!” she commanded before sprinting full speed down the street, a smile on her lips. She knew how she was going to catch the killer.

Chapter 10

Felicity cooked breakfast as she did every morning, but this morning she moved with an excitement that wasn't normally there, the kind of excitement that comes from struggling over a problem and finally having a solution. That relief that comes from having a plan. She just had to wait for the rest of her gang to get done with work, which would be hours from now. Cara slept later than usual since she was off from work. The clouds that had blotted out the moon and stars the night before had turned to thunder and rain. The island would be flooding, as it always did, and the tavern would be packed with people coming in for warm food, cold drinks, and a welcoming atmosphere. It was nothing Felicity couldn't handle. She actually enjoyed the challenge of a busy day. One of the downsides to having super reflexes was that tasks that were difficult for normal people to do were easy enough to become boring. The crowd that the storm brought was enough to put even Felicity's skills to the test.

Gio and Vito's uncle closed the shop early because no one was walking the boardwalk in the middle of a thunderstorm. They went to Cara's and Felicity's house for dinner, mouths watering at the thought of some of Felicity's home cooking. She was happy to oblige. She made tomato and mozzarella topped with her special sauce and toasted Italian bread as an appetizer, and for the main course she served swordfish steaks over risotto with a side of creamed spinach for everyone.

"Felicity, you are an amazing cook," Joey said, his eyes actually tearing up with joy as he ate.

"She's had years of practice," Helen said.

Felicity smiled at her. "Hey, watch it, Helen. You're getting up there yourself."

Helen put on a look of mock offense. "Me? I'm a young songbird compared to you, you old buzzard."

"Wow," Gio said in disbelief.

"What?" Helen asked. "Are you scared of her?" she said with a nod to Felicity.

Cara laughed. "They all are."

Helen waved a hand at Felicity. "Oh, she's a big softie. Nothing to be afraid of."

"That's what I keep telling them Grandma, but they don't believe me," Cara said.

"I was never afraid of Felicity," John bragged.

"That's because you had the hots for her," Sarah teased.

John threw one hand on his forehead and the other onto his heart in an imitation of a swooning Victorian era woman. "Felicity, breaking the hearts of men for generations."

Gio began to cough as his milk went down the wrong pipe, and Felicity didn't have to guess why he looked so embarrassed.

Felicity looked around, desperately hoping someone would change the subject. She hated being the center of attention, especially when it came to her love life. Even more so when a guy she just turned down was sitting next to her. Gio seemed to be reading her mind because he glanced her way and he gave her a small nod when they made eye contact.

"How did you take finding out that Felicity was a vampire?" Gio asked John.

Sarah began to laugh and John turned bright red. "I took it fine," he said.

Sarah shook her head. "If by 'took it fine,' you mean you threw up, then yes."

"Well, it was a big shock! I don't know how you boys all took it in stride like it was nothing," John said, gesturing to the boys with his fork.

"Well we've always been super into paranormal shows and stuff," Vito said.

"Yeah, like these guys watch all the Bigfoot shows," Joey said.

Felicity looked at him quizzically. "Are you comparing me to bigfoot?"

"He means we're open to the unknown existing," Gio said quickly. "Don't get me wrong. We were shocked and I don't think any of us slept the night we first found out, but we had always considered the idea of the paranormal existing."

"Yeah, we didn't have shows like that when I was your age," John grumbled.

After dinner the group hopped into Gio's SUV. The storm had stopped, so Felicity put on long pants and rain boots, then covered herself in a blanket to keep from burning up in the rays of sunshine peeking through. She kept herself covered for the entire ride and managed to keep covered as they entered Penelope's house.

"Ummm?" was all Penelope said as she pointed to the blanket walking into her house.

"We got out of work early," Gio explained. "Sun's still up."

"Uh-huh," Penelope said, still looking vexed.

“So? What’s the big plan?” Cara asked, looking at the still-covered Felicity.

Penelope shot a questioning look at Cara. “She hasn’t told you guys?”

Gio shook his head. “Nope, she wanted everyone together when she told us.”

“Aw Penelope, you’re a part of the team,” Joey said sweetly.

She scoffed at him, but said nothing.

“Penelope,” Felicity said, anxious to stay on task, “my plan hinges on you.”

The displeasure coming off of Penelope was palpable, “Oh great.”

“All I need you to do is convince your dad to get the local news network to do a commercial – to film a commercial, and to make sure it airs before Shark Night,” Felicity assured her.

“Oh, is that all,” Penelope said, sarcasm dripping from each word like a thick syrup.

“Please, Penelope?” Felicity asked, a surprisingly plaintive note in her voice.

Everyone looked shocked, especially Penelope. She sighed. “Explain to me why you need that. And can you people tape some paper over the windows or something? I’m tired of talking to a blanket!”

Vito, Cara, Gio, and Joey scrambled to tape up the windows with pieces of paper, and to draw the curtains where there were curtains to draw.

“You’re good!” Joey called to Felicity as he finished putting the last piece of tape on.

Felicity threw the blanket off and stood up, removing her rain boots and long pants, revealing a pair of shorts underneath. “Thank you. Now here’s what I realized about the killer: We know almost nothing about him or her.

We don't know when they're going to strike, we don't know where, and we don't know who."

"And a commercial will help with that how?" Penelope asked, her usual attitude returning.

"I want to make a commercial for the island, telling people to come vacation here. The one thing we do know about the killer is that they kill using things that people are afraid of, right? It's like they want people to be afraid, to prove that all of those irrational fears are completely rational. If you want people to be afraid, what's the biggest insult you can get?" Felicity looked around the room expectantly but no one had an answer. "The biggest insult would be someone saying that the island is super safe and there's never anything to be afraid of. I figure we could film a commercial where you say how fun the island is. Maybe Gio will say that he loves the food, and I'll say I love how it's so safe and I can walk the streets without fear, or something like that. We release it before Shark Night and whomever this is will hopefully change their target from whomever they were going to kill next, to me. I won't need to track them down since they'll be coming to kill me, and since, of course, I'm a vampire, I'll kill them, instead. It's that easy."

"That's actually genius," Vito said quietly, in awe of her plan but also bitter that he hadn't thought of it.

"That is really smart," Gio said, "but how do you really think we can air a commercial in the next week?"

"I actually do know someone that could help," Penelope admitted. She took out her phone and sent a text. "If we can convince my dad to pay for the commercial to air, then he can get it on the air before Shark Night, but we're going to need to have the commercial finished by morning. Oh, and I'm also going to need a bottle of wine, preferably Zinfandel or this won't work."

"Joey, let's go," Gio said, standing up and taking out his keys. "We'll get the wine. Anything else?"

Penelope thought for a moment, then said, "Not that I can think of. Hurry back, our film crew is on its way."

They didn't waste another second as they ran out the door and sped off.

A few minutes later, the door opened and the group was met with the unexpected sight of Oscar and Stacy.

"Alright Penelope, we have our film stuff. What's the emergency?" Stacy asked, her voice as shrill and harsh as ever.

"Alright guys, so we need to film a commercial that's good enough to air on TV, and we need it done by morning," Penelope said, giving them a cheesy grin and putting her hands together like she was praying.

"We're artists, not miracle-workers," Oscar told her sassily.

Gio and Joey burst through the door with a large bottle of red Zinfandel. "We got it!" Joey shouted.

Stacy snatched the bottle and looked at it. "OK, maybe just this once we can be miracle-workers."

Oscar sighed. "Do you have a script prepared at least?"

Penelope glanced at Felicity who shrugged. Penelope turned back to Oscar. "We have a rough outline."

Oscar and Stacy looked at each other. "Let's get to work," they said in unison. Oscar sat down on the couch with Penelope and Felicity on either side of him and began to type up a script on a laptop. Stacy opened a laptop of her own and looked through stock footage she and Oscar had filmed of the island for a previous project. She began cutting it and arranging it in a video editing program.

"Script's done," Oscar informed his sister, handing her a copy that he had printed out on Penelope's wireless printer.

Stacy read it over and gave a quick nod. "Felicity, what's your last name? I need it for the text I'm going to put under the footage of you, I'm thinking Felicity whatever your last name is, Island Surf Champion."

"Just go with 'Felicity, Island Surf Champion,'" Felicity told her.

Gio looked at Felicity curiously. "Actually, now that you mention it, do you even have a last name?"

Felicity looked at him irritably. "Yes, I have a last name." She walked out of the house, Penelope and Oscar following.

"Boys, grab that camera equipment," Oscar said as he left. "And Stacy, pace yourself."

Stacy grunted as she uncorked the bottle of Zinfandel. She and Oscar both wanted to go into the film industry. They were equal in skill but she enjoyed cutting and editing more while he enjoyed filming more. She took a sip of wine and leaned forward, visualizing the finished product in her head. This was going to be a long night.

Their first stop was Island Village. "First things first, let's get a shot of Felicity walking down the street," Oscar said, scanning the street to find the best spot for what they had in mind. "I like the look of that stretch right over there," he said pointing to a row of shops with large, brightly lit windows.

"Works for me," Gio said. "Just tell us what to do."

"I need three of you on that side and three on this side to keep people from getting in the way of the shot. Felicity, just walk and say your lines, do you remember them?" he asked.

"Yes," she said simply.

"When I say 'action,' walk toward me slowly and say the lines," Oscar instructed.

Felicity walked toward him "I love the island because it's super—"

"Cut!" Oscar called. "You're going too fast. Slower, like a perfume ad."

Felicity went back and tried it again.

"No, no, no!" Oscar said, shaking his head emphatically. "Slower, like a perfume ad," he emphasized each word.

She tried again.

He sighed heavily. "Have you ever actually seen a perfume ad?"

"Yes, of course I have!" she said defensively.

"Then do it like that. You're moving too fast. Take your time with it," he instructed.

"I feel like it looks dumb," she grumbled.

"Look, you called me in because you trust that I know what I'm doing, right? Then trust me that I know what I'm doing," he said gently. "Now do it again. Like in the perfume ads."

This time, Felicity did it perfectly. "I love this island because it's super safe." She did a small twirl as she walked, "I love that I can walk down the streets at night and never be scared!"

"Perfect!" Oscar proclaimed triumphantly. "Let's move on to the next scene."

They walked into the fudge store to find Julia and Andrea finishing up with a customer.

"Hey guys!" Julia said brightly. "We're closing soon but we can help you out."

"Thanks, but we're not here to buy fudge. We actually need your help with something," Felicity said.

"That's never a good sign," Andrea remarked.

"We're filming a commercial and need it done by tonight. Can we film in here, and could you maybe be in it?" Cara asked, clasping her hands together and flashing Julia a cheesy smile.

“That sounds like fun! I’ve never been in a commercial before,” Julia said enthusiastically. “Andrea, do you want to help too or do you want to go home?”

“My shift technically doesn’t end for another ten minutes,” Andrea said as she took off her apron and ran out the door.

“So, what do you need me to do?” Julia asked.

“Just sell fudge to me when I come to buy it,” Cara said.

“Actually, I think we should have one of the guys buy the fudge,” Oscar said, “We need balance. If we have Felicity alone in that last shot, Julia selling fudge, and you buying it, people are going to start asking where all the men are. Don’t you think?”

“Alright, which guy?” Penelope asked, gesturing to Gio, Vito, and Joey.

“Well, I’m going to want one guy now, and then another to be in a couple.”

Oscar looked at Penelope expectantly and she cocked an eyebrow at him. “Why are you looking at me like that? I’m not coupling up for this.”

“We’ll do it!” Cara said, linking arms with Joey.

“You two do make a cute couple,” Oscar admitted, causing them both to blush. “You then,” he said to Gio, “get those muscles pumping; your big scene is coming up,”

“Hey guys, there’s a creepy dude just staring into the store and hiding around the corner whenever I look his way,” Vito said, pointing to a window.

Felicity rushed outside and saw Basil cowering against the side of the building. Gio and Joey grabbed him by either arm and dragged him into the store.

“What? Basil!” was all Julia could muster.

“What are you doing skulking around like that? Here to commit a crime?” Vito asked, sounding like a police interrogator.

"Please let me go. I'm sorry. I was just waiting for Julia to finish up with work and then I was going to try to talk to her," Basil said, genuine fear in his voice.

"Let him go; he's harmless," Felicity ordered, exasperation in her voice.

Joey and Gio complied and Basil slumped to the ground before getting back to his feet.

Penelope took a step forward. "Get out of here; Julia doesn't want to see you."

"Alright," Basil said, sounding defeated, "but Julia, I'm really sorry and you should know that I only did it because I wanted you to like me."

"I already did like you, you dummy!" she exclaimed. "You didn't need to pay some people to pretend to rob us so you could look like a hero!"

Joey snorted and Gio covered his mouth using his hand.

"Is that why you ended things?" Vito asked, his face not quite able to fight off the grin that was trying to break through.

"Yes," Julia and Basil said in unison, both beet red.

"Honestly, it's kind of sweet," Cara admitted.

"Are you kidding me?" Penelope scoffed.

"Yeah, I mean it's dumb, but it's sweet," Cara clarified.

Julia sighed. "Basil, wait. I have to help these guys with a commercial. Can we talk after I'm done?"

Basil's face lit up and he nodded emphatically, apparently at a loss for words.

They filmed the scene of Gio buying fudge and turning to the camera to say, "Great shops," in one take, which worked out well because Julia was anxious to close up and talk to Basil.

Next, they filmed Penelope taking a bite out of an elephant ear and saying, "Great food."

"The two of you are naturals," Oscar said to Penelope and Gio. Penelope flipped her hair and Gio flexed his triceps, both looking equally pleased with themselves. Oscar rolled his eyes. "For the next scene, I want you and your brother, whose name I'll admit I don't know, to sit at that bench."

"My name's Vito," Vito said irritably as he took his place next to Gio at an outdoor table.

"This one is going to take timing and the perfect angle. Ready? Action!" Oscar called.

"Great for family," Vito said, putting an arm around Gio. Oscar turned slightly as he zoomed outward to reveal Penelope on the other side of the table.

"And friends," she said, giving one of the trademark Smith family smiles.

They had to film that one a few times for Oscar to get it right, but eventually he was satisfied with the results. Oscar turned to Joey and Cara to find Joey doing pushups and Cara watching him intently.

"Oh! Our turn," she whispered to him loudly.

Joey hopped up and struck three poses, flexing. "Ready when you are!" he said.

Oscar pointed to a more romantic looking spot with better lighting. "Go over there and do something coupley, then look at me and say, 'Great for couples.'"

They walked over to where he had pointed and looked at each other awkwardly for a moment before they leaned in and kissed. When they broke away from one another, they both looked stunned and breathless.

"Great for couples! Great for couples!" Oscar said angrily. "You didn't say your line! It's one line!"

Everyone else was staring at them in shock and they both looked mortified. Joey began clearing his throat and Cara began to scratch the back of her head.

"You know what, never mind," Oscar said, "I have everything we need here. We just have to go back to the house and do one more scene."

On the way home, Oscar uploaded the footage onto his laptop and began to delete the obvious mistakes. "This way Stacy doesn't have to comb through them herself. She likes to just take the good footage and whittle it down, but she doesn't like to have to delete the mess-ups. She always says, 'I can cut and polish a diamond until it shines but I can't make diamonds out of lead.'" His imitation of her voice was flawless. Once he had deleted all of the obvious duds, he downloaded the footage onto a flash drive. When they arrived at Penelope's house, he handed Stacy the flash drive. "I deleted all the duds for you."

"Good, I can cut and polish a diamond until it shines but I can't make diamonds out of lead," she said, sticking the flash drive into her laptop and uploading the footage. Oscar turned to the group and gave them a small, self-satisfied nod. Stacy poured herself another glass of wine and got to work. "Your dad's home, Penelope," Stacy said, not looking up from the laptop.

All heads turned to Penelope. She looked nervous. "Do I have to do it now?"

"Yes!" Felicity insisted.

Penelope stomped a foot angrily but said nothing as she walked up to the third floor where her father's office was.

"Hey, Dad?" Penelope said as she entered.

He was dressed casually in a large T-shirt from one of her swim meets. "Hi Pumpkin. What can I do for you?"

"I need you do to a me a big favor that you're not going to like, but I think that it'll be really good," she said all in one breath.

"OOOOK, can I have some more details on that?"

"So, we're making a commercial to bring tourists to the island, and we need you to get it on TV. It'll be ready by tomorrow morning," she told him. She knew this much he would be on board with.

"Well that's great, yeah I can do that," he said enthusiastically.

"Thing is, we need it to be on TV before Shark Night," Penelope added.

"What?"

"We need the commercial to be on the air before Shark Night," she repeated.

"Penelope, I can't do that. People book slots in advance and—"

"Do you have any slots already booked?" she asked, interrupting his protests.

"No, I don't," he told her firmly. "Why does it need to be before Shark Night?"

"It just does. I can't explain why, you just need to trust me," she told him.

"Penelope, I can't just—"

She looked at him with big, beseeching green eyes. "Please."

"Penelope, I trusted you to host a party here and you destroyed the gutter and a door on the third floor," he protested.

"And I'm asking you to trust me now."

He sighed and put his head in his hands. "I'll make some calls in the morning," he said at last.

She hugged him. "Thank you so much. I promise this is for the best." He kissed her forehead and she went back down to where the others were. "This had better work," she told Felicity fiercely.

"We're out of options if it doesn't," Felicity replied quietly.

"Alright everyone, focus up," Oscar called. "I need the two beefcakes to grab these boxes and come outside. Felicity, you come too,"

"Alright, this is the last scene," Oscar said when they were all outside. Boys, pick up a box. Really strain, like they're heavy." Joey and Gio picked up their boxes, positioning themselves so it looked like the boxes were heavy, but not so heavy that they couldn't handle it.

"Thanks boys," Felicity said, opening the door and then turning to the camera. "So come on down to the safest island with the friendliest people and the best beaches. There's something here for everyone." She winked. "And that's a guarantee."

"Perfection!" Oscar declared.

Penelope went to bed soon after and Gio took Joey, Vito, and Cara home.

"We'll have it done by the morning," Oscar promised Felicity as she walked out of the house. It was out of her hands now. She hated when things were out of her hands, but she would have to trust that the twins knew what they were doing and hope that Archie Smith would come through for them and get the commercial on the air in time.

Archie Smith had managed to get the commercial on TV four days before Shark Night. He even managed to get it in three different time slots. Cara, Felicity, Gio, Joey, and Vito had decided to go to the Wing 'n' Egg to celebrate.

"So, what's the plan now?" Just wait for the killer to come and kill you?" Gio asked Felicity.

"In the spirit of full disclosure, Gio, I hadn't really thought about the after. I figure, it's on the killer to come up with the plan. They have to figure out how to get to me. I went on television and taunted them, told them that I wasn't scared. If they let me live, they're proving me right. It also sends a message to the community, if they kill me. It says the island isn't a safe place, and people should be afraid. They'll come; I don't know how or when but trust me, they will. And when they do, I'll show them that they're far from the scariest thing on this island." Her voice took on an intensity that made the hairs stand up on the back of Gio's neck.

"Hey guys come on, can we get through, like, one dinner without talking about murder?" Cara asked.

"Alright," Joey said, "Since this is pretty much Felicity's solo mission now, do you want to go to Shark Night with me?" Joey asked.

Cara looked surprised, but not unpleasantly so. "Uh, yeah sure. That'll be fun."

"Wait, I still want to go to Shark Night," Felicity said.

"Felicity, I really can't picture you sitting on a beach watching scary shark movies," Vito told her.

"That's good since I don't sit on the beach and watch scary shark movies," she informed him matter-of-factly. "I have a float I use to watch from the water."

"Yeah, it's shaped like a shark. She sits on it like it's a horse the entire night; it's adorable," Cara said, causing the table to erupt with laughter.

"Does the inflatable shark have a name?" Gio asked.

"Let me guess! Jaws?!" Joey asked as he roared with laughter.

"No!" Felicity said, crossing her arms. "It's Finn," she added quietly.

The table laughed even harder and Joey pointed at Felicity. "Cara's grandma was right! You are a big softie."

She glared at him but the smile playing at the corners of her lips betrayed her true feelings. She was happy. Her plan was working so far; she just had to wait and hope the killer saw her in the commercial. Until then, she would try to enjoy herself as much as she could. It was summer, her favorite season after all, she might as well have some fun.

"Hey do you guys want to do something a little wild?" she asked.

"Wild? You?" Cara said incredulously.

"What did you have in mind?" Gio asked.

"Let's go night swimming," Felicity said. "It's summer, let's enjoy it!"

They paid their bill at Wing 'n' Egg and stopped by Gio and Vito's uncle's house so the boys could grab some bathing suits. Felicity and Cara put on suits of their own and they hit the beach.

"This is the beach we first met at," Gio said to Felicity.

"Yeah, I remember. You clowns ruined my surf with your shenanigans," Felicity complained.

"We were just night swimming, which is exactly what you suggested to do now," Vito retorted.

"You weren't just night swimming, you were filming and hooting and hollering like a bunch of monkeys. Back in my day, we just did things. We didn't have an obsession with documenting it all," she told them haughtily.

"Fel, you're really dating yourself here," Cara pointed out.

"You also knocked Joey on his ass that night," Gio reminded her. "You should do it again for old time's sake."

"Or we could not do that," Joey said, taking a defensive stance even though Felicity was fairly certain he couldn't see her. She crouched down behind him and lifted him up, throwing him over her shoulder and diving into a wave with him. The others laughed as they hopped from foot to foot when the cold ocean water washed over their feet.

"Well?!" Felicity called.

"On three?" Gio asked.

"One," Cara said.

"Two," Vito counted.

All at once the three of them on shore yelled, "Three!" and ran into the water, diving under the frigid crest of a wave.

"Ohhhhh it's cold!" Cara whined.

"It's not so bad," Felicity said.

"Can you even feel the cold?" Vito asked.

"Not the way you do. I recognize that its cold, but my body doesn't react to it," she explained.

They all got out of the water and ran back to Cara's house to dry off.

"I'm not gonna lie," Gio said, smiling from ear to ear, "that was really fun."

"Yeah, that was awesome," Joey agreed.

"Good call, Felicity," Vito admitted.

The boys changed back into dry clothes and went home. Cara took a shower and Felicity decided to do the same. She went to the outdoor shower and turned it on. She walked under the warm spray and ran her hands through her hair. She closed her eyes and lathered some shampoo in her hands, then ran it through her hair, inhaling the refreshing scent of coconut. She opened her eyes and looked around. If the killer came after her now, she would be able to fight him off fine. Her vampire hearing would likely alert her to his presence, but now she was naked. She cringed at the thought of having to kill a man while completely naked. She'd feel so gross and exposed. She quickly washed her body with an exfoliating body wash - not that she needed to exfoliate. One of the perks of being a vampire was having flawless skin. She hadn't had a breakout or a dry patch since 1944. She turned off the water and wrapped a towel around herself and exiting the shower, desperately hoping she wouldn't have to fight anyone naked. Fortune smiled upon her and she was able to make it to the house and get changed into pajamas without incident.

The next day went without incident as well and by morning the day after that, she was beginning to get worried. What if the killer hadn't seen the commercial? Or what if her plan was a complete bust and the killer didn't see her commentary as a challenge? She grimaced as she chopped vegetables. No, she shook her head to rid herself of the doubts she was having. She wouldn't know if her plan worked until Shark Night was over. Maybe she threw the killer off their game. They could be sitting at home, scratching their head right now, trying to figure out how they were going to get to her. She actually wasn't sure how she would get to herself. She almost always had people around, unless they showed up while she was night surfing but then they'd just be waiting on a beach for her. She shrugged, that was their problem not hers.

Later that day, just as the sun was setting, she got her answer when the bartender knocked on the door that separated the kitchen from the house. Felicity opened it and he handed her a wireless phone, "Felicity, phone call for you. They say it's urgent."

"Hello, Felicity," a voice hissed from the phone.

"Who is this?" she demanded.

"That's not what you should be asking. The important question, is who am I with," the voice taunted.

"Who are you with?" Felicity asked, genuinely curious.

"I'm with your friend Cara," it hissed.

Felicity's heart sank; Cara hadn't come home for dinner and hadn't answered John's call. Felicity had miscalculated; she hadn't expected the killer to be this bold. "If you hurt her—"

"I haven't hurt her, yet," the voice interrupted. "If you tell anyone, and I mean anyone, that I have her, I will slit her throat and watch her bleed right where she's sitting. Do you understand?"

"I understand," Felicity growled.

"Good, there's a house being built on Iroquois Road. Do you know the one?" the voice on the phone continued gleefully.

"Yes, I know the one. They tore down that beautiful old two-family house," Felicity said, her anger ready to explode.

"Come there immediately, third floor, alone. Otherwise Cara here will be drowning in her own blood. Do you understand me? You have five minutes tops before I lose my patience," the killer hung up.

Felicity bolted for the door, grabbing her large sun hat on the way. John and Sarah looked at her questioningly. "Killer's in the house under construction on Iroquois," was all she had time to yell before she was out the door.

She had to hold her hat on her head as she ran full speed to Iroquois Road. It was close, only two blocks away, and she made it there quickly. The structure of the new house had been built, but it was still only a wooden frame. The floors and stairs were all in place. She entered the dark structure. Her night vision would give her an advantage if the killer tried to ambush her. She made her way up the stairs to the third floor. One of the rooms had a dim light in it and she walked through the frameless doorway. There was a single figure standing in the room, wearing a mask and gloves.

"Where's Cara?" Felicity demanded, muscles taut and ready to pounce.

"Probably on her way home by now," the killer said. He was a man, and his voice didn't have the same hissing quality it had had over the phone. Felicity had heard this man's voice before; she was sure of it.

"What are you talking about?" Felicity asked.

"I lied, you stupid girl. I never had your friend. I just needed to get you here. You need to die."

"Because I said you weren't scary?" Felicity asked mockingly. Now that she knew the killer didn't have Cara, she could relax. She laughed.

"What's so funny?!" he shouted, taking three steps forward.

"My plan worked perfectly," she told him, still laughing. "I knew you were killing people based on things that people are afraid of, so I asked Archie Smith to make that commercial, specifically to get you to try to kill me. You stupid child, this isn't your trap; this is *my* trap," she said, her voice taking on the power of someone who knew they had every advantage.

"You're the child," he retorted, sounding very childish. "I used to be afraid. Afraid of everything, but then I realized the only way to conquer fear is to become fear. I am the embodiment of fear, don't you understand that? You can't trap me; you're going to die, here. Then I'm going to leave your body out to be found, so the whole world knows that I am to be feared."

"Mhm, I've heard enough," she said, sounding bored. He pulled out two knives in what he probably thought was going to be a sneak attack but to her vampire reflexes, he was slow and predictable. She caught both of his arms with the knives and began bending them toward him. Through the mask, she could see his wormy little eyes fill fear as he struggled in vain against her grip, his own blades slowly coming toward him. He jerked to the side and she planted her foot to stop him from moving her, but the board cracked under her and she fell through, scraping her leg down to the knee. She let go with one of her hands and he used it to drive the blade into her chest, just barely missing her heart. He kicked her in the face, breaking her nose with his steel toed boot.

"I came and sanded down that floorboard yesterday, just in case you somehow got the upper hand on me," he told her gleefully, stabbing her in the elbow and causing her to release his other hand. She wrenched her foot out of the sabotaged floor only to feel the two blades pierce her abdomen. He head-butted her in the face, further damaging her broken nose and blinding her with pain. He used that momentary distraction to pull the knives from her abdomen and drive them into her thighs, causing her to drop to her knees. He punched her in the face, knocking her to the ground. He grabbed her by the feet and dragged her to the open space where the deck was going to be installed. He drove the two knives into her back, causing her to yelp in pain, and used the knife handles to lift her to her feet. "Tell me again how there's nothing to fear," he gloated into her ear as he pushed her forward, the knives sliding from her back and sending her cascading downward, face first. She saw the ground as it approached rapidly, and then – darkness.

Chapter II

Earlier that day, Cara had been on the beach, doing her job checking badges as she did most days when Hershel Meyer walked over to her, holding his shoes in his hands. "You're Cara, right? The girl from the commercial, the one Archie Smith made?"

"Yeah? Why?" Cara asked.

"A friend of mine called me up, I used to work for him on a magazine in New York City. He asked who you were and told me he wanted you to model for his magazine."

"Are you serious?! A model?!" Cara exclaimed with joy.

"Nothing's guaranteed, but he approached me and said he likes the look of you and thinks you're perfect for the next ad campaign. When do you get off work?" he asked.

"I get off at six-thirty today," she told him.

He put a hand to his chin thoughtfully. "Hmm, well, he wanted you there at exactly six-thirty."

Cara's face fell, "Oh no."

"I can probably distract him for a few minutes. Can you get to *The Sandpaper* headquarters by six thirty-five?"

Cara thought for a moment and then nodded. "Yeah, but I'll look like garbage."

Hershel Meyer shook his head. "No, you look perfect. He wants to see what you look like on the day to day, not all done up. That way he can tell exactly how to do your hair and makeup. He is a professional after all."

"Thank you so much for the opportunity, Mr. Meyer! I'll be there!" Cara said enthusiastically. She watched him walk away as panic began to set in. She had no idea how she was going to get there. The boys would be working for another hour after her shift at the very least. She whipped out her phone and called Penelope. After begging for a few minutes, Penelope finally relented and agreed to drive her.

Penelope had driven in icy silence. The traffic lights had not been in their favor and it was six-forty when they arrived.

"I'm so sorry I'm late," Cara said, walking up to a small man with a California tank top, cargo shorts and boat shoes.

He nodded and blatantly checked them out with half-closed blue eyes. "Oh don't worry about it, but uh, I don't know who you guys are?"

"We're here for a photoshoot?" Cara said. "Hershel Meyer told me to come at six-thirty?"

"Oh yah, Hershel, right, his office is back there," he said pointing behind him with his thumb.

"Thanks," Cara said as the two of them walked into the back office where Hershel Meyer was waiting with a greasy-looking man who had wild dark hair and a camera around his neck.

"Oh, girls, good you're here. This is Mr. Giresy," he said gesturing to the man.

The girls exchanged a troubled look.

"Nice to meet you Mr. uh, Greasy?" Cara said tentatively.

"It's Guh-reezy!" Mr. Giresy shouted angrily.

"Right, so, I'll leave you to it," Hershel Meyer said as he left the room.

"First things first," Mr. Giresy said in a businesslike tone, "phones off. I will not have phones going off during my shoot, got it?"

The girls quickly turned their phones off. Mr. Giresy clearly was not a patient man.

"First things first," he declared, "I want some stills against that wall, both of you get over there."

Penelope looked confused. "Me too? I thought I was just the driver."

"What, you too good to model for me?"

"No, no," Penelope said quickly.

"Good," he said with a satisfied nod. "Now up against the wall."

This went on for a long time. Mr. Giresy would have them change poses. He then gave them each a sheet of paper to do their modeling bios, which included their names, heights, measurements, and a few fun facts about themselves.

"Now why don't we go out into the parking lot and see how you do in natural light?" he suggested.

They walked outside to find that the sun was beginning to set. "Wouldn't it have been better to do this earlier in the day?" Penelope asked. "The sun's going down."

"Are you telling me how to do my job?!" he demanded.

"No, just curious," she said, as glamorous as being a model for a big magazine in New York sounded, her patience was beginning to wear thin.

They posed and he took a few shots as the sun continued to set. "Be gone, both of you. I've got what I need," he said with a dismissive wave of the hand. The girls looked at each other, wondering if he was being serious.

He walked to a rundown white car and drove away, which told them that he was indeed serious.

"You know what, I'm starting to have my doubts about that guy," Penelope mused.

"I'm sure that car just has a lot of sentimental value to him," Cara said, sounding not so convinced herself.

Penelope rolled her eyes. "Let's just get out of here so I can go home. I'm starving."

"Do you want me to ask Felicity to cook something for you?" Cara offered as they got into Penelope's car and drove toward Cara's house.

"No," was all Penelope said in response.

As they made the turn to go into Cara's driveway, they saw what looked like Felicity in a sunhat sprinting down the street.

"Wait, was that Felicity?" Penelope asked.

Cara nodded. "I think so. I don't know any other girl who would sprint full speed down a road in a sunhat. Drive down to Iroquois; I think she turned down there," Cara said.

They turned slowly onto Iroquois, scanning driveways and yards as they drove down the road until they saw movement and pulled up to the house just as Felicity was falling. They watched in abject horror as she hit the ground with a sickening crunch.

"Felicity!" Cara shrieked as she ran to Felicity's broken body. Her skull was smashed in where it had hit the ground and her head was lying at a grotesque angle, her neck broken.

"Felicity! Felicity!" Cara yelled, sobbing.

"She should be fine, right? I saw her get stabbed before and she was fine," Penelope said, sounding more like she was trying to convince herself than comfort Cara.

"She's not moving," Cara cried.

"What's going—OH MY GOD!" a woman exclaimed. The woman ran back to her home to call the police.

"Fel! Fel!" Cara screamed as she cradled Felicity's broken form. "Please get up, please."

Felicity didn't move. She lay there like a corpse, bent and broken.

Penelope's eyes filled with tears as she put a hand to her mouth. In time, Gio's SUV parked behind Penelope's car and the boys got out.

"Hey guys, did she get him?" Gio asked brightly. His face fell as he saw Felicity's body. "No," he said quietly. He felt like he had been punched in the stomach. Joey threw up in the bushes next to him.

Vito took a few steps forward. "How is this possible?" he said and a moan escaped his lips as he fell to the ground bawling. Joey leaned against a fence as he continued to heave and Gio simply stared. He couldn't look away. The Felicity he knew, so fierce, so full of life, was gone. She had walked the streets of this island for ninety-three years and now she was gone. Just, gone. He punched the side his SUV, denting the driver's side door. He opened his trunk and pulled out a large security flashlight. He turned it on and ran into the house; at least Felicity had led him to the killer. He owed it to her to finish what she had started.

There was no sign of anyone on the first floor, but there was a hole in the ceiling with light dimly shining through. Gio charged up the stairs and into the room with the light. He saw the hole where Felicity's leg had punctured through but no sign of the killer. He ran out of the back door the house and saw no one. The killer had gotten away. "No, no, no, NO!" Gio bellowed. He took a few breaths to settle himself, his heart beating so hard he thought it would burst through his chest. He swallowed his anger. His friends needed him. He walked back out of the house to where Cara was still cradling Felicity's body. Joey had made his way over to her and had an arm wrapped around her. Vito was still on the ground where he had fallen to his knees and Penelope was standing farther back, looking like she wasn't sure if she should leave or not. He wanted to tell the others that the killer had gotten away but he decided that it might be best to wait. He walked over by Penelope.

"He got away, didn't he," she said, quietly.

He nodded, his expression troubled. She hugged him and he let out a breath he didn't know he'd been holding.

The police arrived soon after with an ambulance and one officer made everyone back up and stand in a line for questioning while two other officers checked Felicity's pulse and breathing and declared her dead.

"Why were you here?" the officer who had lined them up asked sternly.

"Where are you taking her?" Cara asked angrily, tears still pouring down her cheeks.

"We're bringing her in for an autopsy. It might help us find out who did this," the officer said, softening his tone a little. "Now please we need to know what you were all doing here."

The woman who had called the police took a small step forward. "I called you here. I heard that girl scream and came outside and saw, well, you know. So I called you."

"I was driving her back from a modeling gig for a magazine," Penelope said, pointing at Cara. "We saw our friend running on the street and so we came to see what was going on."

Gio nodded. "And we went to her house to hang out like we always do but then her dad said she was coming here, so we came too."

The police officer looked at them. He couldn't tell if they were being intentionally vague or not. "What's her name?" he asked.

"Felicity," Cara said.

"Island surf champion Felicity?" the police officer asked in surprise.

They all nodded glumly.

"Do you know who might have done this?" he asked them.

"No. Truthfully, we have no idea," Vito said bitterly.

"I want you to stay together on your way home, and lock your doors tonight just to be safe," the police officer told them, "but don't worry, we'll sort this out so there's no need to panic. Oh and uh, sorry about your friend." He gave them a small nod and walked into the house to investigate.

Penelope drove home and Gio drove Cara back to her house. She had turned down their offered to stay with her; she just wanted to be alone.

"I'll come back tomorrow with food for you guys," Gio assured her and her parents before he left.

"What are we going to do, man?" Joey asked in dismay.

"What can we do?" Vito exclaimed anxiously. "We've got no leads, our trap backfired, and we have nothing to guarantee that the killer won't attack one of us next time. We were all in the commercial."

"I wish Felicity was here," Joey said mournfully.

Gio nodded solemnly. "Me too. Me too."

Chapter 12

Felicity woke up to a pounding headache in some kind of dark, cold box. She wanted to move and figure out where in the world she was, but her arms and legs couldn't quite follow commands yet. She assumed that was because she'd broken her neck during the fall. There was also the small issue of her many knife wounds that she would have to deal with. She decided to sleep until she healed. She was awoken a few hours later when her box was opened and she was put on a table. Now that she was awake and healed somewhat, she was able to look around and realized that she was in some kind of medical examiner's office. A short, pale, portly, older man tottered around as he gathered his equipment and looked at her chart. She was getting an autopsy, she realized. She cast her eyes down toward her body and realized with horror that her worst fear had come true: She was completely naked. She was going to have to kill this man while completely naked. He seemed nice enough but a medical examiner meant someone looking into her anatomy. It also meant being cut open and having your organs removed, which as a corpse would be painless, but as a vampire, it would not be pleasant. She closed her eyes as he ran a hand over her head.

"That's odd," he said, feeling around where her head had hit the ground. He picked up her chart again. "It says her skull was crushed in, killing her. I'm not detecting that. Hmm, let's see, knife wounds on the thigh are present, as is the elbow wound, and the chest wound. Hmm." He walked to the doorway and called for his assistant.

"What's up?" the assistant, an unremarkable dark-haired man asked.

"Have they uploaded the pictures from yesterday onto the computer?" the medical examiner asked.

"I don't think so," the assistant replied.

"I need you to get me the incident report, the death certificate, and the camera from last night. I've noticed a discrepancy and I want to make sure they're all accurate." A few minutes later the assistant came back and handed the papers and camera to the medical examiner who spread them out on a table, comparing the information. "Cause of death: head injury, cause of death: head injury and broken neck, cause of death: head injury and broken neck. In the photos the head is injured." He walked back to Felicity and ran a gloved hand over her head. "I feel where it was smashed in but it almost feels like it healed. Perhaps an X-ray is in order." He wheeled her to what she assumed was the X-ray room and took some images of her. He wheeled her back out and examined the pictures. "Remarkable, absolutely remarkable. The subject appears to have fangs of some kind."

She heard him walking toward her, no doubt to look into her mouth. This was bad. The longer she was here, the longer this doctor would have to make notes and save his findings. She only had one option. One risky, stupid option that she would have no choice but to pray worked. Just as the doctor leaned over her to part her lips with a gloved hand she opened her eyes. "Boo!" she shouted. He jumped back and screamed, collapsing to the ground and clutching his chest. Success. The portly and vitamin-deficient doctor was having a heart attack. The assistant walked cautiously into the room to see what all the screaming was about and saw the medical examiner on the ground. The assistant ran out of the room to call an ambulance. Within minutes, the medical examiner was being moved to a hospital. Felicity closed her eyes. That was one problem out of the way. Now she just had to wait for her bones to heal enough for her to stand up and delete the X-ray of her skull. Luckily, he was the police station's only medical examiner and everyone was so busy getting him to a hospital that they forgot about her. She tried to sleep but unfortunately the pain of her knife wounds was coming in strong now that her nerves had healed. She gripped the cold metal table under her. She couldn't risk damaging her neck any further by wiggling in pain like she wanted to. This was going to be a long couple of hours. She wanted to sleep, but couldn't quite muster it. She decided to try distracting herself by doing something practical, making a plan. The big issue was not the killer - she knew exactly where to find him and could deal with him at her leisure. The big problem was the fact that she was here, which meant she was reported dead, which of course meant that panic was about to follow. Ironic, she had tried to catch the killer to prevent panic and ended up being the one who caused it. There was also the other issue of being reported dead. The police would have a record of her death. Both issues would need to be remedied. There was also the issue of getting home. She didn't relish the idea of running home, possibly through a police station, naked. She wasn't actually sure where she was, which was also a problem. She was starting to think she had miscalculated the number of issues at hand.

"Ahhh," she groaned. Her wounds were causing quite a bit of pain. She glanced around the room and saw nothing that she could use as clothing. She did spot some sharp objects which might come in handy if things didn't go according to plan. As the hours went by, her plan came together. She stood up tentatively. She was mostly healed, enough to escape at least. The key to the plan working was timing. If she made her big escape too soon, she would end up getting fried by the sun, which would put a damper on phase two of her plan.

Felicity tentatively stood up. Her wounds were healed as far as she could tell. She walked over to where the medical examiner had gone to call for his assistant and stuck her head out the door. There was a small room with a sink, surgical masks, goggles, hairnets, and plastic aprons. So far so good.

She took two aprons. The first one she slid her arms through, and the second she used the arms to tie around her back, making a sort of plastic dress. At least she wouldn't have to do this naked. She slipped on a hairnet, gloves, and surgical mask, just in case she had to pass any cameras. She walked into the hallway and was happy to see the assistant had gone home. She walked up a staircase to a small room with three doors, the door to her left had a window and exit sign above it, the other two were plain wood. She opened the one directly in front of her, it turned out to be a broom closet. She was about to open the door to her right when her ears picked up the sounds of the police station. Just as she had suspected, the coroner's office was in the same building as the police station. She was grateful that she wouldn't have to walk through it to escape. She doubted the side door had an alarm. She guessed that it was used to discreetly bring bodies in for examination without having to walk them through the station itself. She walked quickly back down the stairs to check the computer hooked up to the X-ray machine. According to the time on the computer, the sun was just beginning to set. Perfect. She deleted her X-rays from the system, careful to make sure they were deleted from the deleted files bin on the computer as well. Once that was taken care of, she went to the camera and deleted all the photos they had taken of her. Then, moving to the table where her clipboard was hanging, she took her paperwork off of it and grabbed her death certificate and incident report. She walked back up to the doors and opened the exit. She took off in a full sprint. Even if someone had seen on the camera outside the side door she had run out of, they wouldn't have been able to catch her. She was too fast and too endurant.

It was twilight when Felicity got home. She opened the door and walked inside as she removed her hair net and surgical mask. Cara was walking miserably to her room with a cup of tea. She dropped the tea and screamed, tears coming to her eyes as she ran and threw her arms around Felicity. Burying her face in Felicity's chest, she sobbed heavily. Felicity hugged her back, smiling awkwardly. "Uh, hi?" she said confused.

"I thought you were dead," Cara cried, still not letting Felicity go.

"Felicity! You're alive!" Joey exclaimed, standing up and looking her up and down. "Are you naked?"

She narrowed her eyes at him. "Yes, they strip you for an autopsy."

He continued to stare as everyone began to crowd into the room. Vito, Gio, John, Sarah, and Helen all gawked at her as Cara continued to hug her.

"We thought you'd died," Sarah said, tears falling from her eyes as she threw her arms around Felicity as well.

If Felicity was still capable of blushing, her face would have been bright red. "Guys, I appreciate all the concern, really, but I'm fine. I am a vampire after all."

"Yeah, but we'd never seen you like that before. You weren't moving," Vito said.

"And you didn't have a pulse. You weren't even breathing," Gio added.

Felicity reached a gloved hand out and grabbed Gio's wrist pulling him toward her with Sarah and Cara still holding her. She put his hand on her wrist. "What's my pulse right now?"

He looked troubled for a moment before realization bloomed in his eyes. "Ohh, you never have a pulse."

"Wait a minute!" Felicity exclaimed as she shook off Sarah and Cara and looked sternly down at Cara. "Where were you?!"

Cara's bloodshot eyes looked at her with confusion. "What do you mean?"

"I mean the killer called and said he had you so I rushed to that house looking for you. Where were you?"

Penelope spoke up. "She was with me."

Felicity wasn't particularly thrilled to see Penelope there. "Why?"

"I asked her to," Cara admitted. "I got an offer to try out to be a model. They said they saw me in the commercial we made and liked my look, so I called Penelope for a ride. We were there for a few hours and they didn't let us use our phones. Then they let us go and we saw you running toward Iroquois so we went over. Gio found out from Dad where you were going, so he drove over as well," Cara explained.

"Where was the shoot?" Felicity asked.

"At *The Sandpaper*," Penelope said, confirming her suspicions.

"Great. He outsmarted me," Felicity said ruefully.

"The killer?" Vito asked.

Felicity nodded. "It's Hershel Meyer."

They all looked shocked as their brains tried to piece together all the evidence and information.

"That makes sense," Gio said at last.

"Wait a minute, what are you all doing here?" Felicity asked, now that the initial shock surprise of her return had worn off.

"I figured since you usually cooked and you weren't around, I should bring food for everyone," Gio told her.

"And since we were all pretty bummed thinking you died, it was nice to be together, even if everyone was just sad and mopey," Joey said.

Penelope scoffed, "I didn't care. I was just being supportive."

Gio laughed at her. "I saw you crying your eyes out yesterday."

Penelope crossed her arms and turned bright red. "That's in the past. Besides everyone was crying but you."

Felicity looked at Penelope. She certainly wouldn't consider Penelope a friend, but she was surprised to realize she also no longer considered her an enemy.

"OK, right, sorry. Right now I have a plan and I need all of you to help," Felicity said, shaking her head to get her thoughts back in focus. "I need someone to make posters for an open mic event here at the tavern for next Friday."

"I'm on it," John said.

She nodded in acknowledgement as he ran off to grab his computer. "I also need someone to run to the store and grab me three different colored flash drives."

Sarah grabbed the keys off the counter. "I'm on it," she said, mimicking John's tone.

"OK, I need two people to write big newspaper articles," Felicity continued.

Cara raised her hand. "I can do one."

"I'll do the other," Penelope volunteered.

"Awesome, I need one of you write an article about how Gully was murdered by Hershel Meyer and how he was innocent. One of you write about how the killer was made up by Hershel Meyer to sell newspapers and that Gully was innocent. Finally, I need someone to make a document that looks like Hershel Meyer himself wrote it about how he paid someone from the mainland to come and pretend to be Gully when they mugged Penelope to sell papers, and another about how he killed Gully and framed him while he tried to kill Penelope.

"I'll do the documents. They can do the articles," Vito said.

"Perfect, I'll get changed and come down to give further instruction," she said as she walked upstairs. Helen was waiting by her door.

"I wanted to give you time with the kids, so I came up here to wait," Helen told her.

Felicity hugged Helen. "Did I have you worried too?"

Helen shrugged. “I had my doubts about you coming back, but a part of me thought you might be. I’ve seen the letter, remember? The one that lists all the ways you can die.”

Felicity nodded. “I know the letter. If that building was another two stories higher I might have actually cracked my head open enough to die.”

Helen laughed. “I guess being an old bat has its advantages.”

Felicity chuckled. “You’re one to talk.”

Helen struck a pose. “Compared to you, I’m a spring chicken.” The two of them laughed. They’d had the same banter for years but Felicity never grew tired of it. They were each other’s oldest friends. “Truly, I’m very glad you’re OK, Felicity.” Helen hugged her tightly before tottering off down the stairs.

Felicity quickly changed into a bikini. She covered up with a pair of black track shorts with white trim and a crop top hoodie. She walked downstairs and began giving everyone more detailed instructions on what she wanted on the posters and in the articles and documents. When Sarah got back, she uploaded everything onto their respective flash drives and John printed out the fliers.

“Alright, we’re ready. First things first, we need to get to the bay,” Felicity said. “Penelope, go to the police station and wait for them to get a call. When they do, tell them to check his computer.”

Penelope nodded and drove off in her car as Gio, Joey, Vito and Felicity went to the bay. They arrived just as the movie was starting.

“Hand out those fliers,” she ordered as she took off her clothes and waded into the water in her bikini. Vito stopped the projector and everyone began to protest and shout.

“Attention! Everyone, if I could have your attention please! My name is Felicity. I’m the local island surf champion,” she called. Most people didn’t hear her but one of the people who did turned and yelled to the crowd that

Felicity was there and to be quiet. She heard her name spread slowly through the water and down the beach as everyone turned their attention to her.

"Hello, everyone. As many of you have probably realized, reports of my death have been greatly exaggerated, and I am very much alive. I would like to make an announcement that, like me, there will be live music at Lorraine's Tavern all day next Saturday. My friends are passing out fliers now. Tell your friends! If you bring a receipt with a date ranging from tomorrow to next Friday from any of the local businesses sponsoring me in this year's surf competition to the live music event, you will get half off all appetizers and drinks. It's five dollars to come and you can stay as long as you'd like. Also, it is open mic, so if you'd like to sign up, come to Lorraine's tavern and throw your name down! I hope to see you all then!" Felicity walked out of the water and people kept shouting words of encouragement to her. Most of them had never even seen her face before, but her name was well-known throughout the island. There were also quite a few whistles but she kept walking. She knew if she stopped, at least three people in her immediate vicinity would start flirting with her. The shark movie began playing again and most people's attention went back to the big inflatable screen but a few people did continue to stare as she left the beach.

"So, what's the plan now?" Gio asked as she wrapped a towel around herself and got into his SUV.

"Now we pay Hershel Meyer a visit," she said slyly.

Gio parked and Felicity sauntered into *The Sandpaper* headquarters. The tired-looking woman typing at a desk didn't even look up as Felicity passed her and entered Hershel Meyer's office.

"Hello Hershel," she said provocatively. He looked up and she saw the blood drain from his face. "What's wrong? For the embodiment of fear, you look pretty scared," she taunted.

"Y-you-you— But I— But," he stammered, hyperventilating.

"Aww you look like you've seen a ghost. I'm no ghost but I assure you," she leaned over his desk slowly, her lips parting in a hungry grin to reveal her deadly, inhuman fangs, "I am much, much worse."

Hershel Meyer began to scream, a true scream, a primal, visceral scream of pure terror. He fell from his chair and frantically backed up until he hit the wall, clawing at it like a caged animal. His screams continued as he soiled himself, and the woman from the desk ran in to see what was going on.

"I don't know what happened!" Felicity shouted over his unhinged screaming. "I walked in and said hello and he started screaming. You need to call the police." As the woman ran to her desk to make the call, Felicity slipped on gloves and grabbed Hershel Meyer's laptop. She plugged a blue flash drive into the USB port and uploaded the document from the flash drive. She saved it as a document, deleted it from downloads, checked the trash bin and then ejected the flash drive, putting it back into her pocket. She slid the laptop back into its original position and put her hands in her pockets as the woman came back in. Felicity walked toward the woman and pulled out a red flash drive. "You're going to need to change an article or two. My friend wrote up a replacement article," she shouted.

The woman brought her outside where they could talk without the noise. "What are you talking about?"

"You guys were going to publish an article about me, Felicity, island surf champion," Felicity said as she saw recognition suddenly light up the woman's features.

"Yes! You - You're supposed to be dead!" the woman exclaimed.

"Yeah, that was a mistake. I'm not dead, and I came to tell him that," she said, gesturing back to the building. "He freaked out. My friend wrote an article to replace the one about me dying. Here, it's on this flash drive." she handed it to the woman.

“Thank you so much. I’m sorry for the confusion. I’ll get to work right away. Oh! The police are here!” the woman said, looking at flashing lights in the distance.

Gio’s SUV pulled up and Joey opened the door. Gio didn’t even come to a full stop as Felicity jumped in. By the time the police were pulling into the parking lot, the teens were on the road and driving away.

“That went perfectly,” Felicity proclaimed triumphantly.

“Great, so what now?” Gio asked.

“We meet Cara and Penelope at the Wing ‘n’ Egg to celebrate, obviously!” Felicity said.

Cara and Penelope already had a table for them and they all took their places at it.

“So? What happened?!” Cara asked excitedly.

All of them leaned in; the tension in the air was palpable. Felicity smirked. She had no choice but to give them what they wanted; they had earned it after all. “Alright, I’m only going to go through this once so pay attention. Gio, Joey, Vito, and I went to Shark Night to announce open mic night at the tavern. Shark Night’s a big deal for the town and reporters from all over the area are there to cover it. By being there, I let the community know that I am alive. The reporters hopefully went scrambling to their editors to let them know that the papers are wrong and should be fixed. Then we went to *The Sandpaper* headquarters where I talked to Hershel Meyer. I had Vito write me two documents, one admitting to killing people so Hershel Meyer would go to jail, which I didn’t use, and one about how Gully was innocent and Hershel Meyer hired an actor to use his phone after they found it on the ground, to stage a mugging of Penelope. That’s the one I used. It also said that he had misreported all the murders so he could sell papers. Then I gave the woman a flash drive to replace what would no doubt have been a front-page article about my death with one of Gully's innocence. Penelope, did you tell the police to check his computer?"

Penelope scowled. "Of course I did. They'll find the article, don't worry. But if all it says is that he paid someone to pretend to kill me in order to sell papers, doesn't that mean he'll go to jail for like a year and then come back and kill more people?"

"That's why I had the second article made, just in case, but as I suspected, his sanity snapped. He'll probably be spending the rest of his life in an institution," Felicity said matter-of-factly.

"What? How?" Gio asked.

"He killed people because he was a coward. He used the bullying logic: If people are scared of me, I don't need to be scared of them. So, when someone he killed walks in perfectly fine and then reveals that vampires exist, it was too much for him," Felicity explained.

"How did you know that would happen?" Vito asked, again in awe that she was able to plan all of this.

"I've had a few people find out that I'm a vampire, and some of them had similar things happen. To have your whole worldview shattered like that is too much for some people's minds to take," she said with a shrug.

"So you knew that it could happen to us and you told us anyway?!" Vito exclaimed angrily.

"I did, but you had figured out something was up and seemed to be holding it together fine. My guess is because you were open to the possibility of the supernatural, it didn't damage your psyche too much to find out."

"And me?" Penelope asked, a small, amused smile on her face.

Felicity looked sheepish. "Well, I had planned on killing you after you found out so I was willing to take the risk. My guess is because you already had something unbelievable - like one of your friends trying to kill you - happen, your mind was already sort of in shock so it processed all of it differently? I don't know! I'm not a mind doctor!"

"A psychologist?" Vito said condescendingly.

Gio shook his head. "No, that would be a psychiatrist."

"I'm not either of those! I didn't even graduate high school!" Felicity said in dismay.

Joey snorted, "Wait, seriously?"

"Yes, seriously," Felicity said defensively, "Back in my day, you didn't need all of these dumb degrees. You just worked and read books."

"So, you just taught yourself everything you know?" Gio asked, impressed.

Cara scoffed, "Being a vampire gives you a super good memory. She wouldn't be this smart if she was a human."

Felicity wanted to protest but Cara was correct.

"So, you cleared Gully's name, drove a serial killer insane, brought a ton of customers to the local businesses, and kept the island from panicking all in a single night," Penelope said, sounding both impressed but also like she was leading up to a negative. "What are you going to do about the fact that the police are going to come for you?"

"Oh man, yeah, she's right!" Joey said, as the realization hit him. "They put you in a body bag and brought you away. They're going to be asking questions."

Felicity couldn't help giving a self-satisfied smile. Truly, every phase of her plan had gone perfectly. "They put me in a body bag which means when they brought me to the medical examiner's office, I was in the bag, which means no cameras saw my face, with the exception of the one they used to photograph me. I deleted my pictures from there and I wore gloves when I touched everything and I put on that crazy getup to cover my face and hair when I left so they have no physical proof of me being there. I even took my death record. The only thing they can do is say they saw my body but clearly I'm right here, so how can I be dead?"

They looked at her in stunned silence for a moment before Vito whispered, "You thought of everything."

"I had a lot of time to plan while I was healing," she admitted modestly. "Oh! I almost forgot the best part!"

"Wait, let me guess," Cara interjected, "you said something cool before you drove Hershel Meyer out of his mind?"

Felicity was once again grateful that she couldn't blush. "Yes."

"What?" Penelope asked, completely lost.

Cara looked at Felicity. "Do you want to tell her or should I?"

Felicity decided she would explain. "So whenever I kill I always try to think of a cool line to say. Kind of like an action star, something witty and pithy."

"And she's awful at it," Cara added.

"I'll admit I'm not the best at it, but this time I said it looks like you've seen a ghost, but I assure you I'm much much worse," Felicity told them, looking around expectantly.

They all looked at her silently for a moment before Penelope snorted, then Joey cracked, and Cara, Gio and Vito all broke at the same time. The entire table was laughing.

"You're adorable," Cara said, clutching her side as she laughed.

"It's not supposed to be adorable! It's supposed to be scary," Felicity whined, which caused them all to laugh even harder.

Joey threw an arm around Cara, leaning on her as he doubled over in his chair. "Your grandma was right, she is a big softie!"

Felicity crossed her arms and tried to pout, but their laughter was contagious and soon she found herself laughing along with them.

Chapter 13

Felicity was stressed; she had made some big promises and she wasn't sure she could keep them.

"You're the one who came up with the idea of having live music all day," Cara reminded her.

"I know that!" Felicity said as she moved two kegs.

"The open mic idea was smart," Vito said as he set up the speakers. "Now you don't need to pay for a band."

"I'm just worried that we won't have enough people to fill all the time slots," Felicity said anxiously.

"Don't worry, we all signed up, and Penelope told everyone to sign up. Pretty sure everyone on the island will be here," Gio told her.

"Which means everything has to be perfect," she said, pulling her hair into a ponytail.

"I'm sure it will be! Everyone loves music. Plus, I heard the twins are showing a movie?" Cara asked.

Felicity nodded. "It's more of a short film, but yes. I'm letting people do pretty much anything. I know a boy is doing a magic show at one point. His mom came in and asked if it was allowed."

"We'll perform for you, don't you worry," Joey assured her.

“Oh, we’ll perform alright,” Vito said, a mischievous note in his statement.

“Oh, lovely,” Felicity said sarcastically.

The next morning people began pouring in bright and early. She had covered up the windows to create a theater-like atmosphere, which had the added effect of allowing her to move about the tavern without burning to a crisp, although she still had to avoid the rays of daylight that poured in whenever someone opened the door.

“How many songs am I allowed to play?” Carl, a short white-haired man, asked her.

“You can play as many songs as you want, Carl,” she told him. Carl was a Vietnam veteran and a very talented musician. He was also the only person to sign up for the time slot this early in the morning. Luckily for her, Carl had enough material to last an entire hour and even called up a few of his buddies to come join him. Even though they lacked his talent, they had enough enthusiasm to ensure everyone had a good time. A few more people came in to perform and although most of them lacked real talent, they were all enjoyable. At noon, Stacy and Oscar came in with Penelope.

They set up a projector and played a short movie they had filmed on the island. It was beautiful, perfectly capturing what it’s like being a child down the shore. She even saw a few tears from the crowd as they re-lived their fondest childhood memories through the film. After it concluded, they packed up and prepared to leave. “We’ll be back later, around sixish,” Penelope promised.

As they walked out, a nerdy looking man in his late twenties walked up to the stage for a comedy act.

“Is everyone doing alright?” he asked.

“Yes!” A few audience members yelled.

A mischievous glint flashed in his eyes as a grin slowly spread across his face.

He wouldn't, Felicity thought. *There's no way he would say it.*

The grin grew wider, as his eyebrows knit together. "No..."

Please no, she thought

"You're all left!" he said, practically shouting. The audience all groaned. The man continued with bad pun after bad pun. Each was worse than the last.

After his act, the mood was high and the expectations were low. John and Sarah came to the stage.

"Hello everyone, we're the owners of Lorraine's Tavern. I'm John."

"And I'm Sarah. We've been married for twenty-one years." The tavern broke out into applause. "Thank you thank you," she said smiling graciously. "Today we're going to be singing a duet." The crowd cheered again.

John laughed. "I'm glad you're cheering now because you probably won't be after you hear my singing." After the laughter died down, they began. Neither was a particularly talented singer but the love that emanated from the pair was so overwhelmingly sweet that it more than made up for it.

People came and filled spots throughout the day and around six, all eyes were drawn to the roar of thirty people entering the tavern, led by Penelope.

"As promised, I have brought the party to you," Penelope said, spreading her arms and turning from side to side as if she was displaying a magnificent collection.

"Impressive," Felicity said.

She flipped her hair. "I try." She sauntered back to the group.

Two minutes later, Cara, Joey, Gio, and Vito came into the tavern and walked over to Felicity. "How's it going?" Gio asked.

"It's going well, but we're out of acts after this lady," Felicity said, gesturing to an old woman who was tap dancing surprisingly well.

Cara waved over Felicity's shoulder. "Looks like you just got another act."

Julia ran up and hugged each one of them. Basil walked up shyly and Felicity hugged him. "We got back together," he told her.

Felicity smiled at him. "I'm glad. You two are a cute couple."

Julia practically jumped up and down. "Aw thanks." She turned to Basil. "You ready?"

He swallowed nervously and nodded. She hugged him before he walked up to the stage and set up a stool in front of a keyboard.

"Hi everyone, my name's Basil."

"Hi, Basil," the entire tavern said.

"I learned how to play piano specifically so I could come here and dedicate this song to my beautiful girlfriend, Julia." Julia's jaw dropped and she turned bright red. Basil began to play and Felicity couldn't believe he had learned how to play in just a week. He was no Mozart, but he played like someone who had been taking lessons for years. Julia walked on stage as he finished and kissed him. Now it was his turn to look surprised and turn red. The tavern cheered and the two of them smiled at each other.

"Fine," Joey conceded. "They actually are kind of a cute couple."

"Right?!" Cara exclaimed excitedly. "If a guy did that for me, I'd probably marry him on the spot."

"Next up, is Joey, Gio, and Vito!" Felicity announced. She had no idea what the boys had planned but she knew already that it was going to be ridiculous.

"Hello everyone, my name is Gio," Gio said.

"I'm his brother, Vito," Vito added.

"And my name is Joey. And I would like to dedicate this next performance to a very special lady, who's going to have to marry me now." He made eye contact with Cara who burst into laughter.

"We decided that since we're down the shore, there was only one appropriate song to sing," Gio said as Vito began to half-hum, half-sing a tune. They all began to sing the pirate shanty "Shiver My Timbers." None of them were good singers. In fact, Felicity would have called each on their own a bad singer. She would have even gone as far as to call Gio a very bad singer. That being said, somehow they sounded good together. Joey took the higher notes, Vito, whose voice was the best of the three of them, carried them musically, while Gio sang the low notes in deep almost savage grunts. Their energy was contagious and when they finished, the entire tavern began to hoot and cheer.

"So wifey, where are we going for our honeymoon?" Joey asked Cara when he came back from the stage.

She laughed and elbowed him. "How about we start with dinner and work our way to the honeymoon from there?"

"Sounds good to me," he said.

"It's about time!" Gio said, punching Joey in the arm. "You know this guy was supposed to ask you out the same day I asked out Felicity."

"The same day you what?" Penelope asked, startling Gio.

"Penelope!" he said in surprise.

"Oh, hey Gio, I just came by to ask why you haven't come over to say hi to me yet," she said sassily.

He glanced over at the crowd of Penelope's friends. "You seemed busy. I wasn't sure if you wanted me to…" He struggled to find the word. "Interrupt," he finished.

She grabbed his hand and dragged him out of the tavern. Once they were outside, she turned to him, crossing her arms and looking up at his face. "Alright, spill," she said.

"Spill what?" he said, trying not so convincingly at sounding confused. "Oh, you mean about how I asked out Felicity?"

"No, I'm not surprised about that. She's really pretty," Penelope admitted.

Gio laughed. "It's funny; she said the same thing about you that day."

"Yeah, I always looked like a two-year-old, and now that I'm nineteen and look like I'm four, I'm doing really well for myself," she joked. "But no, that's not what I'm talking about. What's up? Why didn't you come say hi to me?"

"Is it really that big a deal?" he asked.

"It shouldn't be, but I get the feeling that it is," she countered.

He sighed. "I just, well, we took down Hershel Meyer and stuff ya know? Like, that's over and done with and I just didn't think you'd, ya know."

Her brows knit together briefly as she made sense of his words and realization dawned on her. "You didn't think I wanted to see you anymore now that I don't have to!"

"Well, yeah. I didn't really think you liked us that much," he admitted.

She laughed. "OK, you got me there. I actually really don't like the others, but, like, I like you,"

"Really?" he asked, "I always thought you were kind of neutral on me at best."

"No, I actually really enjoy spending time with you," she told him, looking a little unsure if she should elaborate. "I trust you. With most people, I always have to put on a show. With you, though, it's different. I don't really know how to explain it; I can relax around you. I feel safe, I guess."

"Is it because I tackled a serial killer for you?" he asked.

She laughed. "It helps for sure, but no, it's more than that. I just feel like I can open up more with you, I guess. It's hard to put into words, I know, but my point is, I like you, and I consider us friends so don't be afraid to talk to me if you see me somewhere, OK?"

"Deal," he told her, extending his hand for her to shake.

She looked amused. "Seriously? We're going to shake on it like we're making some sort of big friendship pact?" He smirked and gave a little shrug. She rolled her eyes and shook his hand. "Fine." She laughed. They went back inside just in time to see a middle schooler produce a card from out of someone's shoe. The night went on without any problems and Felicity was grateful for it.

The rest of the week was uneventful as well. Felicity saw her friends most nights, but every night before sunrise, she made sure to take time to surf, because the big island surf competition was coming up the following week, and she was both nervous and excited.

It was the big day. Felicity's favorite day. The day of the big island surf competition. She had won every year since 1957, and wasn't planning on losing today. She had her gear ready but had to wait for the official to arrive. Because no one could see her face in her wetsuit, the competition sent someone over to her house to escort her to the beach to ensure that she was truly the one surfing. The official, a short woman with frizzy red hair and purple framed glasses, looked at a few pictures of Felicity, making sure she truly was who she said she was.

"Alright sweetie, you can suit up now," she said.

Felicity wasted no time putting on her specially-made polarized goggles. They limited her vision but kept the sun from frying her eyeballs like eggs in a hot pan. She pulled on her specially made wetsuit, making sure her toes were all in their proper places, pulling it over her head and sealing it shut. She hated the restrictive suit. It made her feel claustrophobic and restricted some of her movements, but it was the price she paid. The official drove her to the beach and when she walked on, the entire beach erupted in cheers. On competition day, she was a superstar. Which was saying something, considering an actual surf superstar was there on the beach as well. He was a man in his early forties, blond, tan, and fairly muscular.

"I'm Brocko Fry, bruh, nice to meet you," he said, his accent was very Californian.

"You're a professional surfer, aren't you?" she asked, "What are you doing here on our little island?"

He laughed. "I'm retired now and only do small local stuff now. Not as much competish. Na' mean?"

"That'll be a shame then, when I beat you," she said with a shrug.

He laughed again. "You're on little lady."

"Alright everyone, places!" one of the officials called.

She walked toward a group of women competitors. There weren't as many women in the competition, but Penelope was one of them.

"Good luck," Penelope said, surprising her.

"Thanks, you too," Felicity replied. "I'd better be seeing you in the final round. You don't get to lose to anyone but me, got it?"

Penelope actually laughed. "If you insist. Just don't blame me when I have a better ride than you and end up breaking your record."

One of the officials pulled a name from a bowl. "Mary Haiffer!" A woman in her late twenties who Felicity remembered from the year before grabbed her board and ran into the water. She had a good ride, but nothing special. "Dave Wilson!" Dave, the local surf instructor, grabbed his board and went out for his ride. He was good. Really good. Felicity wasn't worried. On the contrary, she was excited. "Our Current Champion! Felicity!" the official called. She smiled, not that anyone could see, and grabbed her board.

"Woo! You can do it Felicity!" she heard Cara call. She turned her head and saw Julia, Basil, Cara, Sarah, John, Helen, Gio, Vito, Joey, and Andrea all cheering for her. They were all together, but as she looked around, she saw most of the beach was cheering for her. Most of the locals, especially the small business owners were screaming her name. She ran into the water and waited for her wave. She could feel the apprehension of the onlookers as she sat and waited. She passed up a wave that would have given her a respectable ride. She wasn't here for a respectable ride; she was here to win. The officials gave her a signal telling her that her time was almost up. She had already known this. A younger surfer may have begun to panic, but she was not a younger surfer. She had been surfing these waters since 1957. She closed her eyes and counted to six, then began to paddle. She could feel it: The wave, her wave, was coming. She stood up and began to shred, her vampiric athleticism was muted by the restrictive wetsuit and limited vision, but it didn't matter. Surfing wasn't something her vampirism had given her; surfing was something she had given herself through hours of practice, each year, each day, all leading up to today. Her ride was flawless. She performed moves that shouldn't have been possible, but she performed them all the same. When her ride was finished, she heard the entire beach go wild. As she exited the water, she cast a glance over at Brocko Fry. Even though she knew he couldn't see her eyes, she got the feeling that he knew she was looking at him.

"I thought your last move was a bit of overkill," Penelope said crossly.

"Penelope Smith!" the official called before Felicity could respond. The crowd on the beach hooted and hollered for Penelope as she hit her wave. Felicity was a tough act to follow and Penelope's ride fell short by comparison.

Name after name, surfer after surfer, the competition raged on. Vendors walked the beach selling drinks and Penelope finished her strawberry juice in a matter of seconds. Felicity, of course, didn't drink anything, but she wasn't in any danger of heatstroke.

The judges gave the results of the first round to the officials. “In the final round for the men’s, we have Brocko Fry and Dave Wilson!” The crowd cheered and then quickly died down. The official continued, “And for the women’s, we have the current champ, Felicity and Penelope Smith!” The crowd went wild. Felicity saw Dave and Brocko shake hands and wish each other luck. Dave went first and definitely earned himself a few new students. He was fantastic. She heard a few people in the crowd murmur about how he may actually beat a professional surfer. These murmurs were very quickly quieted as Brocko Fry took to the water. His demeanor changed from the lazy surfer bro she had spoken to earlier. He had a hunger to him. He was in this to win. Dave Wilson had had a fantastic ride, but Brocko Fry cut through the water like a barracuda. The crowd was silent as he finished his ride; they were stunned. As he sauntered out of the water, he stuck a fist in the air. The stunned silence transformed immediately into applause.

“Fickle crowd,” Penelope noted. “You want to go first, or should I?”

“Up to you,” Felicity told her.

Penelope flipped her damp hair over her shoulder and ran into the water. The waves had picked up in size and intensity since her first ride and Penelope took full advantage of it. She was about to pull out her big finisher, the one she had been working on all summer, when her foot slipped. She went careening off of her board and into the water. A combination of groans and shocked gasps came from the crowd.

Penelope walked slowly from the water and Felicity expected anger. Instead Penelope picked up her board and planted it into the ground next to Felicity. “You’d better beat that guy,” she said. Felicity gave her a nod.

Felicity walked over to the official. She turned to face Brocko Fry, and he extended a hand. “I was hoping to see you here. It wouldn’t feel right to take your title if you’re not the one defending it in the end.”

She shook his hand but remained silent. The official turned to them. “Which one of you wants to go first?” he asked.

"Ladies first," Brocko Fry said, gesturing to the ocean.

She shook her head. "You said it yourself, I'm defending my title. If you want it, go take it."

He smiled, his perfectly white teeth standing out against his bronzed skin and ran into the water. He was confident, close to cocky but not quite. He had the skills to back up the confidence he felt, and he demonstrated every one of those skills out on that wave. *So, this was what a professional surfer could do,* she mused. They were truly impressive. When he finished, the crowd was once again stunned silent. No one had ever beaten Felicity, just as no one had ever beaten her mother, or her grandmother, or even her great-grandmother. Of course, her mother and grandmother and even her great-grandmother had actually been her, but as far as the crowd knew, her family had won this competition every year since it began. They may have been witnessing history. This retired pro may have dethroned the island's surf queen. Brocko Fry rammed his board into the ground and threw his fists in the air, beating his chest and letting out a guttural roar. The crowd roared just as loud. *This man should run for mayor somewhere,* Felicity mused. He certainly knew how to work a crowd. As she walked toward the water, time seemed to slow down. He passed her as she went and for a brief moment, their gazes met. An electricity crackled between them. The kind of electricity that comes when a strong young lion challenges an older one for his territory. Brocko Fry had come to win.

Felicity paddled out to the waves and unlike her first ride, there was almost no time before her wave arrived. Brocko Fry had come to win, just as he had done at countless other small town surf competitions. He had made one, tiny miscalculation in his plan. He hadn't just come to any small town surf competition. He had come to the island's surf competition. He had come to *Felicity's* competition. She was here to remind him, and everyone in the crowd that she was champ for a reason. And remind them she did. The wave swelled as if the very ocean itself was on her side. It was perfect. She hit each turn, each trick with a perfection that was indescribable until it was time for her big finish. The competition this year had been fierce. More fierce than it ever had been. She honored that ferocity by performing Penelope's big finish. Unlike Penelope, Felicity executed it perfectly and when she did, there was no stunned silence, there was only cheers. Applause, hoots and screams, and as Felicity exited the water, she looked about her kingdom, and knew that she was the surfing queen of the island.

"We have a winner!" the official exclaimed, lifting Felicity's free hand over her head like a boxing champion and the applause grew louder than she thought possible.

Her friends all crowded around her, congratulating her. She caught Penelope's eye and gave a small nod. Penelope gave her a half smile and a nod in return before walking over to join her father and the twins. She still didn't like Penelope, and she knew Penelope didn't like her, but they had grown to have a mutual respect for one another.

"You're all coming to my party after this right?" Felicity asked the group.

Joey made a big show of looking shocked, collapsing to the sand like a Victorian era woman while Vito put his hands to his cheeks in a rough approximation of the famous painting, *The Scream*. "You're throwing a party?!" Joey asked as he got off the ground and brushed sand off of himself.

"Yeah, I have one every year, all of my sponsors are invited," Felicity said, ignoring their shock.

"We'll be there!" Julia said excitedly. "Wait, am I allowed to bring a plus one?"

"Is your plus one Basil?" Felicity asked. Julia squeezed Basil's hand and nodded. "Then of course you can bring a plus one. You know I was going to invite you anyway right?" Felicity said to Basil, who beamed with pride.

"Do I get a plus one?" Gio asked.

Felicity turned to him, and although he couldn't see her eyes through the goggles, he knew that she was rolling her eyes. "Fine. You can bring her."

He smiled at her and winked before walking off to find Penelope who was collecting her prize money. The second place competitors from the men and women's competition each received two hundred and fifty dollars while the overall second place winner received five hundred dollars. Felicity, as the overall competition winner, received a trophy and one thousand dollars. Felicity would get her check later. Right now, she just wanted to get home and take off her wet suit. She walked with the family back to the car as people congratulated her.

Once she was back home, she brushed out her hair and put on a white sundress with tropical flowers printed on it. She walked downstairs and into the tavern. The windows were all covered and there was a big banner that said, "Congratulations!" Everyone cheered when she entered. One by one, each of them walked up to her.

"Felicity, you look so pretty!" Julia said excitedly.

"So do you," Felicity told her.

"Ayyy there's the champ!" Greg proclaimed as he waved his hands like a gospel singer.

"I did promise you I would be winning again this year, didn't I?" she told him with a sly grin.

"And you are a woman of your word," he said with a theatrical bow.

The next person in line was Gully's father. He stood silently for a moment before speaking. "Thank you."

"For what?" she asked, genuinely unsure what he meant.

"I lost my son and the papers were all calling him a criminal, and we started losing business over it and you, well, people flooded into my restaurant to get receipts for your live music day. And they cleared Gully's name and I just wanted to thank you for all of it. You know you meant a lot to him."

Mr. McMahon's eyes began to fill with tears and Felicity put a comforting hand on his arm.

"I know. And for what it's worth, I made sure that they put the news that he was innocent on the front page."

He swallowed and smiled at her. "Thank you."

Her congratulations continued in this fashion. All of the business owners who had sponsored her were there and each one gratefully shook her hand and thanked her. A representative from the competition was also there to deliver her check and give her the trophy she had won. They also always wanted a picture of her with it and had long since accepted that she, like her "mother," "grandmother," and "great-grandmother" before her, didn't take photographs outdoors. All of the local newspapers also sent people to take her picture and she welcomed them all. As they were leaving, Penelope arrived.

"You should kick her out," Basil whispered and Felicity laughed hard enough to make a few heads turn.

"It's weird to think that if I hadn't been kicked out of that party, I never would have met Gio, Vito, or Joey," Felicity mused. "And actually, now that I think about it, I wouldn't have gone to the party at Penelope's so I never would have introduced you to Julia."

"So really I should be thanking Penelope for indirectly getting me and Julia together?" Basil asked incredulously.

"Everyone should be thanking me for everything. I'm a giver you know," Penelope said as she walked up to them and looked up at Felicity. Even in heels she was significantly shorter. "You surfed well. Congratulations on the win."

"That must be killing you to say," Felicity teased.

Penelope shrugged. "You've got more experience than me. Way to steal my finishing move, by the way."

Felicity shrugged, mirroring Penelope's gesture. "I figured I should pay homage to another great surfer."

Penelope gave her another half-smile and the two of them sized each other up.

"I'm glad you came," Felicity said at last.

"Me too," Penelope said before walking away to find Gio.

"Wow, that was, something," Vito mused.

"You're telling me. But I meant it, I am glad she came," Felicity told him. "By the way, do you think you can distract her long enough for me to steal Gio for a minute?"

"That's more of a Joey job," he told her, gesturing for Joey, who was holding hands with Cara, to come their way.

"What's up?" he asked.

"Felicity needs you to distract Penelope so—" Vito began.

"Say no more! One distraction coming up," he said walking toward Gio and Penelope. "Penelope!" he yelled, throwing his arms around her.

Gio looked at Felicity questioningly, and she nodded her head for him to follow her. She led him through the kitchen and into the house.

"What's going on?" he asked.

"I wanted to thank you," she told him.

He looked at her, confused, "For what?"

"When everyone thought I'd died, you stepped up and made sure everyone was OK. That's why you were the only one who didn't cry, right? You had to keep it together for everyone else?"

He looked shocked, "How did you know?"

She leaned against the counter. "I lived through World War II; I know exactly what that's like. I just wanted to thank you for it. You're a good friend, Gio, and I'm really happy that I met you."

He looked at her fondly and took a deep breath through his nose. He wasn't crying but she could tell what she had said meant a lot to him. She hugged him and he hugged her in return. "Come on," she teased, "your girlfriend will get jealous if I keep you too long."

He looked flustered. "She's not my… Oh, never mind. I'm right behind you."

The party continued for the rest of the afternoon. There was tons of food and even a cake with a wave of frosting being surfed by a little plastic girl on a surfboard. The sun had just begun to set as people started saying their goodbyes and by the time it had dropped below the horizon, all her guests were gone. Felicity decided to go for a walk. She slipped out the door and headed toward the beach.

Felicity walked toward the water, stopping just before the wet sand. The sun had set but it wasn't dark yet. In the bluish gleam of twilight, she looked out at the ocean. The wind whipped through her long dark hair. There was a storm coming in the distance. She closed her eyes for a moment and took a breath through her nose, savoring the scent that the ocean spray let out. Over the crashing waves, she could just make out the sound of a seagull laughing in the distance. She opened her eyes. This was a scene a painter was more qualified to capture than a photographer. The shore had an aura to it, a life that no photo could replicate. This was her home. She smiled and for the first time since she had been human, no melancholy rose to meet it. She threw back her head and her laughter mingled with that of the gulls. She thought of all she'd been through, all the friends she'd made. The walls she had built over the decades had come crashing down, and she realized that although she was by herself on this beach, she was no longer alone.